SHORT STORIES BY
CHRISTIAN CANTRELL:

"Farmer One"
"Venom"
"The Epoch Index"
"Anansi Island"
"Human Legacy Project"
"Brainbox"

CONTAINMENT

Published by 47North
P.O. Box 400818
Las Vegas, NV 89140

ISBN-13: 9781612183626
ISBN-10: 161218362X

CONTAINMENT

CHRISTIAN CANTRELL

b20113808

*For future generations
who must question everything
about the worlds they are born into.*

PART I

CHAPTER ONE

TOTAL EARTH ECLIPSE

THE FIRST THING ARIK NOTICED when he opened his eyes was that he couldn't move his head. He was immobilized from the neck up by a complex and bristling steel vise. Although there was a curtain draped over his forehead, he somehow knew that a portion of his skull had been removed and that his brain was exposed. There wasn't any pain—just tingling. There were questions from someone he couldn't see, and the sounds of tiny electronic motors making thousands of minute adjustments. Then more tingling. Eventually the questions ended and the sensation was gone, and when Arik opened his eyes again, he was looking up at Dr. Nguyen.

"Blink if you can hear me," the surgeon said. He waited for the series of twitches, then leaned down toward Arik's face and shined a bright white diode into one of his eyes, then the other. "Good. Welcome back. You've been out for eighty-nine days, believe it or not."

Arik had the sensation of being inside a heavy inanimate shell rather than his own body. He was entirely paralyzed except for his eyes and the ability to take deliberate, laborious breaths. His head had been recently shaved, and there was a neat hairless incision—precisely cauterized with a laser rather than crudely sutured—above his right ear like an intricate musical note. His immature beard had been allowed to grow in, forming sparse black patches that added an edge to his boyish face.

"Don't try to move or talk. Just relax. Your father is on his way. He'll explain everything."

Arik did not feel the same level of awe and reverence toward doctors and surgeons as most people outside the medical field. He felt like they mostly focused on treating symptoms in order to buy themselves some time while the body eventually just healed itself. In his current position, however, Arik was confused and vulnerable, so he did exactly what Dr. Nguyen asked and resisted the impulse to try to sit up and ask questions. What he really wanted was to see his wife.

They were in the Doc Pod. The small hospital and adjacent laboratory were officially the Medicine Department, but the younger generation, eager to express their individuality and imprint themselves upon the colony's culture, christened it the "Doc Pod." The name stuck.

The room was cubic and cramped, as were most rooms in V1 (the official name of the colony was Ishtar Terra Station One, but it was almost always referred to by its call sign). The outside of V1 was a substantial inert metal alloy shell designed to stand for at least a thousand years against the harsh Venusian atmosphere, but the inside was all about customization and flexibility. The walls of the hospital room were thick but configurable conductive polymethyl methacrylate, or "polymeth," all of which produced a soft warm light and were electronically fogged for privacy. The wall above Arik's head was a virtual dashboard indicating every detail of his physiology. He couldn't see it directly, but he could see the colors reacting to his heartbeat and breathing reflected in Dr. Nguyen's almond eyes.

"If we could have gotten you into a hyperbaric chamber, we might have been able to avoid surgery," the doctor told Arik, "but we couldn't get the specifications from Earth to build one, and we didn't feel like we could wait. Every minute of restricted blood flow was increasing the risk of more brain damage."

He rolled himself down to the end of the bed and raked the bottom of Arik's foot with a thin metal implement. Arik did not react and the doctor frowned.

"Anyway, one of us was going to make history," Dr. Nguyen continued. He recorded something on a luminous polymeth tablet. "Either you were going to be the first human to die on Venus, or I was going to perform the first successful off-Earth brain surgery." He chuckled at his observation, then composed himself. "Considering we actually had to build several surgical instruments from scratch, and the fact that we were right *smack* in the middle of a total Earth eclipse, which meant I had no medical consultation from the GSA whatsoever, I'd say it went pretty well."

The term "total Earth eclipse" was used to describe a period of time during which communication between Earth and Venus was impossible. When there was a direct line of sight between the two planets, communication was easy—it was just a matter of picking the right satellites on either end, aligning transmitters and antennas, and timing the broadcasts. But when Venus was on the opposite side of the solar system, obscured by a violent ball of nuclear fusion and plasma 1.3 million times the size of Earth, sending a radio signal from one planet to the other was like lining up an incredibly complex billiards shot on a table billions of square kilometers wide. You could bank the signal off one of the many communications satellites distributed throughout the solar system, or you could try to bounce the high-frequency microwaves off Mercury's iron-rich surface. You could even direct the broadcast through just the right point in the sun's gravitational well that it bent back around toward the planet behind like a golf ball catching the rim of the cup on its way past. But sometimes everything was just fractions of a degree out of alignment all at the same time, or signals were being scrambled by solar flares, or satellites were busy with higher-priority tasks, and the only thing to do was nothing at all. The only solution was to simply wait for the solar system to realign itself into a simpler and more auspicious configuration.

Total Earth eclipses tended to put people on edge.

"Now technically you did suffer *some* brain damage, but we expect you to recover almost completely—except for some minor memory loss, perhaps." The doctor teased some fibers out from a cotton ball and brushed them across Arik's eyelashes. Arik squeezed his eyes shut—relieved to be able to react to his environment, even in a seemingly insignificant way—and when he opened them again, the doctor looked satisfied. "Good. Your reflexes are coming back. The paralysis you're experiencing is only temporary. We just did that to keep you calm when you woke up."

The fact that Dr. Nguyen was just now getting around to addressing the paralysis was a true testament to his bedside manner. Although Arik had no memory of what happened to him, he assumed whatever it was had caused severe trauma to his spinal cord. Since the moment he realized he couldn't move, he had been trying to imagine a completely immobile and dependent existence—a life expressed entirely through robotic prostheses and computers. The first quadriplegic on Venus. History was always being made here, for better or for worse.

The door in the wall across from the bed began to glow. All the inside doors in V1 were identical prefabricated units. Because space was limited, swinging doors were shown to be impractical in early designs, and because almost all inner walls were made of transparent conductive polymeth, the pocket sliding door design was also rejected. The proposal the Global Space Agency eventually approved was a louvered concept consisting of six long, thin pieces of polymeth standing together vertically. The doors opened almost instantaneously by pivoting the slats ninety degrees, then flinging them on tracks to either side— three to the left and three to the right—where they slapped against one another in a crisp and unmistakable announcement of someone's arrival or departure. Not only were the doors very compact, but they were also airtight in order to help balance the distribution of oxygen throughout V1. And since they were conductive, they could perform handy tricks like glowing as someone approached.

Something changed on the display above the bed, and Arik heard his father's voice. Dr. Nguyen looked up and tapped the wall with one finger. The door snapped open and Arik's father ducked into the room. Arik's young wife entered a moment later, a beat behind, just long enough to let Arik know that she had almost changed her mind. He knew that there was significance in her hesitation; in the fact that his father was taking the lead; in the conspicuous absence of his best friend, Cam.

Darien was older than one would expect the father of such a young man to be, and having been one of the original settlers on Venus, the years of stress and exhaustion showed. There was little resemblance between Arik and his father; Arik's expression, even when relaxed, tended to be intense. Conversely, Darien's expression had the perpetually contented and affable look of a proud grandfather. He put his hands behind his back as he approached the bed as if resisting the urge to reach out and touch his son.

"Can he hear me?" He was looking at Arik, but talking to the doctor.

"Yes. He's reacting normally to stimuli. He just can't move yet."

"Thank God you woke up," Darien said. His normal, easy smile had to be forced, and was incongruous with his worried eyes. He looked at the doctor. "How much have you told him?"

"No details, just as you requested."

Darien watched his son while he paused, selecting his next words with noticeable care. When he was ready, his father leaned forward. "Arik, you had a very serious accident." He spoke slowly and deliberately, a little too loudly. "Your environment suit failed while you were outside. We got you back in, but not before you developed a very prominent embolism in your brain. You're extremely lucky to be alive."

"The technology for this kind of surgery didn't even exist here," Dr. Nguyen reminded Arik.

"But you're going to be fine. Everything went smoothly."

"Well, *mostly*," Dr. Nguyen corrected. "We'll know more in a few days."

Darien looked at the doctor, then back at Arik. There was obvious contention in the room between the optimism of a father and the brutal objectivity of a physician. The net effect was frightening Arik even more than any possible truth could.

"Your mother really wanted to be here when you woke up," Darien said, but he didn't finish the sentence. He gave his son another sympathetic smile instead, then quickly turned his attention back to the doctor. "Yun, when are we going to know how much he remembers?"

"As soon as he can talk. There's no other way to know."

"When will that be?"

"It's impossible to say right now. We're no longer restricting his movements, so he should be fully mobile again in a day or two. The question is how much brain damage he suffered. As you know, we had to remove some lesioned tissue, but the brain is an amazingly resilient and adaptable organ. I don't believe he'll have any permanent disabilities, but it might take some time for him to regain his speech and fine motor skills."

For the third time, the term "brain damage" startled Arik. The doctor used it as casually as if they were discussing a cavity or a sprained ankle. Arik was torn between trying to follow the conversation as carefully as possible and trying to assess his mental capabilities. Telling Arik he might have suffered brain damage was like telling a concert pianist he might have lost his hand.

Darien's lips had tightened at the doctor's explanation and he was nodding. Cadie appeared beside the bed between the two men, and Darien wrapped his arm around her narrow shoulders.

Cadie was a smallish girl who fit well within the scale of V1. Although her parents were both Japanese, she had curiously prominent Western features: round eyes, full lips, freckles—a little elfish. She was smiling with compassion and nervousness as she looked down at her husband, her straight black hair hanging beside her face, the tops of her ears peeking out. Arik could tell that she was very close to crying, and he wondered why she didn't reach out to take his hand, or run her fingers along his cheek. He could see that she was struggling with one of the great paradoxes of human interaction: sometimes the more important it was to communicate something, the harder it was to say. When it was clear how much she was struggling, Darien took over.

"Arik," Darien said, "there's something you need to know."

Cadie was wearing a dark, synthetic, long-sleeved dress that, when flattened out, revealed a subtle roundness that was not there the last time Arik saw her. But even to someone who had never seen a pregnant woman before, the shape was unmistakable.

His wife's transformation suddenly made the passage of time real. Arik felt like he had just been flung into the future—or rather that the future had just abruptly and rudely displaced the present. His eyes were wide as he strained to see his wife's tiny hands clasped over the gentle rise in her middle. He struggled to comprehend the life growing inside her that he knew would be born into a world of containment, of constant and exact calculation, of oxygen levels that everyone knew could not safely support any increase in population.

"As you can see," Arik's father said, "we're going to need you back at work as soon as possible."

CHAPTER TWO

THE PINNACLE OF HUMAN ACHIEVEMENT

THE FIRST PERSON TO BE born on another planet was Arik's best friend, Cam. Three weeks later, Arik became the twenty-ninth baby to be born on another planet. After Arik, seventy-one more babies were born in a two-month period. This off-Earth population explosion came roughly nine months after it was definitively determined that V1 could maintain enough oxygenated air to support exactly one hundred additional lives. No more.

These one hundred babies become known as Generation V, or just Gen V. Several of the original Founders of the V1 Colony (anyone not born on Venus was considered a Founder) claimed credit for the clever moniker; the *V* obviously stood for Venus, but Gen V also happened to represent the fifth wave of humans on the planet, the previous four having arrived via rockets and large capsules known as "seed pods."

The first person to be born on another planet also turned out to be the tallest. By the most accurate instruments available on V1, it was determined that Cam was exactly two meters tall (which meant he was not a big fan of the compact prefabricated doors). The theory was that since Venus was only 81.5 percent as massive as Earth, the weaker gravity allowed Cam to grow taller than the average human. The fact that none of the other ninety-nine children ended up significantly surpassing the average human height on Earth was not enough to disprove the hypothesis in most people's minds. For all intents and purposes, it was fact.

The first hundred babies to be born on another planet made history again by becoming the first class to graduate on another planet. School in the V1 colony was much less structured than the Earth equivalent. Parents were responsible for the basics: reading, writing, math up through calculus, a little history, and introductory biology, chemistry, and physics. Since everyone in V1 was smart enough to make themselves useful on another planet, homeschooling, with the help of curricular software, seemed to make the most sense, up through at least a high school education.

But eventually the kids needed more time than their working parents could afford, and the benefit of disciplines outside their parents' fields of expertise, so they were split up into ten groups of ten and distributed throughout the colony for an hour or two at a time. Topics of study were narrowed down to various forms of biochemistry, physics, engineering, and, of course, computer programming, which was as essential to every branch of science as learning to use a knife was to cooking.

The Education Department didn't take up any physical space. The "Brain Pod" was wherever the small administrative staff happened to squat since anyone's virtual workspace could be called up onto any interactive polymeth surface in V1, allowing for a great deal of flexibility and adaptability. All the Brain Pod really did was shuffle classes around, create schedules, and assign teachers. Eventually, after taking a vote, they determined that the students were ready to graduate, but in order to provide a little closure, they decided that each student should submit a final project. The most impressive, as determined by a specially appointed committee, would be presented during the commencement ceremony in the Public Pod in front of the entire V1 colony (and anyone on Earth who cared to tune in). In order to reduce the number of projects that needed to be judged, the Brain Pod encouraged students to work in groups.

It was no surprise to anyone that Arik and Cadie's project won. They tested their equipment up on the stage of the Venera Auditorium the morning of the graduation ceremony and rehearsed several times. The logistics of demoing what basically amounted to a computer program executing on a piece of custom hardware were not complicated, but Cadie and Arik had never presented anything before (when you grow up on Venus, there isn't a lot of time for things like Christmas pageants and talent shows). Looking out at all the seats from the perspective of the stage made them feel anxious and important, and brought out the obsessiveness in both their personalities. When it was time to take their seats, rather than sitting with the rest of their class, Arik and Cadie sat in the front row in order to give them easy access to the stage. While they waited for the lights to dim, they nervously turned to wave to friends and to search for their parents and favorite teachers among the crowd.

The Venera Auditorium (Public Pod) was one of the first structures built on Venus. At one time, it housed all the colonists (there were only twenty back then) and every piece of their equipment. As the colony expanded, it was to become a warehouse; however, it was successfully argued that, for the sake of morale, the colonists would need someplace where they could all occasionally gather for events like this. A new, much larger warehouse was constructed almost next door as part of the Infrastructure Department, and the Public Pod was officially established. The crumpled and corroded remains of the Venera

14 probe launched by the Russians in 1981 and later recovered during the early days of Venusian exploration were on display in the back corner beside an interactive piece of polymeth tirelessly preaching its significance.

There were exactly one thousand seats in the Public Pod. The morning of the commencement ceremony, it was filled beyond capacity at 1,098 (there were actually a total of 1,100 people in the V1 colony, but apparently two posts were too critical to be abandoned). The back of the auditorium and the aisles were easily able to absorb the overflow, but it was evident that someday they would need to find a new solution for the half dozen or so times a year they all congregated. There was talk of converting the dome—by far the most voluminous structure in V1—into a mixed-use public space as soon as the hundred-thousand-plus ferns it housed in order to provide V1's oxygen were replaced with a more efficient solution.

Kelley almost always spoke at public events like these, but he was usually introduced by someone else. A woman who worked in the Juice Pod (Energy Department) had somehow assumed the role of default master of ceremonies, and had gotten good at building up a little suspense before calling him out on stage. But today, Kelley hosted the event alone. Everyone knew that Kelley took a very special interest in Gen V, and particularly in their education. To him, this was personal.

Kelley was the boss. That was the best way to describe the air of authority that he projected. He didn't hold any official political office (V1 was entirely administered by the GSA), but he was in charge. He was seldom seen, which was a clear indication of his importance. It was assumed that he spent his days coordinating the complex affairs of V1, constantly on the horn with Earth, negotiating on behalf of his people, making a case for more supplies before the next launch window. When he walked out on stage, the wall lights dimmed and the room settled down into a hushed deference.

"Good morning, Ishtar Terra Station One." The conductive polymeth walls captured and amplified his voice evenly throughout the room. No need for a mic. "Today is a very special day—a day I've personally been looking forward to for a very long time."

It was already quiet, but the sincerity in Kelley's tone somehow settled the room still further. Kelley had the air of a used-car salesman sometimes, but he also had an authentic and vulnerable side to him that even his detractors admired. He was roughly the same age as Arik's father but looked much younger. His dark skin and short hair helped conceal his age, though his big, kind eyes could sometimes look impossibly tired.

"Once again, we acknowledge and celebrate the *Pinnacle of Human Achievement*. You've heard me use that term before, but never has it been as relevant and as true as it is today."

He looked down at the stage and took a few wandering steps while gathering his thoughts.

"It's hard to overstate the significance of this day." Kelley raised his head and looked around the audience. He seemed to be addressing each member individually. "Let's take a moment to consider what this ceremony means. Today is not just the day that these hundred students graduate. Today is the day that we hand the reins of the first off-Earth colony over to the first off-Earth generation. Today is the beginning of a new future, not just for us, but for all of mankind. Today will mark the dawn of new ideas and fresh creativity. Someday when we're all marveling at the advancements of the human race, when the technology we use today seems hopelessly obsolete and even comical, we will think back to this day, to this very moment. Generation V is the foundation on top of which the future of V1, and therefore the future of all mankind, will be built."

Kelley paused, indicating a transition, and the audience took the opportunity to get in some light applause. The graduates seemed a little stunned and unsure as to whether they should applaud themselves or not.

"But don't just take my word for it," Kelley continued. "You're about to see for yourselves. Right now I want to bring up two people who I believe represent the very embodiment of the spirit of V1—two people who saw past all the limitations and all the impossibilities of life here, and instead found inspiration and opportunity. Ladies and gentlemen—friends—it is my pleasure to introduce to you the winners of our very first student innovation contest: Arik Ockley and Cadie Chiyoko."

There was a fresh round of applause. The woman from the Juice Pod was sitting next to Cadie and stood up to help usher them to the stage. By the time they got up the steps, Kelley had already stepped down. When Arik turned toward the audience, he was thrown off by how little he was able to see in the glare of the spotlights. They had rehearsed with the house lights up, and now the experience felt completely unfamiliar. Without being able to monitor the audience's reaction, he would have no way of knowing how their presentation was being received.

"Hi, I'm Arik and this is Cadie," Arik began, a little too fast, seemingly startled by the amplification of his own voice. "Today we're going to show you a project we've been working on called ODSTAR, or Organic Data Storage and Retrieval. ODSTAR was the result of extensive research in the fields of DNA nanotechnology, DNA computing, biochemistry, and genetics."

He was unable to sense any reaction at all. He suddenly had the feeling that he was wasting everyone's time, and that the entire colony would resent him for the backlog of work the presentation was inevitably creating. Did anyone really care about ODSTAR? Was it going to make their jobs any easier, or their lives any more fulfilling? Were they genuinely interested, or were they just listening out of respect for Kelley?

"The theme we were given for our final projects was 'maximizing minimal resources.' There are a lot of things we don't have in V1, but rather than dwell on what we didn't have, we decided to focus on two things we have plenty of: computing power and DNA."

When they first began rehearsing, Cadie tried to get Arik to do all the talking, but Arik equated talking time with credit for the project, and refused to take it all. Cadie was a brilliant biologist, and Arik repeatedly reminded her that he couldn't have done the project without her. Although Arik wrote all the software and designed and built the hardware, he wouldn't have known what to build without her. Cadie finally agreed to co-present, and they wrote their talking points together, alternating passages. Now it was her turn.

"There are a total of approximately a hundred quadrillion human cells in V1," Cadie began. Her pace was more appropriate than Arik's, and it was evident that she had memorized her lines word for word. She was standing up very straight with her hands laced together in front of her, speaking into the glare with no hesitation whatsoever. "Each one of those cells contains strands of human DNA, and each strand of human DNA contains about three billion base pairs, or seven hundred and fifty million bytes of information. That's a total of approximately seventy-five septillion bytes, or seventy-five yottabytes, of information inside us—almost as much data storage as a portable solid quantum storage block."

The presentation shifted back to Arik.

"We also have an abundance of processing power in V1. Since replacing the parallel cores in our computing cloud with electron cores, each resident of V1 now has more computing power available to him or her than the entire history of the human race combined up until the creation of the first electron computer."

"And the more computing power you have," Cadie continued, "the more you can understand and work with DNA. Modifying and improving our DNA, and even adding entirely new chromosomes to the human genome, is already so common that in the next fifty years, there won't be a single human left who doesn't contain extensively engineered genetic material. In fact, we've gotten so good at scrubbing our gene pool that over ninety-nine percent of the cases handled by the Medicine Department relate to acute physical injury rather than disease."

There was a short, awkward pause before Arik realized it was his turn to speak again. He was supposed to make a joke about removing the gene responsible for clumsiness, but he suddenly had the feeling that it wouldn't go over.

"As good as we've gotten at modifying and manipulating DNA, no one has ever tried using the human genome for storing and retrieving nonbiological instructions and information. While not nearly as efficient as inorganic quantum storage, encoding data in our own genetic structures can literally allow us to pass information down from one generation to the next, which we believe might someday even be accessible to us on a conscious level, dramatically increasing our own capacity to store and retrieve information with one hundred percent fidelity."

As Arik spoke, a podium with a sloped transparent surface emerged from the stage floor. Arik removed a small dark box from one pocket and stepped toward the podium. Cadie produced a thin red cylinder from a pocket in the front of her dress. Arik presented the box to the audience.

"This is the ODSTAR interface," he said, and placed it deliberately on the podium. A red square flashed on the surface directly beneath the box as the device interfaced with Arik's workspace. Arik looked at Cadie.

"This is approximately one milliliter of Arik's blood containing DNA that we modified to include a specialized twenty-fourth data-storage chromosome."

She handed the blood sample to Arik, and Arik pressed it against the surface of the box. The red square began to flicker, and they both turned to watch the huge polymeth wall behind them. Pixel by pixel, a giant blue sphere began to assemble.

"On one of the very first flights to Earth's moon, the crew of a ship called Apollo 17 took what is still one of the most breathtaking pictures of our home planet. This picture turned out to be the most famous image in human history, and has been reproduced tens of millions of times. But this is the first time it has ever been reproduced from human DNA."

The picture was a stunningly clear photograph of Earth, fully lit, showing the arid desert of northern Africa with its horn jutting up toward the Arabian Peninsula, and the sapphire-blue southern Atlantic and Indian Oceans lying beneath thick white swirls of clouds merging with the southern polar ice cap.

"This is *The Blue Marble*."

Arik's fear that the audience might not be following exactly what was going on, or that they might not appreciate the significance of the experiment, turned out to be entirely unfounded.

From inside the glare, an immense wave of applause erupted. Arik and Cadie hadn't expected such a reaction and weren't sure what to do next. Arik stepped back from the podium, and he and Cadie stood beneath the enormous blue sphere and smiled. Kelley appeared between them and put a hand on each of their shoulders. His grasp was firm, and for the first time, Arik realized what an enormous man Kelley was.

"The Pinnacle of Human Achievement!" Kelley announced triumphantly above the noise. Through the glare, Arik could see that the audience was rising as the intensity of the applause increased. When Kelley spoke again, his voice was calm, but it resonated steadily from every wall of the room. "And with that, we turn V1 over to a new and eminently capable generation."

CHAPTER THREE

THE HISTORY OF V1 PART 1
THE END OF THE SPACE AGE

AT KELLEY'S REQUEST, THE FOUNDERS painstakingly compiled
an enormously comprehensive history of V1. The project took
over two years to complete and ended up being a sort of interactive multimedia documentary containing hundreds of news and
encyclopedia articles, interviews, written and recorded personal
journal entries, and dozens of hours of news broadcasts. The
assumption was that Gen V (and beyond, eventually) would be
immensely curious about their miraculous and unprecedented
circumstances—that with their scientific and analytical back-
grounds, they would one day become obsessed with researching
and learning every last detail of how they came to be born and
raised on Venus.

That assumption turned out to be wrong. Naturally, the
Founders were looking at V1 from their own perspectives. The
fact that they were the first humans to permanently colonize
another world was still sometimes difficult for them to fathom.
They still dreamt of Earth; they still knew plenty of people on
Earth; they sometimes talked about Earth as though they had
never left, then caught themselves and laughed awkwardly.
The fact that they would very likely never go back to the planet
on which they were born and raised was something all of the

Founders occasionally struggled with, and would probably struggle with for the rest of their lives.

But not so with Gen V. In fact, Gen V rarely gave Earth much thought at all. Having been born on Venus, they never wondered about the slightly weaker gravity, never questioned the level-zero oxygen lockdown emergency drills, never complained about the things they didn't have. The Founders eventually had to come to terms with the fact that Gen V was just as accepting of their circumstances—and just as disinterested in their history—as pretty much any other teenage member of the human race since the species' inception.

To Gen V, life on Venus was simply normal.

In retrospect, it was clear that the *History of V1* documentary was really more for the benefit of the Founders than for Gen V. It was a welcome distraction during some difficult times. It helped them maintain perspective, deal with the isolation, comprehend their place in history. But since it didn't really speak to Gen V, the Brain Pod decided to take a different approach to instilling a sense of the past in the younger generation. A small committee was assembled and assigned the task of reducing the entire history of V1 to three succinct parts: the beginning and the end of the world's first Space Age, the Earth Crisis (including how it almost led to the extinction of the human race), and finally, the birth of the second Space Age, and how it gave rise to the first (and so far only) successful permanent off-Earth colony. After being approved by both a subcommittee and Kelley himself, each document was stored in a public place on the central solid quantum storage grid, and a short message was sent around requesting that Gen V review the material on their own time. That was it. As far as anyone in Gen V was concerned, those three documents represented the definitive history of V1, and quite possibly all they would ever know of their parents' home planet.

• • •

Part One of the *History of V1* began: "It all started 13.73 billion years ago with a very Big Bang." According to the logs, that part was inserted relatively recently, and was a good example of the kind of thing that passed for a practical joke on Venus.

The document actually began with the 1957 launch of the first satellite: a shiny aluminum-alloy beach ball called Sputnik 1. The very first living Earth creature was launched into space only a month later aboard Sputnik 2: a dog named Laika (a.k.a. *Muttnik*) who, despite the Russians' great care, died from excessive heat and stress. At the time, it was entirely unknown whether it was possible for any form of life to survive even a relatively short trip into lower orbit, much less the long and arduous journey to other planets.

Sputnik was a wake-up call for the Americans, who were unaccustomed to having their technical and engineering prowess challenged. After revamping the entire American education system to counter the impending scientific threat and forming the National Aeronautics and Space Administration, the United States finally responded to the Russians by launching Explorer I. The Space Age had officially become the Space *Race*.

For a time, the Americans and Soviets traded victories, though the Soviets had a definitive early lead. They got the first man into space (Yuri Gagarin) and the first spacecraft to land on another world (the moon). The Americans fired back with several of the first functional satellites (weather, communication, navigation, spying) and ultimately claimed victory for the first humans to set foot on another celestial world (Neil Armstrong and Edwin "Buzz" Aldrin, on the moon's Mare Tranquillitatis, or Sea of Tranquility). But even back when the moon was the prize, the world was already taking an interest in Mars and Venus. The American Mariner 4 flew within ten thousand kilometers of Mars in 1965, and the Soviets actually crashed a spacecraft into Venus in 1966. Back then, just aiming for and hitting another planet was a major accomplishment, never mind actually landing on it.

But it wasn't until the 1970s and '80s that planetary exploration began in earnest. The Americans achieved the first flybys of Mercury, Jupiter, Saturn, Neptune, and Uranus, and got the first photos of the surface of Mars along with a rudimentary soil sample. The Russians, apparently preferring harsher environments, focused on Venus, achieving the first Venusian orbit, and even successfully landing a few very robust spacecraft on the surface. In 1981, Venera 13 managed some pictures, a soil sample, and even the first sound recording on another world before being destroyed after 127 minutes by the immense heat and atmospheric pressure. It was during this time that Venus was declared the most inhospitable planet in the inner Solar System, and the least likely to ever be inhabited. You'd be better off vacationing on the sunny side of Mercury, it was said, than in the shade on Venus.

The space shuttle years finally began to break down international borders in space. It was a joint mission with the European Space Agency that successfully landed a probe on Titan, Saturn's largest moon, and the People's Republic of China became the third nation to independently launch a person into orbit. The space shuttle also gave rise to the International Space Station, which was an immense achievement in human history, but in terms of public perception, suffered from the fact that it looked nothing like any space station anyone had ever seen in a movie. The Americans continued their obsession with Mars, landing several rovers and probes on its surface since evidence of life on another planet—even ancient, fossilized, microscopic life— would all but guarantee decades of generous funding. In 1996, American scientists even announced the discovery of Martian bacteria found fossilized within a meteorite recovered from Antarctica, though it was never determined whether the micro-fossils originated on Mars, or postimpact on Earth. In 1990, the first orbiting telescope was launched but promptly failed because the main mirror was ground one-millionth of an inch off speci-fication. The astronomy community watched anxiously as an optical component designed with precisely the opposite flaw was installed in the telescope in-orbit, successfully compensating for the error and turning an international embarrassment into an unprecedented triumph.

The Americans made the mistake of attempting to replace the overworked space shuttle fleet with the Orion spacecraft and Ares families of rockets, which, to the public, were indistinguish-able from the command modules and launch vehicles used in the 1960s and '70s. By then, most of the world had become bored with the space program, which primarily revolved around pro-viding the ISS with fresh crews and supplies, incomprehensible experiments, and probes whose discoveries were lost on the aver-age taxpayer. Going from the closest thing the world had ever seen to a real spaceship back to seemingly old-fashioned rockets did nothing to improve NASA's PR situation.

The Russians, on the other hand, chose to abandon their much more powerful and advanced shuttle program after only a single unmanned, unpublicized flight in 1988, opting instead to stick with more conventional rocket systems because of budgetary restrictions. Although the *Buran-Energia* was the most sophisticated spacecraft of its day—more sophisticated, even, than the mighty American space shuttle—it never had the opportunity to imprint itself upon the world's psyche. Therefore, while the Russian space program was seen as stagnating, the perception of the American space program was that it actually took a giant step backward, especially considering the number of times American astronauts had to bum rides into orbit on Russian *Soyuz* rockets.

NASA was eventually forced to get out the manned space exploration business altogether because of massive spending cuts, and to begin looking to private industry for more practical and economical forms of innovation. Unfortunately, private industry rapidly discovered that there simply weren't enough eccentric thrill-seeking million- and billionaires in the world to fund the really serious work, and no priceless minerals, gems, or resources had been discovered within reach to entice the volume of funding needed to take mankind much past low-Earth orbit. There was still money to be had from the government, but most of it was controlled by scorned ex-NASA program managers who had warned the administration that it was a huge mistake to rely on private industry and were henceforth determined to prove themselves right.

Unnerved by steady advances by the Chinese in satellite, rocket, and robot technologies, an entirely new White House administration decided to sink billions into helping NASA recapture their glory days by returning to the moon, which, as it turned out, was more or less as they'd left it almost a century prior. Rather than another national triumph for which the president at the time had hoped, the series of missions were mostly met with mediocre television ratings, general consternation, an excess of merchandising, and a resurgence of the theory that the original lunar landings had been a hoax. The telescope assembled on the far side of the moon succeeded in capturing some stunning images, including a few faint pixels of possible light pollution originating from a small rocky planet in the habitable zone of a nearby solar system, but on the whole, the moon base the Americans began constructing was seen as a poor substitute for the manned mission to Mars that the public felt it had been promised.

Worse than the perceived lack of innovation were the environmental concerns of the world's space programs. The average temperature of the earth was gradually rising during this period as a result of the same greenhouse phenomenon that keeps the temperatures on Venus so astronomically high. But rather than large amounts of carbon dioxide occurring naturally in the atmosphere as it does on Venus, Earth's increasing CO_2 levels were caused by the ceaseless combustion of ancient carbon-based organic materials buried deep inside the earth. The rising temperatures caused widespread climate change, which, as predicted, led to severe global weather anomalies, drought, famine, disease, and, indirectly, increasing rates of genocide and several large-scale wars. Suddenly, images of American, Russian, European, and Chinese rockets launching amid massive plumes of exhaust became symbols of flippant disregard rather than bold exploration. Eventually, the billions of dollars spent servicing the ISS and moon projects fell victim to the prevailing slogan of the time: *Earth First.*

With the exception of China, every nation with any sort of space program abandoned nearly every initiative they were funding. Hundreds of thousands of scientists and engineers lost their jobs and discovered the hard way that PhDs in astrophysics and aerospace engineering didn't transfer well to other fields. Chinese *Shenzhou* rockets helped keep the lights on in the ISS by shuttling a few astronauts, cosmonauts, and taikonauts back and forth, but even this had to be done in relative secrecy.

Less than three years later, funding for anything but the maintenance and replacement of the most critical military satellites had completely dried up. The Chinese were the only bidders on a series of contracts for bringing the last of the ISS and moon base personnel back to Earth, and for disassembling the dilapidated and failing International Space Station into small enough components that most of it would burn up in the atmosphere during a controlled de-orbit.

The world's first Space Age thus ended with a series of spectacular fireballs above the eastern Pacific Ocean.

CHAPTER FOUR

EARTH ELEVATOR

GRADUATES OF THE V1 EDUCATION system didn't exactly have a wide array of career opportunities, but it wasn't in anyone's best interest to make them do jobs they didn't want to do. The Department of Education, along with representatives from every other department, decided they would form a committee of three panelists to hear any specific requests the graduates might have, discuss options, acknowledge their concerns, and ultimately determine whom they would report to the next day. Most of the graduates knew exactly where they were going, and in fact had been groomed for service in a particular area since the time they first showed the slightest proclivity or demonstrated any talent at all. No one expected any surprises.

The Career Committee was to hear ten cases per day for ten consecutive days, starting with the oldest graduate. Cam, who possessed the very rare combination of intelligence, coordination, and great physical strength, was assigned to the Infrastructure Department (Wrench Pod), and was expected to ascend quickly into an administrative role, if he chose to do so. His talents were perfectly suited for things like repairing robots, planning the construction of new pods, and long, arduous EVAs (the GSA still used the term *extravehicular activity* even though it made no sense in the context of V1).

Because of the amount of work that went into maintaining and expanding V1, about half of the graduates could expect Wrench Pod assignments. The Infrastructure Department had consistently lobbied the Education Department over the years to steer as many students as possible toward careers in the Wrench Pod because they were so understaffed and overworked. During the formation of the Career Committee, representatives from the Wrench Pod showed up to meetings only long enough to proclaim that they had no time for such diversions, and to remind other participants how important things like pressure balance valves and air-circulation systems were. You really didn't want bitter, overworked, exhausted staff in charge of them.

All the graduates took a great deal of interest in the first few Career Committee hearings. Cam was mobbed as soon as he was far enough away from the doors of the Public Pod that the committee panelists couldn't hear the inquisition. Who was on the committee? What did they say? Where did he get assigned? When did he have to start? Cam reported that the whole thing went very smoothly and professionally; they had simply asked him where he thought he could be of greatest service to V1, and why. They gave him a few minutes to respond, then asked him to elaborate on one or two things, at which point the decision was swiftly made that he would report to the Wrench Pod at 0700 the next day. The whole thing had taken only about twenty minutes. Since they had to get through nine more hearings that day and still attend to some of their regular duties before going home, nobody saw any reason to drag the process out.

Subsequent graduates reported similar experiences, and by the time Arik's hearing came up, interest had waned. Eventually, nobody wanted to spend the little time they had left before starting their careers interrogating their peers. Initially, Cam was considered the luckiest of the graduates since he was able to get his hearing over with first, perhaps even guaranteeing him the position he wanted, but then the youngest graduates were considered the most fortunate since they were enjoying the longest vacations any of them would probably ever have.

Arik didn't follow all the drama, but he did know that Zaire had been assigned to the Wrench Pod along with Cam. The couple were warned by their friends and families that spending too much time together might not be good for their relationship, but they seemed excited about being able to see each other at work. Besides, if it got to be a problem, they could always request different shifts. Hani was going to the Play Pod, Syed to the Code Pod, and Cadie, as expected, was assigned to the Life Pod, where it was assumed Arik would be joining her shortly (she was a day older than him). They, too, would have to be conscious of their personal relationship, but there was no way the ODSTAR team was going to be broken up. Apparently Kelley himself had seen to that.

Arik's was the ninth hearing on the third day. He waited outside the Public Pod until the next-oldest graduate—a boy named Seth whose self-confidence Arik had always admired—emerged and held the door open for Arik. The Public Pod had the only traditional physical swinging door in V1, since it was built before the prefabricated polymeth doors arrived. Nobody saw any reason to swap it out.

"Good luck," Seth said blandly as Arik passed. He seemed entirely unimpressed with the outcome of his hearing, and suddenly, for the first time, Arik felt apprehensive. He was accustomed to having a great deal of freedom in his research and in the topics he chose to pursue, but he was starting to realize that such indulgences were the special privilege of childhood. For the first time, he realized how much of what he took for granted was going to change. He was about to become a resource—assigned specific tasks that were to be completed in specific and prescribed manners. His creativity and productivity were to be constrained and directed toward only those problems that his superiors deemed worthy of his effort. Arik was about to become an adult.

The Venera Auditorium was probably the least appropriate setting for the Career Committee hearings, but it was the only space in V1 nobody else was using. There was a portable polymeth desk set up on the stage, behind which the three panelists sat with their workspaces open in front of them (they were no doubt trying to keep up on comms as much as possible between hearings in order to minimize the amount of work they would have to get caught up on later). There was a single chair set up opposite the desk, placed just far enough away that its occupant would feel excluded from the group. The process of traversing the long aisle, passing in front of the rows of seats, ascending the steps, and crossing the stage seemed like absurd pageantry, but it helped that the three panelists were busy tapping on and muttering into their workspaces until Arik sat down.

The panelist on the left was Fai, a stocky Chinese man who was one of the initial twenty colonists. He had been in charge of V1's very rudimentary computer systems and went on to found and head up the Technology Department (he disliked the informal "Code Pod" designation). Fai was one of the few who could keep up with Arik's computer skills, although he had long since lost the intense curiosity and passion for discovery that was so apparent in Arik. Arik had always sensed in Fai a complicated intermingling of admiration and resentment toward him.

In the middle was a tall, thin, balding man named Zorion, whom Arik knew very little about, except that he was high up in the Energy Department, and that he knew as much about nuclear fusion as anyone on Earth or Venus. He seemed particularly sensitive to the awkward position that Arik was in, and was trying to comfort him with a deliberate but warm smile.

Nobody would have guessed that the rightmost panelist was Arik's mother. L'Ree seemed the least engaged of the three and still hadn't taken the time to look up from her workspace. Arik wondered if Fai and Zorion were conscious of L'Ree's behavior. They might assume that she had lost track of the schedule and didn't realize it was her son who had just taken a seat in front of them, but Arik knew that very little escaped his mother's attention. Arik did not dislike his mother, and as far as he knew, she did not dislike him, but their relationship had always been curiously distant. Perhaps now she was adding a little extra distance so that nobody would think she was giving her son preferential treatment. Then again, perhaps she was just being herself.

L'Ree was considered one of the most beautiful women in V1, but her beauty was tempered by her fiercely serious nature. Although Arik was considered an intense young man, and everyone assumed he inherited his ambition and intelligence from his mother, their personalities were somehow entirely different— even at odds. Arik had once told Cadie that he and his mother simply never understood each other, and both had long since stopped trying.

Zorion was the chairman of the panel and, according to all the accounts Arik had heard, was supposed to do most of the talking. He seemed to be giving L'Ree the opportunity to speak first, but when she insisted on remaining disengaged, he commenced the meeting himself.

"Hi, Arik. Would you please tell us where you think you can be of greatest service to V1, and why?"

Arik had played out dozens of scenarios in his mind, searching for the right way to present his proposal, but he couldn't think of any form of preamble or preface that would make what he wanted to say any less jarring, or make him seem any less like a dissenter. So he decided to just be blunt and direct, and ultimately to improvise.

"I want to go to Earth."

L'Ree looked up. Fai became instantly annoyed as if Arik had personally insulted him, but Zorion's expression told Arik that there was something in the response that he appreciated. Maybe he was just bored with the hearings and welcomed a departure from the routine. Arik addressed him directly.

"I want to start building the Earth elevator, and I think it should be our top priority."

The term *Earth elevator* was used to refer to a series of processes, vehicles, and launch sites that would someday make bidirectional travel between Earth and Venus not just possible, but practical, and hopefully even routine.

"Why?" Zorion said. He wasn't skeptical or judgmental. He seemed genuinely curious.

"Because if we don't stay politically and culturally integrated with Earth, we'll become increasingly isolated, and if we wait until that happens, I think it'll be too late to build it."

"We're not *isolated*," Fai said. "We're in *constant* communication with Earth."

"I'm not."

"Everyone who *needs* to be is."

"Anyone who wants access to Earth needs to have it," Arik said. "And anyone on Earth who wants access to Venus should have it too. If we allow ourselves to develop dramatically separate cultures, it will inevitably lead to conflict. We have to start think-ing about that now rather than waiting until it happens."

"This is ridiculous," Fai said with great exasperation. "This isn't even worth discussing."

"I'd like to hear him out," Zorion said. "That's what these hearings are for, aren't they? Go ahead, Arik."

"I think we have to stop thinking of V1 as a colony. Colonization inevitably leads to only one thing: *de*colonization. History has taught us that over and over again. The Earth eleva-tor will turn V1 into an extension of Earth rather than a colony of Earth. People need to have the freedom to travel back and forth, and to share knowledge and culture. And most importantly, peo-ple need to be able to decide on their own where they're going to live and what they're going to do. They can't have those things imposed on them, at least not for their entire lives."

L'Ree shifted in her seat and cleared her throat to let every-one know that she was about to speak. "Right now we do what we *have* to do, not what we *want* to do. When we need the Earth elevator, we'll build it."

She looked back down at her workspace. Arik knew that in her mind, the matter was resolved.

"It'll take years to build," Arik said. "Decades, probably. If we wait until we need it, it'll be too late. That's what I'm trying to tell you. We have to plan ahead. We always talk about it like it's inevitable, but if we don't make it a priority, it'll never happen. I don't believe the Earth elevator is a luxury or a novelty. I believe it's essential to the long-term success of V1, maybe even to the long-term *survival* of V1."

"Do you have any idea what the escape velocity of Venus is?" Fai asked Arik. He seemed to be taking a different tack toward shutting this down and getting the hearing back on track.

"Ten point four six kilometers per second."

"And how do you propose we achieve a velocity of ten point four six kilometers per second without fuel?"

"Obviously we would need some form of renewable propellant. And spacecraft. And hundreds of other things that we need to start planning for now. I'm not saying it's not a lot of work, but I actually think it's going to be easier than most people realize."

"*Easier*?" Fai was simultaneously amused and offended. "You call building a rocket out of materials we don't have, fueling it with propellant we have no way to refine, and launching it from a site that doesn't exist *easy*? Just the heat shield alone for surviving reentry into Earth's atmosphere is impossible for us to build."

"You're focusing on everything we *don't* have rather than what we *do*," Arik said. "That's the difference between your generation and mine."

Fai was clearly not accustomed to being spoken to in this manner. Arik knew he was an extremely well-respected computer scientist, and although nobody would describe him as mean, he always insisted that his students and subordinates address him with due respect. But Arik wasn't being spiteful or intentionally irreverent; he was simply stating the relevant facts.

"Tell us what components you think we already have," Zorion said.

"First of all, we're not talking about building a two-way system. We obviously already have the launch sites, vehicles, and the knowledge and experience to get from Earth to Venus. Second, we're not even talking about getting from Venus to Earth. We just have to get from Venus to the moon since we already have a proven system for getting back and forth between the moon and Earth. That means we won't even need a heat shield."

"What about fuel?" Fai said.

"Until we figure out how to make our own propellant, we could easily get enough fuel from Earth to get us into orbit around Venus."

"Orbital velocity *maybe*," Fai conceded, "but *escape* velocity? Doubtful."

"All we have to do is get ourselves into a parabolic orbit, and we can use a gravitational slingshot to get us to Earth, and another gravitational slingshot to slow us down once we get there. Since we'll be moving away from the sun, we'll steadily lose speed, which means we should be able to slow down enough to get into lunar orbit without aerobraking. We can use physics to do most of the work."

"Arik, we all know you're smart," L'Ree said with exasperation. "Nobody here doubts your intelligence, and I don't think anyone here even doubts your ability to figure this out given enough time. But that's not the point. The point is that we need you working on other things. We have to solve the air problem before we can do anything else."

Arik knew that he was unlikely to get approval from the group, but he realized now that just having the support of his mother would have been enough. Seeing her stand up for him—even if she'd been ultimately overruled by Zorion and Fai—would have been enough of a victory for him, and he would have dropped it. Instead, her disapproval only added to his resolve.

"You know that the environmental systems are stable," Arik told his mother. "They've been stable for years."

"They're stable, but we aren't. We can't support a single additional human on Venus right now. Doesn't that strike you as problematic? Don't you think Gen V is going to want to get married and start having children someday?"

"We can get additional air from Earth," Arik said. "We have hundreds of tanks we've never even used."

L'Ree leaned back and looked at Zorion, seemingly reluctant to continue. Arik could tell that something needed to be said that she didn't feel she had the authority to say.

"Arik," Zorion said, "we fully appreciate that you and your generation have a unique perspective on life here. That's why we're so anxious for your contributions. But you have to realize that *we* have a perspective that *you* don't."

Zorion paused. He appeared to be gathering his thoughts, choosing his next words cautiously. He leaned forward and looked up at the heavy closed door at the back of the auditorium before continuing.

"Arik, it is extremely important that we reduce our dependency on Earth as much as possible. If our environmental systems fail, or if they can't keep up, we'll be dependent on Earth for the most basic of human necessities. That's not a very strong position for a colony to be in, is it?"

Arik suddenly realized that the discussion wasn't about whether decolonization could happen—they were already debating what to do about it. The committee had accepted the premise of his argument before he'd even sat down; it was his conclusion that they were calling into question. Arik was arguing for proactive measures while they were already thinking defensively.

"I'm not trying to scare you, Arik," Zorion continued, "and there's certainly no cause for concern at the moment. But you have to understand that things need to be done in a specific order here, and right now, we *need* to solve the air problem. Arik, we need you in the Life Pod."

"But we won't *have* an air problem if we can avoid decolonization," Arik said. "That's the whole point."

"Arik, what was the first thing you said about colonization?"

Arik took a moment to recall his words, then suddenly realized the trap he had laid for himself. "That it inevitably leads to decolonization."

"The definition of *inevitable* is that which is certain to happen and cannot be avoided or prevented. That was your word, not mine. Now, being a colony of extremely limited resources, does it make more sense to apply those resources toward trying to prevent something that cannot be prevented, or toward preparing for it instead?" Arik knew that the question was rhetorical, and that the hearing was over.

CHAPTER FIVE

REEDUCATION

NOT COUNTING DR. NGUYEN, ARIK had received only a single visitor. His father came to see him almost every day, but because Arik's white blood cell count was inexplicably low, leaving him susceptible to infection and disease, Cadie, Cam, and Arik's mother had been asked to communicate via video stream rather than in person.

The hospital bed had been turned ninety degrees from the position it was in when Arik woke up, so that it faced the largest expanse of uninterrupted polymeth in the room. His workspace filled the entire surface in front of him from just above his feet all the way to the ceiling. The wall was alive with diagrams, video feeds, and hundreds of lines of scrolling code.

Arik watched the movement in front of him, deadpan, his hands flat on the bed beside his body. He was wearing the BCI that his father had brought him. A BCI was sometimes referred to as a mindmouse, wavecap, NP (neuro-prosthetic), or, probably most descriptive of all, a headcrab. It consisted of a white polymer hub that sat on the back of the head with wide, flat fingers reaching forward above all four lobes of the brain. Technically, it was an NIBCI, or a Noninvasive Brain-Computer Interface, meaning that it sat on your head as opposed to being embedded inside it.

Not everyone could use a BCI. Most people preferred soft polymeth keyboards and multitouch surfaces, or to stand and trace out commands on a horizontal polymeth surface, or if they were really committed, to train themselves on a Prehensile-Computer Interface. PCIs were usually long glove-like devices that could sense a wide array of movements, impulses, and gestures, and translate them into various commands (gestures could, of course, be tracked without the use of additional hardware, but most people preferred the tactile feedback of a physical apparatus). And all these methods could be augmented with eye tracking and voice input. But a BCI was by far the most efficient method ever conceived for communicating with machines—if you were able to master it.

For most of its existence, the field of BCI research had been considered "fertile," which is a scientifically polite way of saying that it had a long way to go. The problem was the learning curve. Researchers had a fair amount of success with invasive BCIs since they were able to pinpoint regions of the brain associated with very specific tasks; subjects were literally able to just think about doing certain things and watch their intentions realized on their workspaces in front of them. However, as scar tissue built up around the implants, the signal tended to degrade, and neurosurgery was not something you wanted to undergo on a regular basis. There was also the small matter of occasionally needing to upgrade the hardware in order to accommodate more sophisticated software—a process that required sixteen hours of brain surgery.

The focus gradually shifted to noninvasive BCIs like the one Arik used, but the problem was that, in most cases, they required unrealistic levels of training. Since sensors on the outside of your brain picked up far more noise, the subject had to learn to focus and control thoughts in order to increase the signal-to-noise ratio. Additionally, it was very difficult to pinpoint precise signals when reading brainwaves so far away from their origins. It was more like trying to understand what someone was saying to you from across a noisy room as opposed to having the person whisper it directly into your ear.

Arik's parents had introduced him to BCI technology at a very early age because of the work of a brilliant African neurobiologist named Kainda Nsonowa. At the time, BCI researchers generally fell into two camps: those who believed it was up to hardware and software to extract precise patterns from noise, and those who felt it was the subject's responsibility to learn how to produce cleaner signals. Nsonowa showed that the answer turned out to be somewhere in the middle. Her team helped reinvigorate the field by constructing systems that enabled computers and humans to grow and learn together.

Nsonowa theorized that this coevolution needed to start at as early an age as possible. She discovered that seven-year-olds who had been training on BCIs since they were three could interact with machines as efficiently as any adult using any other method or combination of methods of human-computer interaction. By the time subjects were twelve, they were at least twice as proficient as adults, and by the age of fourteen, children were able to perform complex tasks between ten and twenty times more efficiently than any adult in the world.

Nsonowa had proven that people who grew up with BCI technology could control machines as easily as their own limbs.

The challenge of using a BCI fascinated Arik, and he and the computer mastered each other very quickly. Most of the training programs were in the form of games that Arik devoured, and by the age of six, he was more proficient with a computer than any adult in V1. At the age of ten, Arik began modifying the learning, acclimation, and adaptation algorithms, and by twelve, his parents suspected he was several times more proficient with a BCI than anyone in human history. He was often asked how he did it, but Arik honestly didn't know. He understood how both the hardware and the software worked, but it was the organic part of the equation—his own brain—that he didn't understand. He described it to people as being able to punch a code into a keypad, but not actually being able to recite the sequence of numbers. The knowledge was stored in a part of his brain that conscious thought could not access directly.

Arik's parents were also familiar enough with Nsonowa's work to stop Arik's research into building a two-way BCI. It didn't take Arik long to realize that once the process of a human communicating with a computer using a BCI was mastered, the bottleneck became the process of the computer communicating with the human. After processing input, the computer had to convert its output into some sort of graphical form, which it normally displayed by exciting molecules of polymeth at specified X, Y, and Z coordinates. The X and Y coordinates were needed to arrange the output into a coherent pattern, and the Z coordinate specified the depth of the event, which helped determine which wavelengths of light were allowed to escape, resulting in billions of possible colors. The photons then had to span the distance between the polymeth and Arik's eyes, strike the rods and cones of his retinas, and get converted into electrical impulses that were carried by the optical nerve to the visual cortex in the occipital lobe all the way in the back of his brain. It was only then that Arik could even begin the process of making sense of the visual input that, depending on the task, was done in one or more completely different parts of his brain.

Arik imagined a far more efficient process of computer output. If a BCI could allow you to communicate with a computer more efficiently by bypassing primitive input methods, why not build a BCI that could bypass primitive output methods as well? Why not skip the visual representation, the polymeth, and the eyes entirely, and send information directly into the brain? Nsonowa refused to do any work with two-way BCIs. She fit her own definition of wise in that she knew what she did not know, and she did not know the risks of bypassing all the safeguards evolution had seen fit to install between your eyes and your brain. What she did know, however, was that using your brain to control a computer was entirely different from using a computer to control your brain. The tiniest software bug, hardware malfunction, or physical miscalculation would have repercussions that she did not want to be responsible for. She admitted that the technology was intriguing, probably even inevitable, but she insisted that it would not come from her, and Arik's parents made sure that it would not come from him either.

The first time Arik had the BCI placed on his head after the surgery, he was terrified that he would no longer be able to use it. Since he still didn't have a clear idea of what the embolism and the surgery had done to his brain, there was no way for him to know whether his neurological conditioning had been affected, and whether his relationship with the BCI's software had been damaged. To Arik, computers were prostheses. When he needed more storage capacity and processing power than he had in his own head, or when he needed to extend his ability to communicate, he put on his BCI, opened his workspace, and came closer than any other human in history to mentally merging with a machine. He knew if that relationship were ever to be damaged, he would probably never be able to fully repair it, and that an integral part of who he was would be dead.

Arik hypothesized that he would either have no trouble communicating with the computer at all, or that the computer would behave completely erratically. Either the portion of his brain that was conditioned to interact with the BCI was fully intact, or it had been irreversibly damaged. But what actually happened was, as Nsonowa herself would probably have predicted, somewhere in the middle. He seemed to be able to communicate with the computer normally, though there were occasional "lapses." In a typed-out explanation (Arik still wasn't completely comfortable talking yet), he described it to Dr. Nguyen as having a normal and fluid conversation with someone, then suddenly not being able to come up with the next word in a sentence. Or like punching in a code on a keypad that you've done thousands of times before, but suddenly not being able to remember the next number in the sequence. Arik realized that there wasn't one specific part of his brain that knew how to use the BCI; rather, the knowledge was distributed throughout its neural structure. But it wasn't just stored once. There seemed to be some redundancy, since with enough practice he was able to recover the knowledge to fill in the gaps. It was just a matter of subconsciously locating the redundant information and resequencing the damaged routines. It took about a week of exhausting and repetitive practice, but Arik felt he had again become as proficient with the BCI as he had ever been.

In the corner of his workspace, Arik could see Dr. Nguyen approach his room with someone behind him—Raakesh Priyanka, a friend of Arik's father. Dr. Nguyen never bothered to knock, so Arik never bothered to open the door for him. Arik saw the surgeon reach out and touch the wall beside the door, then the slats slid apart. Both men entered the room unannounced.

"Hi, Arik," Dr. Nguyen said. He was studying the summary of Arik's physiology on the wall above the bed. "How do you feel this morning?"

Arik had already cleared his workspace and brought up a large blank canvas on which he could type in letters large enough to be read anywhere in the room.

FINE.

"Still not talking?"

Arik was starting to talk again, but his speech was thick and slurred. He preferred to type, although *typing* wasn't quite the right word for it. His sentences appeared instantly on the wall rather than letter by letter, word by word, and they appeared in much less time than it would take to speak them.

STILL WORKING ON IT.

"Good. Keep practicing. Of course you know Priyanka."

Priyanka was a stocky and handsome Indian man in his early forties. He would occasionally come to visit when Arik was growing up. If Arik was around, Priyanka always asked him about what he was working on, and unlike other friends of his parents, genuinely seemed interested. Arik didn't know where Priyanka worked, which struck him as strange because everyone knew where everyone else worked in V1. How you contributed was an important part of your identity. Arik wasn't sure whether he never knew, or whether he was simply unable to recall. He clearly remembered other details, like the fact that Priyanka never stayed for dinner when he came over to visit, always leaving just before they sat down, waving to Arik from the door.

YES. HI, PRIYANKA.

"Hello, Arik."

"Arik, Priyanka has some things he needs to talk to you about this morning. Is that OK?"

YES.

"Good. Let me know if you need anything."

Dr. Nguyen left the room as abruptly and unceremoniously as he'd entered. Priyanka looked around for a place to sit. The only chair in the room was positioned so that he could see Arik's face but not read the wall. When Arik realized that Priyanka was trying to work out how to make the conversation feel as normal as possible, his workspace shifted to the wall to the right of the bed, thereby allowing it, in addition to Arik's face, to be easily visible from the chair. Priyanka smiled.

"Thank you."

Priyanka was holding a piece of silicon paper. It was partially folded in half, but Arik could see that there were several lines of handwritten text on it. Silicon paper consisted of two very thin sheets of plastic film with several billion tiny magnetically charged beads about a micrometer in diameter pressed between them. The beads were white on one side and black on the other. A magnetic pen was used to apply either a positive or negative charge, which caused either the black or white hemispheres to rotate into view depending on whether you wanted to write or erase.

"Yun tells me that you'll be ready to go home soon."

I HOPE SO.

"So do I. Have you had any trouble with the BCI?"

A LITTLE AT FIRST, BUT NOT ANYMORE.

"Good. That's an extremely rare talent you have."

ALL IT TAKES IS A LIFETIME OF PRACTICE.

Priyanka smiled. He glanced down at his notes, then refolded the paper. Arik could tell that he was ready to transition from pleasantries to the actual purpose of his visit, and he wondered why someone like Priyanka was suddenly allowed to visit when his own wife and best friend were still being kept away.

"Arik, before you can go home, I need to ask you some questions."

OK.

"Do you remember anything about the accident?"

NO.

"What's the last thing you do remember?"

MY MEMORY ISN'T LINEAR. IT'S MORE LIKE AN APPLE WITH WORMHOLES IN IT.

"Interesting. In that case, why don't you tell me what you *don't* remember?"

I DON'T REMEMBER MY ENVIRONMENT SUIT MALFUNCTIONING. AND I DON'T REMEMBER WHY I WAS OUTSIDE.

"But you remember going outside?"

PARTIALLY.

"Do you remember ever being outside before?"

NO, BUT I BELIEVE I HAVE BEEN OUTSIDE MANY TIMES.

"Why?"

BECAUSE I DON'T REMEMBER FEELING NERVOUS.

"Has anyone told you what you were doing outside?"

YES.

"What?"

I WAS DISPOSING OF AN EXPERIMENT.

"What was the experiment?"

I DON'T REMEMBER. I KNOW IT WAS RELATED TO MY INVESTIGATION INTO THE FEASIBILITY OF TERRAFORMING VENUS.

"Do you believe that terraforming Venus is possible?"

IT'S PROBABLY POSSIBLE, BUT NOT PRACTICAL.

"Explain that, please."

IT'S THEORETICALLY POSSIBLE TO REPLACE THE EXISTING VENUSIAN ATMOSPHERE WITH ONE THAT WOULD SUPPORT LIFE GIVEN THE PROPER EQUIPMENT AND ENOUGH TIME, BUT THERE'S CURRENTLY NO KNOWN PRACTICAL TECHNIQUE FOR DOING SO.

"But at one time you must have believed it was practical."

I DON'T REMEMBER. I CAN ONLY ASSUME I BELIEVED IT WAS WORTH INVESTIGATING.

"Why don't you believe that it's practical anymore?"

I READ THE RESULTS OF MY EXPERIMENTS.

"What do they indicate?"

GROWING GENETICALLY MODIFIED FLORA IN INDIGENOUS SOIL IS CURRENTLY THE ONLY PRACTICAL TECHNIQUE FOR TERRAFORMING VENUS. HOWEVER, THE VENUSIAN SOIL IS STERILE.

"Does it surprise you that the Venusian soil is sterile?"

NO. THAT'S WHAT I WOULD HAVE HYPOTHESIZED.

"Why would you have formed that hypothesis?"

WE KNOW THAT THE VENUSIAN ATMOSPHERE IS FAR TOO HARSH TO SUPPORT OR PERMIT ANY FORM OF LIFE. EVEN THE MOST ROBUST MICROBIAL LIFE AS WE UNDERSTAND IT CAN'T SURVIVE HERE.

Priyanka nodded his head. He seemed satisfied with Arik's answers. Arik hadn't yet put all the pieces together, but it was clear to him that Priyanka and several others were not happy about the fact that he had been outside. Arik wondered if there was something he should be trying to hide, and if there was more to his isolation than just his depressed immune system.

"Can you tell me what AP is, Arik?"

ARTIFICIAL PHOTOSYNTHESIS.

"What do you think of artificial photosynthesis?"

IT'S A DIFFICULT PROBLEM.

"Would you say that it is a challenge?"

YES.

"Do you believe it is a challenge worthy of your attention?"

YES.

"Do you believe that AP is possible?"

IT IS POSSIBLE. THE QUESTION IS WHETHER IT IS PRACTICAL.

"OK. Do you believe that it's practical?"

YES.

"Do you believe that AP is more important than terraforming?"

YES. I DON'T BELIEVE TERRAFORMING IS CURRENTLY PRACTICAL.

"Do you recall that your job at the Environment Department is to solve AP?"

YES.

"Do you feel like you're ready to return to work?"

YES.

"Good." Priyanka folded his piece of paper in half again and pushed it down into his breast pocket. "I have one more very important question for you, Arik. Can you explain to me *why* AP is so important?"

THE ENVIRONMENT DEPARTMENT IS ALREADY PRODUCING OXYGEN BEYOND ITS INTENDED CAPACITY. WE CURRENTLY CAN'T SUPPORT ANY MORE HUMAN LIFE ON VENUS.

"Why can't we just get tanks of compressed air from Earth?"

WE NEED TO REDUCE OUR DEPENDENCY ON EARTH AS MUCH AS POSSIBLE.

"That's right," Priyanka said. He pushed himself up out of his chair, then smiled. "Well, your memory seems perfectly fine to me. I will recommend that you return to work as soon as possible." He started to move toward the door but caught himself. "Oh, your father told me the news about Cadie. Congratulations." He watched Arik steadily. "I hope you're not concerned. Sometimes all we need to hasten a breakthrough in our work is for something to lend it a bit of urgency."

Arik's response did not appear. Priyanka looked at the wall for a moment, then back at Arik. Arik forced a smile, then did Priyanka the favor of snapping open the door.

CHAPTER SIX

THE HISTORY OF V1 PART 2
EARTH CRISIS

THE HISTORICAL RECORD KELLEY HAD compiled showed that the climate crisis on Earth eventually became known as the "Earth Crisis" in order to encompass the prodigious pollution and other environmental problems that had coevolved alongside climate change. Grassroots movements successfully penetrated most political institutions, but world leaders found themselves in impossible situations; just about every option available to them for addressing the Earth Crisis had serious repercussions on the world's economy. The age of skepticism had long passed—there was hardly anyone alive who didn't have firsthand experience with the hardships of living on a hopelessly polluted planet, and news organizations concerned themselves with little else—but it was nearly impossible for an elected official to pass laws and enforce the kinds of sanctions that could have dramatic and measurable effects. There were a few decades of "phased reductions" and "economic incentives" that had so many exemptions and loopholes that everyone knew they never had any real hope of delivering actual results.

But then two things happened that made managing the Earth Crisis both technologically and economically feasible. The first was nuclear fusion, the process of combining atomic particles as distinct from nuclear fission, the process of dividing them. Nuclear fusion occurs naturally in stars as gravitational forces become strong enough to fuse hydrogen atoms, and it also occurs unnaturally in thermonuclear weapons when the energy from a smaller fission bomb is used to ignite a much more massive fusion reaction.

Despite its association with nuclear warfare, fusion is a much safer process than fission. Fusion reactions require such precise conditions that they are inherently self-regulating; should anything at all go wrong, the process simply ceases with very little risk of a runaway reaction. Fusion also produces far less radioactive waste than fission, which means less reprocessing of spent fuel, and a lower security risk. But the trick with nuclear fusion is starting and maintaining a reaction in a controlled way that, over time, generates more energy than is required to maintain it. Artificially recreating conditions typically found only in the cores of stars is extremely resource-intensive, which means that until the fusion reaction is self-sustaining, there is actually a significant net loss of energy.

But once methods for safely and efficiently starting and maintaining reactions were perfected, nuclear fusion power plants began sprouting up like shopping malls all over the industrialized world. The process was then made millions of times more efficient by two discoveries: the first enabled nuclear waste to be reprocessed back into usable fuel, and the second was the discovery of a technique for capturing the energy released by a fusion reaction directly as opposed to using that energy to boil water in order to produce steam that was then used to turn turbines. Over the course of just a few decades, an incredible amount of cheap, pollution-free energy was available almost everywhere in the world.

As a perfect and timely companion to ubiquitous nuclear fusion power, the Nobel Prize–winning concept of "End of Life

Plans," or ELPs, was adopted by most of the industrialized world. ELPs were simply instructions included with absolutely everything bought or sold that explained what should be done with the item and its packaging in order to discard it. There were, of course, strict guidelines as to what constituted a valid ELP, and strict oversight of those guidelines. Legitimate ELPs included things like returning the item to the manufacturer where it could be refurbished, dropping the item off at a local ELP station that specialized in recycling its components, or, if the material were benign enough, the right colored bin to toss it into.

Consumer adherence to ELPs was also strictly enforced. Anyone caught violating an item's ELP faced fines or community service, and sometimes even very imaginative forms of public punishment involving bright green jumpsuits or yard signs with short shameful slogans. No item could be bought, sold, or imported without a valid and approved ELP, which meant that even countries that weren't particularly interested in saving the world needed to comply in order to have access to markets that did. Consumers started selecting products based on the attractiveness of their ELPs, which meant that as much thought and engineering had to go into disposing of a product as producing it. Products that weren't easily recyclable, reusable, returnable, renewable, compostable, convertible, or biodegradable languished on shelves beside their more eco-friendly counterparts. People wanted to feel as good about getting rid of something as they did about acquiring it.

It was initially feared that ELPs would ruin the already-fragile world economy. The theory was that raising costs associated with research and development would cause the prices of goods to increase beyond what the market could bear. In reality, however, ELPs ushered in an entirely new era of sustainable economic growth and prosperity. Even the sharpest and best-paid economists underestimated the guilt that the media had gradually installed in consumers for buying goods that were designed to exist in landfills for centuries but only function for anywhere from a few seconds up to maybe a year. It was true that prices rose, but temporarily; costs were more than offset by the dynamics of guilt-free consumption, and by manufacturers' ability to refurbish and resell end-of-lifed goods. Entirely new industries sprang up around ELP stations. Manufacturing costs gradually decreased as more recycled components were used and fewer raw materials had to be purchased and converted. Many manufacturers transitioned into what became known as re-manufacturers. The quality of products even increased so that their components could be reused in future versions. It was common for electronics manufacturers to build very fast processors for their devices but underclock them so that when they found their way back into their factories through their ELPs, the chips' constraints could simply be removed, and the entire device resold as the next generation, new and improved. ELPs allowed even the biggest and most powerful of multinational corporations to participate in sustainable and responsible manufacturing practices while still feeling like they were being suitably devious.

The costs associated with manufacturing, packaging, and shipping goods was further reduced by On-Demand Automated Manufacturing Plants. ODAMPs were initially described as being similar in concept to printers. A printer could produce any conceivable image no matter how complex, provided it had just a few basic colors and the correct instructions. Similarly, ODAMPs could produce, package, and ship thousands of different and even highly customized products given nothing but schematics, specifications, and the necessary raw materials.

ODAMPs were extremely simple in theory, but in practice, they constituted the most complex man-made systems ever conceived of and built. A typical ODAMP encompassed dozens of square kilometers of factory space filled with thousands of highly diversified robots and pieces of equipment along with hundreds of metric tons of raw materials. Once an ODAMP went online, the only subsequent interaction humans had with the factory was delivering new shipments of raw materials and picking up items ready to be shipped. Everything else was performed by highly adaptive, self-sufficient, self-organizing machines. The entire process of scheduling and coordinating the production of items was completely automated, including receiving and confirming orders, locating appropriate schematics and specifications, converting raw materials as needed, constructing individual components, and finally, assembling and packaging final products—all as quickly and efficiently as possible. ODAMPs even prepared shipping schedules and routing instructions before placing items on a loading dock to be picked up and hauled away.

Even the creators of ODAMPs had only a very dim notion of what actually went on inside the massive unlit electronic hives.

ODAMPs resulted in an almost unimaginable level of manufacturing efficiency. Just a few dozen ODAMPs manufactured over 90 percent of the products in the world, and not a single product was manufactured that wasn't needed. ODAMPs were eventually even able to perform diagnostics and repairs that human labor costs had previously made impractical, and over time, each ODAMP was upgraded so that it had the ability to accept almost anything as a raw material—even truckloads of end-of-lifed items. Everything manufactured had the potential to eventually become almost anything else through an ODAMP, and almost nothing was wasted. And, of course, the entire process was powered by nearly unlimited and completely pollution-free energy.

But even with the cessation of almost all greenhouse gas emissions and pollution, enough carbon dioxide and methane had already been released into the air and dissolved into the oceans that even the most optimistic predictions still showed Earth's mean temperature continuing to rise for hundreds of years. With unlimited clean energy, however, it became possible to split infrared-absorbing molecules in the atmosphere into their more benign constituents without actually creating more waste than you were converting. Clean Air Catalyst Machines were able to remove greenhouse gasses from the atmosphere at rates far faster than Mother Nature herself could have ever achieved, thereby clearing the way for far simpler and cheaper innovations like Ice Paper.

Ice Paper was invented by an undergraduate college student who figured out that the upward-facing surface area of all the cars in the world was almost exactly equal to the surface area of the Arctic and Antarctic polar ice caps, which had long since melted. Rather than writing an academic paper on the concept (which he was certain his professors would scoff at since they hadn't thought of it themselves), he dropped out of school and invented Ice Paper. Thanks to his girlfriend (who was studying political science before dropping out herself), Ice Paper was soon required by international law to cover every hood, roof, trailer, and trunk in the world, almost entirely replenishing the earth ability to reflect solar radiation back out into space in the span of only a few years. By associating radiation reflection with cars, concentrations of Ice Paper were inherently proportional to the amount of industrialization and urbanization in a given region, which actually made it even more effective and efficient than the polar ice caps could ever have been.

With a flourishing global economy and the cleanest, healthiest environment the world had seen since before the Industrial Revolution, the Earth Crisis was officially declared "averted," and it was time once again to turn humanity's attention toward exploration and outward expansion—or as the politicians never tired of repeating, to "get serious about space." The challenges of the previous 160 years had promoted an unprecedented level of global cooperation that carried over into the new space program and led directly to the formation of the Global Space Agency.

The GSA's headquarters were established at the precise juncture of China, Pakistan, and India in a region known as Aksai Chin. Logistically, the site made perfect sense because it was almost entirely uninhabited, received almost no precipitation to delay launches thanks to the ability of the Himalayan mountains to intercept moisture, and was an entirely flat desert of salt, which made it easy to build on (the extreme cold was a concern initially until the Russians convinced the Site Selection Committee that launching in subfreezing temperatures was not only safe, but exhilarating). Politically, the site was a symbol of the world's ability to put centuries-old disputes aside for the benefit of all of mankind.

The GSA needed to warm up a little before tackling the big missions, so they completed the moon base (which was never considered an actual colony because although it was constantly manned, there were no permanent settlers), repaired and upgraded the moon telescope, built and deployed the ISS II (which this time looked like a proper space station with segments that rotated to create centrifugal gravity and large windowed observation decks), and even completed several manned missions to Mars. With a success rate of 99 percent, with unprecedented public support, and with mankind riding the biggest wave of economic, scientific, and cultural prosperity in history, the human race had earned the right to expand into the rest of the solar system.

CHAPTER SEVEN

WATER PRESSURE

THE DAY BEFORE ARIK STARTED work at the Life Pod, he got an audio message from one of his former teachers. Her voice was characteristically elegant and assertive, but with an undertone of apprehension.

"Hello, Arik. Rosemary Grace here. I just heard about your assignment to the Life Pod. Congratulations. As much as I was hoping we'd get you, I knew that wasn't possible. All the best talent must go into solving the air problem right now, as you know. For now, that's our top priority.

"I know you're preoccupied with beginning your new career, but I want you to do something for me. I'd like you to stop by my office tomorrow morning on your way into work. I have a couple of things I'd like to discuss with you. It'll take only a few minutes. Consider it your final homework assignment. See you soon."

Rosemary worked for Arik's father in the Water Treatment Department. She was an environmental and hydraulic engineer by trade, but she taught Gen V about much more than just computational fluid mechanics, flow dynamics, and particle image velocimetry. Those were things that computers were good at, she told them. The next generation of scientists and engineers needed to get better at the things computers weren't good at: creativity, intuition, resourcefulness, and perhaps most importantly, curiosity. Half of each lesson was hard science, but the other half was not so much about learning anything in particular as it was about learning *how* to learn—how to think both critically and creatively in order to solve seemingly impossible problems. Her lessons were some of the most inspiring, engaging, and challenging material Arik had ever encountered.

Early on, she had taught them the real meaning of Occam's razor. Developed by an English logician in the fourteenth century, Occam's razor was usually understood to mean that all things being equal, the simplest solution is usually the correct one. In Rosemary's view, this was, ironically, an oversimplification of the principle, and not an accurate or even useful interpretation. Nothing was simple, she maintained, and there's certainly nothing about a simple solution that makes it inherently more valid than a complex one. In fact, in her experience, the more variables, subtleties, vagaries, and contingencies that a system took into account, the more useful and reliable and realistic it was. Our penchant for simplicity—our need to reduce everything to good or bad, black or white, on or off—could rarely be imposed on the universe, no matter how hard we tried. If something seemed simple, you probably just weren't looking at it hard enough or peeling away enough layers to see what's really beneath.

The real meaning of Occam's razor, Rosemary believed, was that explanations and solutions should be free from elements that have no real bearing on the system in question—that solving problems isn't so much about simplifying them as it is about properly and realistically reducing them to only what's relevant. And one of the best ways to reduce a problem to only what's relevant is to throw away most of your assumptions about it. Nothing has misled researchers and impeded scientific progress more throughout history than incorrect and inappropriate assumptions and preconceptions.

Rosemary's personal aphorism, which she tirelessly worked to instill in her students, was "question everything."

• • •

Rosemary's office was on the second floor of the Wet Pod, above the plant, at the top of an open metal staircase. The smell of the chemicals used in the water treatment process reminded Arik of his father; it was always in Darien's clothes and in his hair, and it made Arik think about when his father used to reach over him to help him with something in his workspace, or the smell of the breeze he made when he walked by. Most people considered the smell unpleasant, but it reminded Arik of home.

When the door opened, the chemical smell was overwhelmed by the aroma of fresh coffee, and Arik remembered that Rosemary always had a fresh pot brewing even though she preferred tea. She used it to cover up the smell of the chemicals (which reminded her of work, not home), and to keep a steady flow of her staff coming and going so she could keep up with what they were working on without having to hold formal meetings. She told her class once that meetings were not actually for communicating, but for fixing breakdowns in communication. In a well-run work environment, communication should be constant and efficient and organic, and formal meetings should almost never be necessary.

"Come on in, Arik," Rosemary said warmly. "Thank you for coming."

She was seated in front of her workspace with her hands around a cup of tea. It was difficult to guess how old Rosemary was because her apparent age varied dramatically depending on what she was doing. When she was focused on something, the lines around her eyes and mouth became much more prominent, and her hair seemed to be more wiry gray than blonde. But when Rosemary was passionate about something—when she was speaking and moving and smiling and gesturing—she assumed an extraordinary beauty and was every bit as youthful as Arik.

The walls of the office were currently transparent, providing a spectacular view of the entire water treatment facility. Below them were complex networks of pipes, valves, pumps, and narrow catwalks woven around still pools of pure blue water. Darien had shown Arik around the Wet Pod several times as Arik was growing up, and some of Rosemary's classes had been held in her office, so none of this was new to him. He was much more interested in the intricate model of an entire pod system on a table in the middle of the room.

"Am I here for one last class before starting my career?" Arik was helping himself to a closer look at the model, bending down and peering at it from several angles.

"In a way. Do you know what that is a model of?"

"No. It doesn't look like V1."

"It's not. It's V2. Or at least it's the current proposal."

"Is this to scale?"

"Yes. What do you see that's different from V1?"

"There's no greenhouse."

"Yes, that's the biggest difference. Anything else?"

As usual, Rosemary was not about to give anything away; as usual, Arik would have to figure it out for himself. "The water tower."

"Exactly. As you know, we use pumps to pressurize our water supply, but pumps use a lot of energy, and they're difficult to maintain. Since there are peaks and valleys in water demand, we have to use several different types of pumps so we can dynamically increase and scale back pressure as necessary. Worse than being inefficient, it's incredibly *inelegant*."

"So V2 is going to use a water tower instead?"

"That's what I'm proposing. Water towers use gravity to create all the pressure you need, regardless of demand. And you only need a single simple pump to refill it once a day from the clean water reservoir. It uses much less energy, and there's very little to maintain."

"Why doesn't V1 use a water tower?"

"There was no way to build one at the time. In truth, there still isn't, but I'll worry about that later. First, I have to prove that it's a good idea. What do you think?"

"I think it makes sense. The fewer moving parts, the better."

"Exactly. No truer words were ever spoken in the context of engineering."

"Why did you build a physical model?" Arik asked. "Why don't you just use computer models?"

"Ah, very good question, and precisely the reason I asked you to come. We do have computer models, but how would we know whether they were accurate without testing them against a physical model?"

"Why wouldn't they be accurate? This all seems pretty straightforward to me."

Rosemary frowned at the model. "I don't know why, but they aren't. Everything having to do with water storage and delivery is identical between the physical and computer models, and the physical model is perfectly to scale, yet the pressure sensors are showing higher levels of pressure than the computer models report."

"There must be a mistake in the physical model."

"Why the physical model? Why not the computer model?" Rosemary was staring at him intently.

"Because hydrostatic formulas are very well understood and proven, so they can't be wrong. And computer models are much easier to analyze, so it's much more likely that the error would be in the physical model."

"True, but on the other hand, the physical model has the advantage of being real, and using actual gravity. Real-life physics is difficult to argue with."

"I guess it doesn't really matter where the problem is," Arik said. "All that matters is that there's an inconsistency that needs to be understood."

"Now you're looking at it the right way. Assuming the error is in one place or the other is more likely to mislead you than to expedite a solution. Unfortunately, I've been looking at it for two days, and I can't figure it out."

Arik realized that he was not here for one last lesson, but that Rosemary—without a doubt, the most stimulating, engaging, and effective teacher he'd ever had—was actually asking for his help. "You want me to try?"

"Please. Not right now, of course, but whenever you have time. I'd give the software models to the Code Pod to analyze, but you know what that process is like. It would take them months to get around to it, and then fifteen minutes to decide there's nothing they can do."

"Don't bother with them," Arik said. "I'll do it for you. Just copy everything I need into my workspace."

"Thank you, Arik," Rosemary said. "I know you have to get going, but there's one more thing."

"Sure."

"I want to give you a little advice about working in the Life Pod."

"OK."

"You're going to be asked to solve some very difficult problems—problems that nobody else has had much luck with yet."

"I hope so."

Rosemary leaned closer, putting down her cup. Arik had the sense she was watching him carefully for his reaction to what she said next. "All I can tell you is to trust your instincts. The reason nobody has been able to solve these problems isn't because they aren't solvable. It's because nobody has figured out the *right way* to think about them. Do you know what Albert Einstein's definition of insanity was?"

"No."

"Doing the same thing over and over and expecting different results."

Arik nodded. He understood what she was telling him. She was alluding to everything she had taught Arik and Gen V about how to think—connecting her unconventional method of teaching with the need for Arik to think unconventionally in the real world. It wasn't his knowledge of software or botany or chemistry that would decide how successful he would ultimately be in the Life Pod; it was more important for him to focus on the things he didn't know. Sometimes knowledge can be a trap, Rosemary once said. It can just as easily obscure the truth as illuminate it.

"I understand."

"Good. Then I'll bet you can guess what my final piece of advice is."

"I think so," Arik said. "Question everything."

Rosemary smiled and nodded. The gesture was meant to be reassuring, but Arik knew her well enough to sense the trace of uneasiness.

CHAPTER EIGHT

THE EMERALD
EYE OF VENUS

ORIENTATION WAS HELD FOUR DAYS after Arik and Cadie started working in the Life Pod. The Career Committee still had two days of hearings left, but the director of the Environment Department had met her hiring quota and wasn't expecting any additional personnel.

Both Arik and Cadie spent their first four days in their labs. Their offices were next to each other, and when the polymeth wall that divided them wasn't fogged, they could see into each other's laboratories. Of course, this was an intentional arrangement; they needed their own spaces so that one might mix chemicals while the other debugged a piece of code, but they also needed to be able to easily collaborate. They could step into each other's offices as necessary, or they could project their workspaces on both sides of the common polymeth wall in order to share ideas. So far they hadn't spent much time together, but they knew that the professional relationship they had established while working on the ODSTAR project would soon be applied to solving the real-world problems of the Life Pod.

New employees were asked not to go into the dome until they had an official tour, so neither Arik nor Cadie had any official duties yet. Arik spent his time learning everything he could about botany, photosynthesis, and human respiration; Cadie, having a strong foundation in biology already, focused primarily on V1's life-support systems. They moved their workspace around the walls of their labs and alternated between standing and lounging as they read, watched video feeds, studied 3-D models, and solved puzzles designed to test their comprehension and reinforce concepts. On the afternoon of the fourth day, all the new employees received an incoming video message. Subha's face appeared in the corner of his workspace and very cheerfully told her new employees to take the rest of the day off, but to be back first thing in the morning for orientation. Playtime was over. The real work was about to begin.

The next day, Arik, Cadie, and the other six new employees stood as a group outside the entrance of the Environment Department. Although all but two of them had already started working and had even been assigned offices, this was their real initiation. There was a very palpable sense of anticipation and wonder among the group—even a sense of pride. Arik realized that this was the first time any of them would be seen as peers by the Founders; from today on, they would work side by side, solve the same problems, complain about the same mishaps, and share the same triumphs. He knew he would need to ask a lot of questions as he got acclimated to his work, but he also knew that it wouldn't be very long before his coworkers were coming to him.

The orientation was really about being given access to the dome. Although the small airlock that made up its entrance was not secured as far as Arik knew, only Life Pod employees were permitted inside. Arik guessed that no more than a hundred people had ever set foot inside the dome, and only a very small percentage of those had any kind of real understanding of what they were looking at.

The dome was the heart of V1. It was located at its very core, and its job was nothing less than to pump V1 full of life in the most efficient and intelligent manner possible.

Arik had initially resented the Career Committee's refusal to allow him to pursue the Earth elevator, but after only a few hours in his new laboratory, and only a few minutes gazing through the hazy transparent barrier between the Life Pod and the dome, he succumbed to the excitement of the novel and the unknown. He realized that it wasn't the Earth elevator itself that appealed to him so much as it was the challenge of the project, the opportunity to think creatively, and the promise of really making a difference. If working in the Life Pod could provide him with those things instead, he was prepared to fully commit himself.

Cadie stood beside Arik as they waited for orientation to begin. The tour was to be given by the director herself. Her name was Subhashini Ramasubramanain, but she liked to be called Subha. Subha was an easygoing woman with an uncommon enthusiasm for her work. She was married to Priyanka, and seemed roughly the same age, but she had a much younger disposition, which she partially expressed through her wardrobe. Everyone in V1 wore practical, lightweight, uniformly colored clothing made of nanofabrics that were compatible with V1's waterless ultraviolet sanitizing machines. Everyone, that was, except Subha. She was never seen without, at the very least, a long, colorful cotton skirt, if not a full-length silk sari. How she got her clothes clean, only she and Priyanka knew.

Today she was wearing a maroon floral skirt with a white synthetic top. She came out from inside the Life Pod to meet her new employees with a wide, welcoming smile, bright against her dark complexion.

"Good *mor*-ning," she sang. "Is everybody here?" She counted them off with her index finger. "Great! Let's get started!"

Everyone arranged themselves into a line and stepped through the door into the Life Pod entrance. Cadie was beside Arik, and Arik instinctively reached over and took her hand before thinking better of it and letting go. They settled for a furtive glace and a smile, instead. Subha was walking backward so she could face the group as they progressed through the tour.

"First of all, I want to welcome all of you to the Environment Department, and congratulate you on being chosen for such prestigious positions. All jobs in V1 are created equal, but I think we all know that some are created more equal than others."

The group liked that. Arik assumed that his peers were all hearing similar prepared remarks in a dozen other departments throughout V1 this week. There was a good-natured rivalry between pods, which sometimes manifested itself as cricket matches in the Play Pod when time permitted. Subha seemed to be ensuring that the tradition would be passed down.

"The Environment Department is divided into two primary sections: the labs and the dome. All of the labs are located on either side of this hallway with two supply rooms in the middle. Because of space limitations, your labs double as your offices, and unfortunately, some of you are being asked to share labs until we finish reconfiguring the space. We were hoping to have everything ready by the time you started, but the Infrastructure Department wasn't able to get it done in time, even under threat of having their oxygen rerouted."

The group was clearly relieved to find that their boss had a sense of humor. Arik looked over at Cadie and saw that she was smiling, absorbed in Subha's narrative. Arik liked Subha so far but decided that he would reserve judgment. In his experience, some of the most vindictive people he had ever known had at one time seemed like the friendliest. It was impossible to know right away whether someone was a genuinely warm person, or whether she was simply comfortable working both ends of the social spectrum. In his mind, Arik heard Rosemary's voice reminding him to question everything.

"Once you're assigned to specific projects, you'll have a better idea of what you need to research and who you'll be working with, so let's not worry about the labs right now. I think our time is much better spent this morning in the dome, don't you?"

Arik watched Cadie join the chorus of agreement, and couldn't help but smile himself. They were standing at the end of the hallway in front of the small polymeth air exchange chamber that made up the entrance to the dome. In a way, this moment symbolized the beginning of their adult lives.

"Excellent. The first thing you'll notice is that you have to go through an airlock in order to get into the dome. The airlock helps maintain the environment inside so that oxygen levels can be more accurately monitored and controlled. Everything is completely automatic, so you don't have to do anything but wait. We're going to go in two at a time, and when you get inside, please stand with the group and wait for everyone to come through." She pointed to one of the new recruits. "René, you come with me."

Subha entered the airlock first, and René followed. They stopped just inside, and the door closed behind them. Their hair moved and their clothing rippled as air was exchanged between the airlock and the dome. When the environment was stable, the door in front of them opened, and they stepped through to the other side. Arik saw René make a funny face as she looked around and sampled the air. Subha motioned for the next two to enter.

Since René had gone with Subha, there was an odd number in the group. Arik would have usually been the one to hang back and forgo a partner, but it seemed natural that he and Cadie should go through together. Arik had always wanted to take Cadie to the dome on a date, and had asked his father on a few occasions if it could be arranged, but they had never been given permission. So they did what all the other couples in Gen V did instead: immersed themselves in interactive 3-D environments, played table tennis in the Play Pod, and idly rode the maglev from pod to pod, howling through the tunnels, hands laced together on the hard plastic seats.

The door closed behind them, and as soon as Arik heard the hiss of the air valves and smelled the gas that was filling the air-lock, he panicked. His first thought was that something was malfunctioning and filling the chamber with some sort of exhaust. Rather than the cool pure smell he was expecting, the air was metallic and burnt, and he suddenly understood the face René had made. Arik and Cadie looked at other, each with a quizzical expression. When the door in front of them opened, Arik found that the atmosphere inside the dome had the same curious tinge, and that the rest of the group had become as perplexed as he was. Subha seemed to be savoring the moment. She was waiting to address it until everyone was inside.

"OK. Now, does anyone know what that smell is?"

"Fertilizer?" Jun guessed.

"No. The nutrient spray we use is odorless. Any other guesses?"

"Carbon dioxide?" René suggested.

"Carbon dioxide is also odorless."

Everyone was anxious to give Subha the correct answer, but there were no other ideas. Arik was forming a theory, but it was Cadie who put it together first.

"These plants aren't producing pure oxygen."

"Ah, very good, Cadie." Subha said. "What you're smelling is ozone, or O_3."

Subha continued walking backward down the hallway toward the heart of the dome. The walls around them were tall, but they were sloped and getting shorter as they progressed, opening up more and more of the dome, exposing the group to more sunlight and an increasingly strong breeze from the air circulation system.

Arik relaxed more and more as he adjusted to the smell of the air.

"The plants we grow here produce O_3, which allows us to yield fifty percent more oxygen than if they produced pure O_2. The ozone is also a critical component in our water treatment and filtration systems. Of course, ozone also happens to be toxic in quantities much more than about one part per million; however, in these conditions, it dissociates very rapidly and reforms into pure O_2. Although the air you're breathing isn't the least bit toxic, our noses are sensitive to quantities of ozone as little as one part per hundred million, which is about the quantity of ozone in here that hasn't been converted into oxygen yet. Fortunately, you get used to the smell pretty quickly. Believe it or not, it even starts smelling good."

By the time they had reached the center of the dome, there were no walls around them, and they stood in the largest open expanse any of them had ever experienced. A collective gasp arose among them. The greenhouse was a tremendous geodesic dome, far larger than what Arik was expecting—larger than what he would have guessed possible considering the limited machinery on Venus. The frame consisted of plastic pipes that interlocked to form thousands of polyhedral triangles, each with a thick translucent plastic panel inside. In the center of the dome was a pit with stairs leading down to a large, black, cylindrical tank. All around them were terraces rising up to meet the edges of the dome like bleachers in a stadium, each covered with perfectly spaced, perfectly formed, beautifully verdant ferns. They were only a few Earth days into Venus's 3,024-hour solar day so there was plenty of sunlight, though it was a thick, yellowish mustard color from passing through the dense Venusian atmosphere. Despite the haze, it was strong enough to cast shadows, and everyone but Subha squinted. This was the first time they had ever felt the sun on their skin, and Arik realized that this was probably the closest feeling to being outside that any of them would ever experience. The sense of amazement and wonder among them was palpable.

"Welcome," Subha said, spreading her arms and looking around her, "to the Emerald Eye of Venus."

The dome was sometimes poetically referred to as the Emerald Eye of Venus because of what it must look like from the sky. The atmosphere was too thick for satellites to get a true-color picture in the visual spectrum, but from just under the clouds, the geodesic dome, with its concentric green circles and large black tank in the center, must look eerily like a giant green eye staring up from the surface of the planet.

Subha gave them some time to experience the dome before she resumed the tour. The group had started to dissipate around the platform that encircled the black tank.

"Let's start with the dome itself, which is a geodesic structure two hundred meters in diameter containing over eight thousand panels." Subha said. Her tone was becoming more businesslike, less like a new friend and more like their new boss. She proceeded to give them the specs.

A dome had been chosen over a more standard quadrilateral design for several reasons. First, domes were the most efficient way to enclose space. Second, the strength of the structure was inherent in its design, which meant that it could easily withstand the pressure of the atmosphere, yet no material and space would be wasted on structural supports. Third, the aerodynamic quality of domes meant they could more easily resist wind and weather. Fourth, domes allowed the capture of more light than any other structure. With 126 Earth days of sunlight followed by 117 days of darkness, the colony needed to capture every last photon of sunlight. The final reason Subha gave for the dome was the simplest: they were surprisingly easy to build. All the materials had been fabricated on Earth, so all the colonists had to do was put them together.

"And domes have the wonderful quality of serving as their own scaffolding as they're being assembled, which means they can be built higher than any other structure without the use of a crane."

The group had reassembled in front of Subha while she spoke, with Cadie and Arik being the last to wander back. Several questions had occurred to Arik, but he felt they were premature. She clearly had more to say.

Subha pointed to the vegetation. "The plants we grow here are called tulsi ferns. They were genetically engineered to produce ozone rather than oxygen, to produce positively obscene quantities of it, and to produce it equally whether in light or darkness. That means as long as they get enough light while the sun is up, they'll keep producing ozone throughout the entire Venusian night."

"How many plants are there total?" Cadie asked. Arik smiled; he had been trying to calculate the number himself.

"Who wants to take a guess?"

"A hundred thousand," Arik said.

"Close. Roughly a hundred and *ten* thousand. If there were only a hundred thousand, you guys would never have been born."

There were narrow walkways that ascended the terraces at regular intervals, and Subha took a few steps up one to allow the group to get a closer look at the plants.

"All our plants are aeroponically grown, which means we don't use any soil whatsoever. The part you can see is called the canopy and must remain exposed in order to gather light for photosynthesis. Below the canopy, the root zone is entirely suspended, and every forty-two minutes, it's sprayed with an atomized nutrient solution. If you look carefully, you can see that the root trays are pentagonally shaped so that the atomized nutrient spray can ricochet at the correct angles to be distributed evenly."

Arik crouched down and could see that the canopies converged at narrow circular openings, presumably leading to the ferns' complex root systems below.

Subha sat on a stair to give the group time to examine the plants. Nobody attempted to touch them.

"Why aeroponics rather than hydroponics or geoponics?" René asked.

"A geoponic system would have been impossible," Subha said. "First of all, soil is heavy, and in the space business, weight is fuel, and fuel is money. You also have to have a way to move the soil once it's here, which takes a great deal of work and equipment, and you have to engineer a far stronger terracing system, which means even more materials and more weight.

"Aeroponic systems are not just easier and cheaper to transport—they're also much more efficient to maintain. Air can be circulated throughout an aeroponic system more efficiently and with less energy than a geoponic or hydroponic system, and nutrients can be delivered far more precisely. That means we need less of it, and it means less runoff to manage and process. You see that tank down there?" She pointed to the black cylinder in the center of the dome—the pupil in the emerald eye. "If we had to deliver nutrients to the roots indirectly by fertilizing soil, we would need a nutrient storage container at least four times that size."

Arik was as impressed as everyone else with what he was hearing. The complexity and the genius behind V1's life-support system was turning out to be far beyond what any of them had expected. Arik realized that this could very well be the most stimulating and unique experience of their entire lives thus far. He wondered what kinds of discoveries and breakthroughs and developments might one day challenge this moment.

"But most importantly," Subha continued, "the roots are more easily contained in an aeroponic system, which means if a pathogen were to be introduced, any affected plants could be quickly quarantined. That's why the plants aren't packed closer together. We could probably generate between twenty and thirty percent more oxygen if we reduced the space between plants, but if we allowed root-to-root contact, a single pathogen could wipe out our entire oxygen supply. That's also the primary concern with pure hydroponic systems. Pathogens travel very quickly through water. Although our system generates very small amounts of runoff, none of it is allowed to come into contact with any other root systems."

"I have a question," Arik said. His hand was raised and Subha turned and looked at him. He hesitated, suddenly worried that what he was about to ask might come across as smug or insulting—or worse, ignorant.

"What is it?"

"Why not just convert CO_2 directly into oxygen? Why use plants at all?"

"That's actually a very good question," Subha said. She stood up, smoothed out her skirt, and started down the walkway toward the center of the dome. "Why even have a greenhouse at all? Why not just use electrolysis to convert carbon dioxide directly into oxygen? Because it's actually significantly less practical than letting photosynthesis do the work for us. It takes a tremendous amount of energy to maintain the necessary environment to promote the conversion of large amounts of CO_2 into O_2, and even if we had unlimited energy, only about twenty percent of CO_2 becomes breathable oxygen. The rest becomes carbon monoxide, which would require still more energy to either safely vent or process again into even smaller amounts of O_2." She looked at Arik and smiled, emphasizing the irony in what she was about to say. "In other words, we could do it, but we prefer to use our energy for things like computing power rather than manufacturing air."

Subha was obviously alluding to the fact that Arik probably consumed more CPU cycles than anyone else in V1.

"Photosynthesis is also much safer," Subha continued. She began leading the group around to the far side of the nutrient tank. "Thanks to the dome, in the event of a total power loss, we would still have air. You see those two lockers?" She pointed out two tall metal boxes below the platform. "Those contain environment suits. If we were ever to lose power and the air circulation system stopped running, everyone could gather in areas with ducts directly connected to the dome, and we could send two people out to fix whatever broke."

This was obviously not a scenario the group had ever contemplated. They had all participated in oxygen lockdown drills, but the scenario Subha was describing was an even more desperate contingency plan. Arik realized they were all looking at the lockers with the same combination of awe and concern.

"But I'm glad you raised that point, Arik," Subha said. "Just because photosynthesis is more practical than electrolysis doesn't mean that a greenhouse is the best way to promote it. In fact, half of you will be researching an alternative to photosynthesis which we call AP, or *artificial* photosynthesis."

"Photosynthesis without the plant," Arik said.

"Exactly," Subha said, pointing at Arik. "How many of you know what stemstock is? I mean where it *actually* comes from?"

"It's meat synthesized from the stem cells of livestock," Cadie said.

"That's right. The Agriculture Department has perfected meat without the animal, and now we need to perfect photosynthesis without the plant. As much as I love our ferns, the day is coming when we're going to need more oxygen than they are able to provide us. Without more oxygen, V1 is as big as it's ever going to get, and it will always be vulnerable to things like pathogens and any number of other events that can unexpectedly destroy plant life."

"What about terraforming?" Arik said.

"Artificial photosynthesis could make terraforming Venus entirely possible," Subha said. "If AP is as efficient as we think it will be, it might be possible to build AP machines and disperse them across the surface of Venus to make the air breathable in anywhere from—oh, I don't know—maybe a few hundred to a few thousand years. Of course, that would be a huge amount of work, and it's likely to be extremely expensive, but it's probably possible."

"I mean by engineering a plant that will grow in Venusian soil," Arik said. "Then you could terraform the entire planet essentially for free."

Subha frowned at Arik.

"Arik, the Venusian soil, as you well know, is completely sterile. If you can engineer a fern that will grow in the soil of the least hospitable planet in the inner solar system, then you should have AP figured out by the end of the week."

The remark got the intended reaction from everyone but Cadie. Subha gave Arik a reconciliatory smile.

"Why don't we start with AP," she said, "and see what happens from there."

CHAPTER NINE

THE HISTORY OF V1 PART 3 THE COLONIZATION OF SPACE

IT WAS ALWAYS ASSUMED THAT the Global Space Agency would establish the first off-Earth colony on Mars. Mars was considered a relatively inviting planet. Somewhere around four billion years ago, the dynamics of the planet's molten core changed, which almost completely eliminated its magnetic field and allowed the sun to blast most of its atmosphere off into space. The remaining carbon dioxide, nitrogen, and argon gas now constitute less than 1 percent of the atmospheric density of Earth. But in the world of planetary exploration, having no atmosphere was considered better than having a harsh atmosphere. Since humans wouldn't have been able to breathe it anyway, the mission engineers viewed it as one less thing to have to worry about in the design of long-term structures. Having almost no atmosphere to trap in heat also meant that Mars had a relatively hospitable temperature range of –140 degrees Celsius to a balmy 20 degrees above zero in the summer.

But the biggest problem with Mars was gravity. Hundreds of experiments had proven that humans could live for extended periods in microgravity, but nobody knew what would happen to people spending an entire lifetime in an environment with only 38 percent of the gravitational force humans had known for their entire two hundred thousand years of existence. Preliminary studies suggested an extensive loss of bone and muscle density, and a weakened immune system—symptoms which were clearly incompatible with a great deal of dangerous physical work and very limited medical facilities.

Raising children on Mars was another major concern. The goal of Project Genesis was not to construct off-Earth outposts or temporary bases where personnel would be rotated in and out on a regular basis like they were on the moon. These colonies would eventually have to be able to replenish almost all their own resources, including themselves. Even though it was accepted that none of the original colonists would be able to return to Earth anytime soon, it was also accepted that someday people would freely travel back and forth. Going from Earth to Mars was fine, but there was serious doubt as to whether a child born and raised on Mars could ever adapt to Earth's much more formidable gravitational demands.

Various forms of artificial gravity were considered. Centrifugal force can create a feeling of gravity inside a structure that rotates with enough speed, and linear acceleration can easily generate a G or more of force for finite periods of time (unfortunately the laws of physics don't allow for indefinite acceleration), but designing permanent planetary habitats around these concepts was never very realistic. Of course, it was theoretically possible to transport enough mass from Earth or elsewhere in the solar system to actually increase gravity on Mars, but no one even bothered to seriously calculate how much mass was required, how long it would take, where it might come from, and how much energy it would take to move it.

Just when the entire project was in danger of being restructured into yet another semipermanent outpost as opposed to a true off-Earth colony, a frustrated French planetary scientist suddenly blurted out that they would have been much better off if they had just chosen Venus rather than Mars. The remark was made during the crestfallen adjournment of a six-hour meeting that had proven the impracticality of using diamagnetism to simulate a gravitational force against any organism much larger than a frog. The entire room was stunned. The answer had been right in front of them the entire time. Mars was simply the wrong planet. Venus, being almost 82 percent as massive as Earth, easily had enough gravity to make the risks of long-term health problems acceptable and manageable, probably even negligible. The incredible pressure of the atmosphere (ninety-two times as dense as Earth's) and the excessive amount of heat trapped by the large amounts of carbon dioxide and nitrogen were certainly obstacles, but unlike the gravitational problems of Mars, they were addressable. Designing and building habitable structures for Venus was much more like building submersibles for countering the pressure of the deep ocean rather than capsules for surviving the vacuum of space. Venusian atmospheric pressure is equivalent to an ocean depth of about one kilometer, which is trivial for deep-sea technology. There were already decades of research, knowledge, and technology relevant to living for long periods of time underwater. Habitable structures on Venus, the GSA realized, were as simple as communities of interconnected nuclear submarines with heat shields.

The meeting was immediately reconvened, and the entire sum of human knowledge pertaining to Venus was retrieved and arranged on the walls around them. By the time the meeting adjourned for the second time early the next morning, the mission objectives had been officially altered and ratified, and a landing site had even been selected. The northern highland region of Ishtar Terra had enough elevation to make the extreme temperatures and atmospheric pressure on Venus slightly easier to manage, and it received more than enough sunlight to make a greenhouse viable.

The management style of Project Genesis was as innovative and risky as the project itself. Rather than telling all the various teams that they had ten years to make living on Venus a reality (at which point all sense of urgency would instantly be lost since who can realistically plan for next month much less the next decade?), the project leaders tried something new. They told their teams that they had exactly one year to figure out how to put a hundred people on Venus with enough supplies to survive for six months. The next year they were told they had another year to figure out how to put two hundred people on Venus for twelve months. Every year, the criteria (and the resources available to the engineers) increased, and every year, each contract and position was reevaluated based on the feasibility of launching the mission that day. Ingenuity, productivity, and even job satisfaction soared, and where it didn't, appropriate adjustments were made. The result was very possibly the most technologically and intellectually impressive feat in human history: in just ten years, man was ready to colonize space.

The process of selecting the first colonists unofficially began the moment the GSA first started kicking around the idea of permanent settlements. Friends and relatives of GSA employees, and even several GSA employees themselves, submitted unsolicited resumes, references, essays, videos, letters of recommendation, and every other conceivable form of self-promotion and endorsement. But with ten years of lead time, the GSA decided to throw it all away and take a chance on a brand-new approach to selecting volunteers for the most dangerous and ambitious set of missions in human history. The problem with the traditional method of opening requisitions, then screening applicants through automated questionnaires, background checks, polygraphs, psychological evaluations, aptitude tests, medical examinations, genetic analyses, and various scare tactics, was that at the end of the process, you usually had a group of people who, in addition to being extremely intelligent and accomplished, were also unbelievably competitive, incapable of forgiving themselves for making even the most insignificant of mistakes, and just a touch insane for actually volunteering to do something so crazy. For short-term missions, such profiles were workable, but the GSA had serious reservations about putting these kinds of people together in a single confined and inescapable space for the rest of their lives.

So the task of selecting the initial thousand colonists and their one hundred alternates fell to the GSA's team of information architects and data miners, who temporarily became the most sophisticated recruiters in headhunting history. Just about every detail of everyone's life (grades, major accomplishments, medical history, employment history, financial history, criminal history, genetic makeup, physiological profile, sexual orientation, marital status, political affiliation, hobbies, and so on) was either directly available for analysis and cross-reference, or could be extrapolated using the right algorithms if you knew where and how to look—and assuming you had the proper authority. It only took four programmers three weeks to come up with a list of three thousand of the best qualified people in the world to represent the human race on another planet, leaving almost an entire decade to train and shape them into precisely what the GSA wanted them to be.

There were four initial phases of Project Genesis executed over the course of four consecutive launch windows. Venusian launch windows are about a year and a half apart and last about a month. During the first thirty days, a total of ten heavy Sagan and Vega rockets were launched. The first nine carried supplies and equipment, and the tenth carried the first twenty Venusian settlers to their new home planet. The next three phases consisted of an astonishing twenty launches each, with fifteen dedicated almost entirely to colonists and five reserved solely for massive amounts of equipment and supplies. At the end of the first four phases, which spanned a total of a little over six years, there were exactly one thousand humans living in Ishtar Terra Station One. Not a single life had been lost, and although there were plenty of emergencies and unforeseen events, hundreds of thousands of the smartest people in the history of the human race were on hand twenty-four hours a day to help solve them.

The job of the first twenty settlers was primarily to establish the site, get a few simple structures assembled, and organize equipment and supplies. With weeks to spare before the arrival of the next wave of settlers, they also found time for a little research in the form of recovering an early Russian probe that sent back some of the first images of the surface of Venus. The question on everyone's mind was whether any microbes from Earth had survived the harsh Venusian environment, but the probe turned out to be as lifeless and sterile as Venus itself. The technology, as obsolete as it was, was still awe-inspiring to the early Venusian settlers, and they kept its remains in the corner of a warehouse as a reminder of the progress and incredible will of the human race.

The second, third, and fourth phases of the project were about expansion and establishing critical systems like water purification and waste management. The third phase brought components for the construction of a massive aeroponic life-support system beneath one of the largest plastic geodesic domes ever built on Earth or anywhere else. There were huge tanks of compressed oxygen on every flight, but it was clear that the V1 colony would need to establish a self-sufficient environment if they were to expand and prosper on their own.

After the first four initial phases of Project Genesis, the amount of fresh supplies and new equipment gradually decreased. The colonists were able to synthesize plenty of food, purify water, and maintain a perfect environment. Everyone worked, and a more or less routine—albeit labor-intensive—existence had been firmly established.

The amount, quality, and flow of air throughout all of the individual pods in V1 was very carefully monitored, recorded, and controlled. Huge tanks of compressed oxygen could automatically be added as needed in the event of a level-zero oxygen lockdown, and redundant systems of pumps and valves were always ready to balance the atmospheric pressure. In the event of a catastrophic failure, there were over twenty-five thousand perchlorate "candles" distributed throughout V1, each one capable of producing enough oxygen for one human for one week once ignited and placed in a special reactor. As a backup plan, the GSA maintained three rockets on three different launch pads in three different parts of the world that could be launched in a matter of hours, all filled with nothing but emergency supplies. Two of the many satellites that orbited Venus were also capable of being remotely instructed to drop capsules of emergency supplies close enough to V1 to be easily retrieved via robotic rover, or with a short trek in an environment suit.

But the life-support monitoring systems weren't designed just for redundancy and reliability. They were also designed to constantly calculate how much air was being used, how quickly it was being recycled, and, most importantly, how many humans the system could support. When it first came online, the readings were in the negatives since all the air in the colony was coming from tanks and none of it was being recycled, but as the Environment Department started using aeroponically grown, genetically engineered ferns to recycle air, and as the valves of the oxygen reservoirs were gradually sealed, the numbers started climbing. At first they crept up slowly as the averages were thrown off by being in the negatives for so long, but it didn't take them long to hit their initial benchmark of one thousand. The predictions and calculations of the GSA's biologists and botanists and engineers had proven almost perfectly accurate.

Now the Environment Department needed to push the numbers past a thousand so that history could be made once again. They added additional aeroponic terraces until the massive greenhouse was actually slightly beyond its intended capacity, and they completely rewrote the airflow algorithms so that they increased or reduced oxygen levels throughout V1 in real time depending on where people actually were and the amount of oxygen they were consuming. Everyone watched the stubborn numbers gradually increase until they peaked at exactly one thousand one hundred. After six months of minor fluctuations in either direction, it was definitively determined and then officially declared by Kelley himself that V1 could support a hundred additional inhabitants.

That night, the conception of Gen V began.

CHAPTER TEN
HOMECOMING

BEFORE THE ACCIDENT, ARIK HAD always thought of people as being more or less static. Of course they were always changing, but the changes typically happened so gradually as to be almost imperceptible, like the erosion of a landscape. But also like a landscape, it was always possible for extreme and unanticipated events to occur that could transform a person instantly and almost beyond recognition.

Cadie looked perpetually tired. Her hair was longer than Arik remembered it, and she wore it pulled back into a simple ponytail. She wore her glasses all the time now, and her complexion was ruddy and lustrous. She didn't fit into any of her dresses anymore, and usually wore synthetic pants with an elastic waist and one of Arik's shirts.

Before the accident, Arik had worn his hair long like most of the males in V1, but it was now kept short enough that his incision could be easily examined. He seldom bothered to shave, and his face was often involuntarily contorted by the pain of his constant headaches. His muscles were atrophied, and the last time he was weighed, he was told that he had lost 13 percent of his body mass.

Cadie was getting bigger, swelling with life, and Arik was being reduced to a thin and brittle shell.

They had hardly spoken in the three days since Arik came home. Cadie hadn't been allowed to see Arik in the Medicine Department after her initial visit because of fear of infection, and until Arik's emotional and cognitive states were better understood, she was asked not to communicate with him via video link. Arik received several recorded messages from her, but they always felt awkward, and rather than bringing them closer together, they only seemed to emphasize the distance between them. He never responded.

The last three days had shown Arik a side of himself that disappointed him. He had always thought of himself as an objective and extremely effective problem solver. He was very good at detecting patterns, tracking down irregularities, getting at their root causes, and repairing them. There was no reason for him to assume that problems with his marriage would be any different. Arik and Cadie always knew they wouldn't be one of those couples that let problems between them fester. They would immediately address any issues that arose, bring them out into the open, and discuss them until they reached a mutually satisfactory conclusion. They felt bad for some of the Founders who they believed had unhappy marriages—couples who were not strong enough to be truthful and open with each other, and even worse, with themselves.

But Arik was discovering that relationships were very different from other parts of his life that were prone to unexpected anomalies. Software could be approached objectively because software itself was objective. Computers were uncaring and, for the most part, predictable, assuming you knew what you were doing. But relationships were made up of complex analog emotions rather than digital logical bits, variables that just led to more variables and unknowns rather than to well-defined constants.

Sometimes *true* evaluated to *false* in the context of human emotion, which meant relationships were not problems that could be worked through using conventional logic. The complexity of relationships had the potential to increase exponentially until the only sane way to approach them was through instinct and intuition rather than calculation.

Arik had tried several times to talk to Cadie about the baby, and he assumed that Cadie wanted to discuss it as well, but there was always something easier to talk about or to do. Arik had daily examinations and physical therapy, and he spent his evenings trying to catch up on work. Cadie was learning everything she could about fetal growth and development while putting in even more hours at the Life Pod. It was easy for them to put their work ahead of themselves because the most obvious and measurable problem that the baby represented was that the dome wasn't producing enough oxygen to safely support an additional human life. But that wasn't the problem that Arik wanted to discuss. Oxygen production was quantitative and constrained. It was a problem with known variables that could be identified, broken down into individual components, and ultimately solved. The problem that neither of them were prepared to address was the fact that there was no way the baby could have been Arik's.

CHAPTER ELEVEN

THE BIGGEST WEDDING
IN THE GALAXY

ARIK HAD PROPOSED TO CADIE several times before she finally said yes. Even at a young age, they all knew that they would grow up and intermarry, so proposals were frequent among the children. In fact, it was no accident that Gen V consisted of exactly fifty males and fifty females. The one-to-one ratio was predetermined; left to chance, the outcome was statistically more likely to be fifty-one males to forty-nine females, which all of the Founders agreed could one day lead to all sorts of unpleasantness.

Gender predetermination was a given, though several Founders proposed much more dramatic forms of genetic manipulation and intervention. What if a small percentage of the population couldn't find a suitable mate? Or decided to be celibate? Or was gay? The term "sexual symmetry" was soon coined and rapidly became a concern among those assigned to research the matter. Life on Venus was tenuous enough without having hormonally disgruntled teenagers among the general population.

But nobody could agree on exactly what should be done, or even what *could* be done. They felt confident that they could manipulate levels of various hormones associated with sexual desire and attraction, and even stop the special auxiliary olfactory sensor called the vomeronasal organ from regressing at the fetal stage, which, in theory, would make Gen V more susceptible than the average human to pheromones. But in truth, funding for human sexual research had been scarce enough over the years that nobody knew for certain what the results of such intervention would be. In the end, they decided that there was nothing evolution favored more than a good hardy immune system, which was already standard genetic procedure, so the rest would have to be left to chance.

Would-be parents were allowed to submit gender preferences. Arik had heard several times the story of Kelley personally guaranteeing parents one of their top two gender choices. The story also went that enough couples didn't have a preference that those who did got exactly what they wanted. Gen V was supposedly the most thoroughly researched, best planned, and most widely anticipated generation in the history of the human race.

Arik was sometimes skeptical about elements of Gen V's little creation myth. Although he had no proof, he suspected that certain couples did not want children at all, but assumed the responsibility for the overall good of the gene pool and advancement of the colony. He suspected that some children were conceived more out of duty than love.

Since everyone in Gen V had known one another essentially all their lives, Arik had no memory of meeting Cadie, but he did remember the first time he felt attracted to her. They were seven years old, and they were drinking hot sweetened soy in the Play Pod where they sometimes spent a couple of hours after school while waiting for their parents to pick them up on their way home from their shifts. The top layer of the soy was aerated with nitrous oxide to make the high-protein treat more of a novelty. Several of Arik's friends were experimenting with drinking from the backs of their mugs, which left white foamy beards on their chins. Unlike foam mustaches, foam beards were out of range of most of their tongues, leaving only their shirtsleeves for getting them off. Nobody wanted to waste precious soy foam, however, so while watching the other kids stretch and strain their tongues, Arik realized a more practical solution was to lick each other's chins. Arik and Cadie teamed up, but Cadie's father happened to walk in at precisely the moment Arik was fulfilling his part of the bargain. Although the two of them were yanked apart amid a flurry of commotion, Arik still managed to get a taste of her salty flesh beneath the sweet foam. He never forgot the sensation.

He proposed to her for the first time the next day. Her only answer was a coy and ambiguous smile, which Arik interpreted as the need to impress her and keep her as close to him as he could. He tried his best to get on her team when they played cricket, and to hide with her when they played ghost in the machine. If she had a problem with her workspace, he would solve it before a teacher could intervene. As they got older, they worked on projects together, ate with each other's parents, and participated in the V1 version of dating.

By graduation, everyone in Gen V had been paired up. The process was long and certainly not without its share of drama, but fears of incompatibility, alternative lifestyles, and accidental death proved unfounded. Most couples had been together since their early teens and had plenty of time to develop strong friendships as well as romantic relationships. As the number of commitments increased, those remaining tended to come together out of necessity. There were certainly fears that a hundred healthy young adults confined to such a small area would eventually lead to some level of mingling and indiscretion, but none of the couples believed that it could happen to them.

The Infrastructure Department used any spare time they had over the years to configure fifty additional double-occupancy home pods. V1 was not a religious environment, and therefore its citizens were not governed by traditional Puritan morality, but when it came to relationships, there were two rules that were considered gospel: first, you had to be married to move into one of the new home pods; and second, you *always* used birth control.

Arik proposed to Cadie again thirteen years after his first proposal. They were in her parents' home pod during a break from their work at the Environment Department. Arik worried that Cadie would be dismissive yet again, but they had reached a point in their lives where marriage was finally realistic, and she surprised him by immediately accepting. They knew from watching old videos from Earth that this was supposed to be an emotional moment, and they were both certainly happy, but there was none of the crying or general commotion of a pivotal and ecstatic milestone. That night, while lying awake in bed, Arik realized that the typical reaction to marriage on Earth was not so much a celebration of a union as it was relief at the avoidance of solitude and loneliness—a fear that seldom occurred to anyone in Gen V.

Rings weren't expected on V1, and neither were weddings, necessarily. Kelley had the authority to marry, but Arik didn't have access to him, so in an attempt to bring his mother further into his life, he asked her for help in making the arrangements. He remembered the long moment when she looked over at his father, and Arik was certain she was going to delegate the responsibility to Darien; however, she eventually smiled and agreed.

Apparently, Arik and Cadie weren't the only couple putting in requests for Kelley's time, and it was decided in the interest of efficiency that Kelley would marry multiple couples simultaneously. Once the couples who weren't yet engaged discovered that their friends would soon be moving out of their parents' pods and into pods of their own, they hastily proposed as well. Kelley then proclaimed that all the marriages would take place at once in what would be, as far as anyone knew, the biggest wedding in the galaxy.

The couples were allowed to move into their new home pods the day before the wedding, since saying good night to your new spouse after the reception and going home with your parents would be unbearably anticlimactic. All fifty couples were able to move in a single day, since moving in V1 basically consisted of carrying a couple of cases on the maglev from one home pod to another. Most of what people owned was clothing, a small amount of equipment, and their data stored in the central solid quantum storage grid. Since the doorways in V1 were too small to cram most pieces of furniture through, all the new home pods came fully furnished.

Arik and Cadie's new pod was almost identical to the pods they grew up in, but it had four rooms rather than three. The largest room combined the kitchen, eating space, and a small sitting area into a single room. There was also a small bedroom, a lab, and a spare room that, for the time being, would probably be used as a second office, but could be converted into a baby's room once the time had come.

Arik and Cam were hoping to get pods in the same section, but they ended up being almost as far apart as they could get. The four-room pods were in Section R, and Cam and Zaire were assigned a smaller pod in Section C since no Wrench Pod employees qualified for home labs. Cadie and Zaire were friends, but Arik knew that Cadie would miss Cam's casual company more than Zaire's. Cadie and Zaire's friendship was based more on the fact that Arik and Cam were best friends than on any type of real connection with each other, or even any common interests.

Cadie and Cam didn't share much in common either, but they had always had an uncommonly open and effortless relationship. Arik knew that Cam was probably Cadie's best friend as well as his.

The wedding was the next evening, and the Venera Auditorium was completely full. The wall lights were down, and the polymeth above the stage showed a panoramic view of a white birch forest with luminous green leaves in columns of sunshine. Music wasn't a big priority in V1, so someone made a simple and obvious choice that even Arik recognized as a movement from Vivaldi's Four Seasons.

The brides wore simple white synthetic dresses and carried long tulsi fern stems. They were escorted one at a time down the aisle and up to the stage by their fathers, who kissed their cheeks and then took their reserved seats next to their wives in the front of the auditorium along with the grooms' parents. Arik was standing in line on the stage, along with the forty-nine other grooms, jostling one another and leaning forward to see friends farther down the line. They wore dark outfits with collars, and held their hands clasped behind their backs in order to keep them out of their pockets.

When the last father exited the stage, all the brides and grooms stood facing each other in parallel lines. Despite Arik's theories about Gen V experiencing more muted emotions around marriage than couples on Earth, when he looked at the girl who was about to become his wife, he felt an unexpected upwelling of joy, love, and pride. What surprised him most about the experience was the sudden compulsion to keep Cadie safe, although from what, he had no idea.

The music faded and Kelley stepped out onto the stage. He stood at the leftmost end of the group facing the audience and delivered an uncharacteristically short speech. He couldn't believe that just six months ago, he stood up there and watched Gen V graduate, wishing them well in their new careers. In another six months, he was sure they would all be back here again while these talented young men and women presented their findings on accelerated stemstock growth, more efficient forms of nuclear fusion, and, of course, artificial photosynthesis. But today he was there to wish them well in an endeavor equally important to their work: marriage.

The ceremony was also short and characteristically secular. Kelley described marriage as a practical contract, a partnership in which both parties were equal beneficiaries, a collaboration resulting in achievements that could not have been otherwise possible. Marriage was not the combination of two entities into one; instead, it represented the creation of a third entity whose sole purpose was to soothe and inspire the two individuals.

Arik and Cadie recited their vows to each other along with everyone else. They promised to support each other in all their endeavors, to promote all aspects of each other's development, and to never yield to selfishness. Kelley then pronounced them legally married, and the two lines came together amid a roar of applause. Arik couldn't remember ever embracing another girl apart from the casual gesture of greeting or congratulations, but he felt as though he were holding and smelling and experiencing Cadie for the first time. Even as he saw those around him separate and wave to the audience or begin to exit the stage, he clung to the moment and did not let her go.

The wall lights changed and the ceremony led immediately into the reception. Boxed meals were carried in along with V1's modest but effective supply of alcohol. The stage was used for dancing (which Arik and Cadie avoided) and part of the center section of seats was removed and replaced with several small tables. The focus of the gathering was initially on congratulating and celebrating the young couples, but the event soon became a much-needed break from the general stresses of the V1 routine. The party spread throughout the auditorium, then out the door in the back. As the night progressed, the aisles became lined with forgotten punch cups and plates, and someone even left a tall half-full mug balanced on the remains of the Venera probe in the back corner. Patches of seats were gradually filled by the usual V1 cliques who were too tired or intoxicated to stand, and a few people had even shuffled their way to the center of a row of seats and fallen asleep. Arik and Cadie sat in the aisle along with Cam, Zaire, René, and Syed, and both Arik's and Cadie's parents sat at a table in the back corner. When everyone's cup was topped off with the last of the evening's punch, Kelley climbed up on stage.

"Everyone, can I have your attention one more time this evening?" He paused to give the room time to get settled. His eyes were heavy and tired, and he blinked as he tried to focus on the room in front of him. "First of all, I've been asked to convey to the brides and grooms the best wishes of everyone on Earth, and in particular, the GSA. I believe the exact message they sent was 'Congratulations on setting a new galactic record, and please remember to take precautions.'"

There was still enough life left in the party to raise a good laugh. Someone shouted, "Hear! Hear!" and everyone with a cup drank.

"But I'd also like to raise a special toast to two people who mean a lot to me. Arik and Cadie, where are you? There they are. Get up here, you two."

Arik had been afraid that he and Cadie would be singled out, but had thought the evening was close enough to being over that they were safe. He looked at Cadie and rolled his eyes. They both had to be pushed to their feet and sent off toward the stage.

"These two kids have been together nearly their entire lives," Kelley said. "They played together as children, grew up together, and as they got older, they worked together to accomplish things that nobody even dreamed were possible." He waited for them to finish crossing the stage, then put an arm around each of them. Arik could see Kelley's cup in the corner of his vision, and he could smell Kelley's breath mixed with his cologne. "You two are the pride of V1, did you know that? You're a symbol of all that's right with humanity."

Arik humored Kelley with a forced smile. Kelley stepped back and brought the couple together in front of him. He raised his cup and everyone remaining in the room drank to the pride of V1, their symbols of the future, a perfect and indivisible union.

CHAPTER TWELVE

EASTER EGG

ALTHOUGH ARIK WAS HOME FROM the Doc Pod, he still had to go in several times a week for physical therapy. He was going into the Life Pod only a few days a week now, partially because of headaches, partially because of Cadie. When they were both at work at the same time, they kept the polymeth wall between their offices opaque, and they made it a point to check to see if the other one was in the dome before going in themselves. If Arik was there during lunch, he usually brought Cadie a boxed meal, but after she thanked him, he carried his own back to his office and ate alone.

Arik swallowed two pain pills, then dimmed the wall lights in his home office to ease the stress on his eyes. He brought his workspace up on the wall and immediately noticed the string of characters in the lower right-hand corner of the polymeth:

2519658000000 922.76 40.002 DELTA

His initial thought was that nothing was going to boot because of an unrecoverable error in the shell program, but when his workspace appeared just as he'd left it the night before, he assumed Fai's team was just doing some debugging on the live system. V1CC (the V1 Computing Cloud) was usually capable of debugging itself either proactively by using idle CPU cycles to look for potential errors in byte code, or in real time by verifying

processor instructions as they were being executed. But sometimes humans were just smart enough to introduce bugs that
even computers couldn't catch, which meant they had be tracked
down manually.

Most software engineers resented having to manually debug
code. It was considered a waste of their time, a task that was
beneath senior engineers and architects, which meant that it
was usually delegated to those with less seniority. But Arik actually enjoyed debugging. He found the process stimulating, even
rewarding. Most errors were predictable and relatively easy to
fix, but occasionally an anomaly was so complex and subtle and
elegant that tracking it down and holding it all in your head at
once actually pushed you to the edges of your comprehension.
Sometimes fully and completely grasping both a problem and its
solution simultaneously felt like stopping time.

To Arik, these moments were euphoric.

The message remained in the corner of his workspace for
the next several hours, and Arik became increasingly curious. It
wasn't uncommon to see diagnostic output for a few seconds or
maybe even a few minutes while someone tried to track down a
problem with the live system, but he'd never seen something like
this remain visible for an entire day. He was thinking of contact-
ing someone in the Code Pod when he got a video message from
his father asking him if he had time to look into what he called
the "anomalous string" that was appearing in the corner of
everyone's workspace. Darien seemed to be in a hurry, and sent
off the message without any additional information or details.
Arik looked at the time and realized that Cadie would be home
from work within the hour. He knew that they would have to
discuss the baby very soon, but now that he had a new problem
that needed solving, it wouldn't have to be tonight.

Arik wondered why the request to debug the problem had come from his father. Darien was a chemical and structural engineer. He headed up the Wet Pod and had designed several of the buildings in V1. Like all engineers, he knew computers well, but he didn't have any obvious stake in bugs in the shell program. He was good friends with Fai, however, which suggested to Arik that Fai had probably asked Darien for his son's help. Fai would have been too proud to ask Arik for help directly, and Arik imagined that the circuitous request through his father was still presented more as the Technology Department simply not having the time or resources to be distracted by such a trivial issue. But if the request did, in fact, originate from Fai, that meant the message was not simply diagnostic output, but probably a series of error codes that were unusual enough that nobody in the Code Pod had any idea what they meant.

Arik stood up in front of the polymeth wall and stretched while bringing up the source code for the shell program. He had been taking pain medication all day, and he needed to stand and move around the room in order to clear his head and stay focused.

Before he even had a chance to begin his debugging ritual, he recognized the first number in the error code, 2519658000000, as a date. Since computers weren't inherently able to distinguish one absolute date from another, they used relative dates expressed as some unit of time since a known epoch. V1CC inherited the ancient convention of expressing moments in time as the number of milliseconds since midnight on January 1, 1970. Since numbers like 2.5 quadrillion didn't come up very often in day-to-day computing tasks, when they did, it was usually safe to assume that they were machine-readable dates. And since the last six digits were all zeros, Arik could even tell that the number probably pointed either to exactly noon, or exactly midnight.

The date was most likely what programmers referred to as a "time stamp." Error codes almost always came with time stamps so whoever was debugging the problem could figure out exactly how long ago it happened, or could try to recreate the conditions that led to the problem. But when Arik did the math of subtracting the error code's time stamp from a time stamp representing the current time, he was surprised to find that the result was a negative number. The computer wasn't reporting a problem that occurred in the past; it was predicting an error 2.75 days in the future.

Although computer models were used to predict the probability of errors and failures all the time, as far as Arik knew, V1CC was not programmed to perform predictive diagnostics on itself. It was far more likely that the computer's clock had wandered prior to printing out the message, or was even wandering now. As powerful as computers were, left to their own devices, they were astonishingly lousy timekeepers. In order to keep their internal clocks accurate, they needed frequent calibration. Every ninety minutes, V1CC received a signal from a satellite, passing overhead, which contained one of the most accurate clocks ever built. The clock used twelve lasers to monitor the optical light emitted by the electrons in a single atom of ytterbium. Counting the tiny pulses of light allowed the clock to break a second down into almost a quadrillion parts. By the time the sun burned through most of its hydrogen gas and expanded to the point that all life in the solar system was destroyed, the ytterbium clock would have likely strayed less than one second. Of course, for V1CC to benefit from the accuracy of their microgravitational optical atomic clock, it would have to successfully receive the time calibration signal.

Arik instinctively checked his watch, which consisted of two separate dials: a digital module that calibrated with V1CC, and an analog mechanical movement that used a steel spring, rotor, gear train, escapement, and about two hundred additional parts to keep time to within about a second a day without relying on any external power source or time calibration signal whatsoever. Although mechanical watch movements were mostly favored by obsessive and anachronistic hobbyists, several of the computer scientists in V1 found them useful for keeping tabs on V1CC. There was no way a mechanical watch could detect a fraction of a second drift in V1CC's timekeeping, but it could detect a loss or gain of time adding up to a couple of minutes or more. When things like the life-support system relied on the computer maintaining almost perfect time, and the computer relied on an atomic clock orbiting twelve thousand kilometers above the surface of the planet, it seemed like a good idea to have some kind of an isolated analog backup.

But both times on Arik's watch agreed to within a few seconds, and a quick review of the logs showed that V1CC had missed only a handful of time calibrations in Arik's entire lifetime, the last one being over four and a half years ago. Whatever the time stamp meant, it was probably accurate.

Arik ran the shell program inside another program that could trace the rendering of each pixel back to the exact line of code that initiated the drawing instruction. He drew a rectangular debug region around the message in the lower right-hand corner of his workspace, and restarted the shell. He found that the message was being rendered by a little over a hundred lines of code interspersed throughout the shell's source, nestled in among other similar lines of rendering code with such apparent randomness that it had to have been done intentionally. Each component of the message was calculated using a long and complex equation. Some of the variables in the equations were even random numbers, yet each formula was orchestrated in such a way as to somehow compensate, always yielding the exact same result.

Now that Arik was sure that the message was intentionally injected into the shell program, he believed it had to be an attempt to communicate with someone inside V1—very possibly him. He looked at the second and third numbers again, and now that he had a fresh perspective, he recognized them instantly. They were radio frequencies. The first frequency, 922.76 MHz, was what the Earth Radio Pod used to communicate with the satellites that relayed signals to and from Earth, and 40.002 MHz was the frequency that V1 used to communicate with the ERP. The ERP was isolated from V1 so that in the event of a catastrophic accident, it might still remain functional. It was a small structure, large enough for only one or two people, and it was located a full kilometer south of V1 where it was well out of range of fires or shrapnel should the unthinkable occur. It had its own computer system, power supply, and miniature life-support system based on tanks of compressed air. The only connection between V1 and the ERP was the 40.002 MHz radio link.

Two radio frequencies and a date three days in the future suggested to Arik that the message wasn't so much a message in and of itself as it was instructions on where and when to find the real message. The problem was that Arik wasn't able to listen in on either of those two frequencies. All communications to and from Earth were highly secured using encryption algorithms that Arik would be hard-pressed to break anytime in the next decade, even with a multicore electron computer. That, Arik believed, was what explained the word *DELTA*. In the context of radio communication, "delta" was usually used in place of the letter D; however, an alternative interpretation—the variation of a variable or function, or the difference between two values—seemed to make much more sense. The difference between the two encrypted frequencies was 882.758 MHz—a frequency which, as far as Arik knew, wasn't being used for anything, and which he should be able to easily tune in to using the V1 frequency scanner.

By this time, Arik was simultaneously disturbed and intrigued by the fact that he was almost positive the message was intended for him. He was also fairly certain that it was either a trick being played on him by a friend of his in the Code Pod, or possibly a test arranged by Dr. Nguyen or Priyanka to make sure Arik was still up to the task of solving AP. He checked the source control system's logs to see who was responsible for the changes to the shell program, and was astounded to find that all of the revisions had been attributed to him.

This was almost certainly not a joke. Embedding "Easter eggs" in code for fun and covering your tracks was one thing, but attributing changes to another user was much more difficult, and in the case of Arik's account, very nearly impossible for anyone except maybe Fai himself. Not only did Arik use the standard DNA identification protocol, but he was probably the only one in V1 who combined biometric identification with gesture identification. Gesture identification required that unique shapes or patterns be drawn in order to verify someone's identity. Even if someone had figured out how to spoof his biometric signature, his gesture ID was complex enough that it couldn't be guessed, and since he almost always used his BCI to draw it, it was unlikely that someone could have covertly recorded it, or deduced it from marks or prints left on a piece of polymeth.

The likelihood that Arik's account had been compromised was extremely low.

It was far more likely that Arik's memory of hiding the Easter egg had been destroyed either by the accident or in the surgery afterward, and that the message was an attempt to pass along information to himself in the future. The theory made perfect sense except for one thing: it implied that he had somehow been able to predict the accident.

CHAPTER THIRTEEN
DIRT

AFTER ARIK AND CAM BEGAN their careers, they very rarely saw each other. They both had so much to learn in their respective fields that neither of them had much time for anything outside work. What little time and energy they had left at the end of the workday usually went into their marriages rather than their friendships. All four of them had managed to get together twice for dinner and a little four-handed chess, but both evenings ended prematurely: one night, Cam kept nodding off in his chair and drooling down the front of his shirt, and the other, Cadie fell into a deep sleep on a convertible futon between turns and had to be carried into the bedroom. She woke up the next morning asking who was ready for dessert.

So Arik and Cam decided that they would get together occasionally during the day. Although they wouldn't be able to spend much time away from work, at least they could spend that time talking rather than trying to stay awake. But lunch proved much trickier to coordinate than dinner. Between emergencies, midday meetings, having to eat with senior colleagues, and simply feeling too overwhelmed to get away, they found that their schedules never aligned. Although Cam was as overworked as anyone in V1, it was usually Arik who sent the terse last-minute cancellation message that Cam had learned to check for on the nearest piece of polymeth before leaving the Wrench Pod and boarding the maglev. Each time a lunch date ended before it even started, Cam responded with a shrug and a "don't worry about it" that made Arik feel even worse.

The fourth time Arik canceled, he sent Cam a long and detailed apology. "Cam, I'm really sorry for the short notice, but I'm going to have to cancel again. I know it seems like I'm taking our friendship for granted, but I swear, I'm not. I'm just under a lot of pressure to make some kind of progress." He checked behind him before continuing. "Subha's practically stalking me and I've barely made any progress at all. I know I need to work on my priorities, and I will, but I really need to make some kind of a breakthrough." He looked away from the camera and shook his head. "I don't know—I'm starting to feel like AP is going to be my life's work rather than just my first assignment. This isn't how I pictured my career. Anyway, I'm sorry. Again." Cam later joked that they could have probably had lunch in the time it took Arik to write the apology. But Cam's immediate response was just a single line that Arik never forgot:

"Let's be the only two people in V1 who never have to say they're sorry."

It was Cam who then came up with the idea of spontaneous scheduling. Rather than the futile exercise of trying to anticipate a day on which they would both be free only to have to repeatedly cancel when something unexpected came up, the assumption would always be that they were both too busy. If one of them discovered that they were able to get away, they would send the other a message by 1145 hours. There was no need to respond if you couldn't make it, and no need to apologize or justify yourself. Just try again another time.

The system worked. They had each sent a couple of unacknowledged messages, and neither felt guilty. And then on a day when Subha didn't come in and there was the light and carefree atmosphere of a holiday around the Life Pod—a day when Arik and Cadie spent the entire morning together in Cadie's lab— Arik went into his office to send Cam a message only to find that Cam had already sent one to him.

"I'm free. You?"

For some reason, it was always assumed that if their schedules ever aligned, Cam would come to the Life Pod and they would eat there. But Cam had seen the Life Pod before and had even gotten a rare personal tour of the dome. Nobody ever told Arik that he wasn't allowed to show people around, so he felt reasonably comfortable pleading ignorance if it turned out to be against department policy. Fortunately, nobody seemed to mind, though it probably didn't hurt that he had conducted the tour at 2300 hours, long after all of Arik's colleagues (including Subha) had gone home. All the automatic lighting in V1 had faded in accordance with sunset in Aksai Chin (coordinating day and night between V1 and the GSA's headquarters meant more sleep for everyone), and Cam was expecting the Life Pod to be dark. But there were still hundreds of hours of daylight remaining in the Venusian solar day, so the mustard-yellow sunshine filled the dome, penetrated the polymeth airlock, and lit up almost the entire Life Pod. Even the hallway was bright enough that they had to squint and shield their eyes as they walked toward the dome. With no windows in V1, it was almost impossible to imagine that the sun did not rise and set with the rhythms of the human race.

Arik replied to Cam's message:

"I'll come there. Leaving now."

• • •

When Arik stepped off the maglev in front of the Infrastructure Department, Cam was waiting for him on the platform.

"Welcome to the Wrench Pod," he said. Although the two of them had known each other their entire lives, it seemed appropriate to shake hands. Cam was grinning, clearly excited about showing Arik something he had never seen before, and maybe even teaching his friend a thing or two. Arik had been past the entrance to the Wrench Pod hundreds of times on the maglev, but he'd never had the opportunity to go inside.

"Sorry I'm a few months late."

"No worries. Stemstock never spoils. Cadie couldn't come?"

"I thought we'd leave the wives behind today."

"Good. Zaire has inventory duty so we probably couldn't find her even if we tried."

The entrance to the Wrench Pod was just off the maglev platform. It was a gaping archway designed to make it easy to move large pieces of equipment from the workshop to the maglev, then on to wherever it needed to be installed. This might have made sense during the early years of construction, but at this point, they'd built so many narrow passageways and installed so many prefabricated doors that they now had to build almost everything in small individual components and assemble them in place.

"When does the tour start?"

"Let's do it before lunch to give the break room time to empty out."

The Wrench Pod was much bigger and busier than Arik expected. There were probably over a hundred people bent over various workbench configurations using every form of saw, electron laser, press, and pneumatic tool against sheets of steel, slabs of plastic, and cylindrical pieces of ductwork. There were sheets of polymeth embedded vertically in tracks in the floor, bright and alive with rotating diagrams and schematics. Arik looked up and saw a complex network of catwalks overhead that provided access to pulley systems and motorized lifts. Cam led Arik along the perimeter of the room where they wouldn't be in the way. He had to raise his voice to be heard above the noise.

"The Wrench Pod is divided up into three main sections. This is the shop where most of the action happens. There's also the warehouse where Zaire probably is right now and the dock where I usually work."

"What do they have you doing these days?"

"Still repairing rovers. But everyone is required to specialize in at least two areas, so I'm also learning welding."

"Welding? What's to learn? Don't you just melt two things together?"

Arik didn't know anything about welding, but he knew enough about soldering to know that welding was probably surprisingly complicated and intricate.

"It's about as easy as growing a fern," Cam said. Even best friends weren't immune to the rivalry between pods. "Actually, I've come to think of welding as the ultimate craft. The concept is as simple as it gets: you want to take two things and join them into one. But to do it right, you have to know chemistry, physics, a little engineering, and you have to have very good dexterity. Besides, because of you, we have to use all the most difficult welding techniques."

"Me?"

"We're not allowed to do oxyacetylene welding since it burns too much oxygen. So because you guys can't keep up with demand, I have to learn resistance, ultrasonic, and plasma welding."

"Now do you see why I never leave work? Everywhere I go people complain there isn't enough oxygen. If you want more oxygen, go live on Earth."

"But then I wouldn't be the 'Pinnacle of Human Achievement' anymore, would I?"

The opening into the warehouse was another massive archway. They entered from the edge and ducked beneath the slope. It was much quieter once they got a few meters inside, and it was much darker because of the sheer immensity of the room, and the massive racks that prevented a large percentage of the light from reaching the floor.

"The Public Pod was the first warehouse in V1," Cam said. "You can see why they had to build a new one."

"I can't even see where it ends. How much stuff is in here?"

"There's at least one of every single thing that went into building V1 in this room with the exception of computer equipment, nuclear reactor parts, and a few custom-built components."

"How can you possibly find anything?"

"That's why we constantly have someone maintaining a running inventory."

"How much of V1 do you think you could rebuild with this stuff?"

"Probably twenty percent. About half of all this will go into maintenance, repairs, and reconfigurations, and the other half is for expansion. One of these days, we may even start building V2, assuming you guys can figure out how to fill it with air."

They began walking perpendicular to the first row of shelves so Arik could see down the massive aisles. Cam motioned toward the indiscernible rear of the warehouse.

"In the back, we have several hundred tons of steel, a little concrete, probably a hundred prefab doors, a few kilometers worth of maglev rail, and somewhere between five hundred and a thousand slabs of raw polymeth."

"Do you guys do the polymerization yourselves?"

"As far as I know, all the polymeth we have came from Earth. I know we can make nonconductive polymeth if we have to, but we don't have the technology to make the conductive stuff." Cam pointed down an aisle that came into view as they walked. "Down there is all the flexible PVC and duct material. Past that is vacuum plumbing, pumps, valves, and purifiers. All those little bins contain every conceivable screw, bolt, nut, washer, pin, and clip you could possibly imagine, though it takes about an hour to find what you're looking for because nobody puts anything back where it belongs. All this is electric and lighting. That stuff stacked over there is fiber and urethane insulation, and all that is old composite insulation that needs to be moved outside since we can't use it anymore. These crates contain a couple of thousand tubes of butyl, silicone, and various types of adhesive, and all those spools on that wall hold pulse optical cabling."

"What happened over there?"

"That used to be a stack of about ten thousand carbon rubber tiles—the things that turn everyone's feet black—until someone backed into it. Nobody will own up to it, though, so everyone refuses to restack them."

"Where do you store things like furniture? Cadie told me to look for a new bedroom set."

"We custom mold almost all furniture as it's needed so we don't have to store it. That's one of the things Zaire is learning to do." Cam noticed two black plastic bundles on a low shelf. "Here's some inside information for you. Whatever you do, don't break your toilet. We have only two spares for all of V1 right now. There were three here yesterday, but it looks like someone stashed one."

"You guys are a bunch of misfits."

"Are you saying we're not as civilized as a bunch of chemists and botanists?"

"Is the dock close by? I have to get back soon, but I want to see it before we eat."

"Yeah, it's back this way."

Cam ducked through a door in the rear of the warehouse, and Arik followed him back out into the din of the shop. They walked along the back wall, and Cam turned his head and talked over his shoulder.

"So how do you like working with Cadie?"

"It's good. We haven't had a chance to collaborate much yet because we've mostly been doing research, but we spend so much time at work, it's nice being able to see each other occasionally. What about you and Zaire?"

"Eh. Let's just say that Zaire is no Cadie."

"What do you mean?"

"I love that woman dearly, but she's not exactly the easygoing type. I'll tell you at lunch. I don't know where she is right now and if she hears me complaining, she'll kill me."

"Where are we going to eat?"

"The break room. It's next to the dock."

"You guys are supposed to have the best stemstock in V1."

"I doubt it's the best, but I can guarantee we have the most. You should see these people eat."

They stepped through a small archway into the dock. The left side of the room was lined with wire mesh lockers, most of which contained limp and grimy environment suits. There were an equal number of helmets strewn across the tops of the lockers, mostly on their sides. The right side of the dock was a small parking lot with three small robotic rovers in the corner and three full-sized manual rovers beside them, all tethered to the wall by thick black cords. Beside the last rover was a small trailer with its magnetic hitch pointed out into the room. The back wall was lined with mesh shelves containing various types of tools. Arik could see picks and shovels, jackhammers, pneumatic tampers, and what looked like the components of a small pile-driving rig. The floor was a giant grid of metal grate tiles that resonated with each step.

"This is where I spend most of my time," Cam said. "And *those* are my babies." He pointed to the rovers. "The big ones are Anna, Betty, and Clara, and the little ones are Malyshka, Kudryavka, and Zhuchka. Obviously they were built by different engineers."

"Evidently. What do they do?"

"The little ones are mostly used for inspections and very simple repairs. They have camera booms, and the six arms in front can be outfitted with just about any kind of tool you want. They can be controlled from any workspace anywhere in V1, and they can even function somewhat autonomously, though I've seen them do some pretty stupid things. The big ones are man-op only. They're mostly used for hauling supplies and personnel around the perimeter of V1, usually when we're too lazy to walk."

"Are they hard to operate?"

"The little ones can be tricky, but the big ones are easy. The stick on the left controls the two left wheels, and the stick on the right controls the right wheels. Push both forward to go forward, pull both back to go backward, and move them in opposite directions to rotate."

"What's the range on them?"

"Probably a hundred kilometers or so, but they never go more than maybe five kilometers in the course of a day."

"How far have you taken them out?"

"Not very far. There's no reason to go any more than a few meters from the perimeter of V1 unless you're going to the ERP, which I'm not allowed to do. Why, are you planning on running away?"

"I'm just wondering how brave you are."

"I'm plenty brave, I'm just not stupid. I know the guy who maintains these things."

Arik was startled by the sudden hiss of rapidly equalizing pressure. He turned and saw a man in an environment suit step into the room through a set of wide steel doors. The man took a deep breath and blew it out as he removed his helmet, and Arik could see that his long gray hair was damp with sweat. His arm reached around behind him and came back with a slender hexagonal tube about fifty centimeters long. He stacked it on top of several identical tubes on the left side of the door, and Arik noticed that there was a similar stack on the opposite side. The man stomped his feet as he walked over to an empty locker. The purpose of the mesh floor, Arik realized, was to catch and contain the dirt from boot treads and rover tires.

"That's obviously the main airlock," Cam said. "All the functional e-suits are over against that wall. They're pretty much one-size-fits-none. You're supposed to do an integrity test on your suit every time you come in, and clean and disinfect the inside of your helmet, but I don't think I've ever seen anyone do either."

They watched the man shove his gloves down in his helmet, then toss the whole thing up on top of the lockers. He groped for something inside the metal ring of his collar, then pulled the suit apart down the front and began peeling it away. He sat down on a bench so he could get his feet out of the integrated boots, then hung the suit on a hook by its stiff metal collar. On his way out of the dock, he took a bottle from a shelf and doused himself with water.

"See?"

"They don't look as well cared for as the rovers."

"They're pretty much indestructible, so nobody worries about them. They're made out of seven alternating layers of some kind of ballistic composite fiber material and all the seams are welded so they can't tear. It would pretty much take a laser to cut through them. The helmets are made out of a hardened glass fiber composite which is supposedly shatterproof. I've seen guys drop their helmets on the metal floor while getting them down, pick them up, put them on, and stroll right out the airlock without a second thought."

"Has anyone ever gotten hurt out there?"

"Not that I know of. Statistically, working in the warehouse or the shop are both far more dangerous than working outside."

Arik walked over to the lockers to get a closer look at the suits.

"Are these things easy to use?"

"They're completely automated. The hardest part is finding one that fits you. Once you get into one, all you have to do is seal up the front, make sure your gloves and helmet are latched, and throw a fresh cartridge in the back. The suit won't activate unless everything is threaded and sealed properly. The cartridges provide both your air and your power, so that's all you need. You can even hot-swap them while you're outside, but I wouldn't recommend it—at least not without a buddy nearby in case something goes wrong."

"Are those the charged cartridges on that side?"

"Spent cartridges on the left, charged on the right. Heaven forbid someone put up a sign or something. Every night someone takes all the spent cartridges and puts them in this huge wall unit we call *the hive* to charge them, and every morning someone stacks them all back up."

"How does the airlock work?"

"I don't think anyone actually knows, to tell you the truth. It's completely automated. The inner and outer doors are physically linked under the floor so it's impossible for them to both be open at the same time. The computer in the airlock can tell how many people are inside, and it won't open the outer doors until the number of people it detects and the number of activated suits are the same. All you have to do is push a button and the computer takes care of the rest. It even does all the necessary decontamination on the way back in."

"How long can you stay out?"

"Four to six hours on a single cartridge, depending on how hard you're working and how much you're breathing."

"What's it like out there?"

"*Hot.* And hazy. That's pretty much it."

"Is there anything to see?"

"Not really. The air is so thick, you can see only a few meters in front of you. If we didn't have strobe beacons along the perimeter of V1, all of us would probably be wandering all over the planet by now trying to find our way back."

"Can you feel the pressure out there?"

"Not at all. The suits completely counter it. They have a microskeletal system that automatically compensates for any pressure changes."

"This is so much more interesting than the Life Pod."

"Any day you want to trade jobs, just let me know. I'd be happy to sit back in a nice cool office and stare at a wall all day."

Arik saw something on the floor and crouched down. There was a tiny mound of sulfur-yellow powder at his feet, perched along the thin metal of the grate.

"So this is dirt," Arik said. He pinched the mound and rubbed it between his fingers. "This is actually the first time I've ever seen it."

"If you like dirt, you're in the right place. Once a month we have to pull up these tiles and shovel it all out."

Arik peered through the metal grate and could see a trail between the lockers and the airlock doors.

"What do you do with it?"

"Just throw it outside so it can get tracked back in."

Arik was still crouched. He found another tiny mound of the fine powder, pinched it, and sprinkled it into his palm. He tilted his hand and watched it fall down through the grate.

"Can I have some of it?"

"You want some dirt?"

"Yeah, why not?"

"I'm not the one who shovels it out usually."

"I mean right now. Can we pull up one of these tiles and scoop some out?"

"Why in the world would you want some dirt? All this stuff does is stain clothes and clog up gears."

"I just want to run some tests on it."

Cam watched his friend for a moment, then smiled.

"I know what you want to do," he said. "Cadie told me about the argument you had with what's-her-name during your orientation. You want to see if you can grow something in it."

"It wasn't an argument," Arik said. "I know it's completely sterile. I just want to see what's in it."

Cam looked out through the archway into the shop, then looked back at Arik.

"Keep your box from lunch and we'll fill it up on the way out."

"Thanks. I'll bring you a fern leaf or a petri dish in exchange."

"I have no idea how my boss would react to this, so don't mention it to anyone."

"Don't worry," Arik said. "I know exactly how my boss would react. No one will ever know."

CHAPTER FOURTEEN

CONCEPTION

ARIK FELT LIKE HIS HEARING had become more sensitive since the accident. Even from outside the bedroom, he could tell that Cadie had just closed her workstation. Conductive polymeth was supposed to be completely silent, but Arik's ears could pick up the infinitesimal vibrations of the excited molecules entombed deep in the thick plastic. It resonated throughout the pod just above the threshold of perception, and he usually wasn't even aware that he was hearing it until it suddenly stopped. Perhaps his hearing had somehow improved, or perhaps Arik was so intent on avoiding Cadie now that he'd simply become much more attuned to her actions. Cadie turned the wall lights out and slid down in bed, and now Arik could hear her trying to find a comfortable position for her unfamiliar body.

He got up and stood in the doorway. Cadie was hugging a long latex foam pillow that went under her swollen belly and between her legs. She sensed him watching her and rolled over.

"What's wrong?"

"Before you came home tonight, I was working on something."

"What?"

"I'm not sure. But I think it was something important."

"The error codes?"

"They weren't error codes," Arik said. "I think it's a message."

"From who?"

Arik paused before he answered. He was still trying to make sense of it himself. "From me."

"From you? What do you mean?"

"I think I sent myself a message before the accident."

"What does it mean?"

"I don't know yet." He paused in a way that indicated that he wasn't finished, but didn't quite know how to go on. "But I think once I figure it out, everything is going to change. I think we need to talk about the baby."

Cadie watched Arik for a moment in the dark, then pulled herself up and leaned against the headboard. She drew her legs up to make room on the bed, and Arik sat down. Neither of them reached for the light.

They each waited for the other to start. Arik had constructed this conversation in his mind dozens of times since he'd returned home from the hospital, and he knew that there was no way to avoid asking Cadie one simple and direct question:

"It isn't mine, is it?"

"It's complicated."

"It isn't complicated. We both know it isn't mine."

Arik's eyes were adjusting to the dark, and he could see Cadie watching him carefully.

"We need to talk about more than just the baby."

"It's Cam's, isn't it?"

"I need you to listen to me. I need to tell you something, and I need to start from the beginning."

Arik could see that Cadie had rehearsed this. He understood his wife well enough to know that she would have to do this in her own way.

"OK."

She took a moment to prepare herself. She looked down and watched her hands while she spoke.

"We all thought you were going to die," she said. "Your father contacted me at the Life Pod and told me to meet him here. When I got here, he said you'd been involved in a very serious accident, and that without surgical assistance from Earth, they didn't think you'd live."

Arik had never even seen Cadie cry before—at least not as an adult. The way her features changed, and the way she moved her head to the side and her straight black hair fell beside her cheeks, made her look like an entirely different person. It suddenly occurred to Arik what an incredibly sheltered life they had all lived up until now. They had never lost a family member or a friend, and until Arik's accident, nobody they knew had ever been seriously injured. There weren't even any pets in V1 to run away, or to get old and die. Living in such a carefully controlled environment had a tempering effect designed to keep emotions as well-balanced as the atmosphere.

"The next day, Priyanka came to see me. He said there wasn't a lot of time, and that if we were going to save any part of you, we were going to have to act quickly. He said I had a responsibility to V1."

"A responsibility to do what?"

Cadie looked up. "To replace you."

"Why would I need to be replaced?"

"You have no idea who and what you really are, do you?"

"What are you talking about, Cadie?"

"I'm talking about your purpose," she said. "You were born to solve problems that no other human being can solve. All of us were."

"Who's all of us?"

"Gen V," Cadie said. She wiped her eyes and took a deep breath. "Our parents were selected. Our genes were selected. We were taught math and biology and physics and computers and every other science practically since the day we were born. We knew the scientific method before we could even feed ourselves. Everything from the formula we were given to the amount and types of stimulation we got to the games we played were all designed to make us the best problem solvers the world had ever seen."

"We were raised by engineers and scientists," Arik said. "Of course we were taught to solve problems. I doubt we were raised any differently from kids on Earth with parents like ours. In fact, kids on Earth have access to a lot more resources than we do. Their education is probably much better than ours."

"Arik, think about it. V1 is an entirely isolated and controlled environment. Food, oxygen, stimulation, genetics, even lighting. Everything here is controlled. There are no distractions, and there are no options. Our housing is taken care of for us. Our meals are taken care of for us. Our careers were assigned to us. Even our marriages were practically arranged. Whether we like it or not, our lives are entirely dedicated to nothing but scientific advancement."

Arik knew everything Cadie was saying was true, but he had never thought of his upbringing as being in any way malicious or exploitive. It was no secret that they were being groomed to inherit V1—to help improve and expand the colony—but Arik had always thought of this expectation as a privilege.

"What do they want us to do?"

"Expand, of course," Cadie said. "Colonize the rest of Venus, then the rest of the solar system, then other solar systems, and eventually other galaxies."

"That's not even possible," Arik blurted out. "You're not making any sense."

"It all makes *perfect* sense. The human race has already learned how dangerous it is have our entire population on a single planet. It's far too vulnerable. If we don't destroy ourselves, we'll eventually be destroyed by a comet or an asteroid, or some sort of solar prominence, or a nearby gamma ray burst, or a pandemic. There are an infinite number of scenarios that could lead to human extinction. Everyone agrees it's not a question of *if*—it's a question of *when*. The GSA has one single directive: preserve the human race by promoting self-sustaining colonies throughout the solar system, galaxy, and the universe. And they can't do that without us."

"Cadie, you're talking about technology that's hundreds or even thousands of years away, if it's even possible at all. It's completely unrealistic. We've barely left Earth, and we're already struggling."

"It's not technology that limits us. *We're* the limitation. Our technology is an expression of our intelligence and creativity, so the limitations of our technology are a reflection of our own limitations. We can't fundamentally advance technology until we fundamentally advance ourselves. That's what Gen V is all about."

"But the whole point of technology is to push us beyond our own limitations and capabilities. That's why we have computers that can perform calculations quadrillions of times faster than the human brain."

"Arik, you know as well as anyone that computers are capable of far more than even the most complex tasks we give them. Computers aren't limited by hardware. They're limited by the software that humans write. That's why you're so important. I don't think you realize this, but you're already considered one of the best computer scientists in history. At your age, you're already far beyond Fai, and nobody here or on Earth can use a BCI like you. You have the potential to solve problems that nobody else has even dreamed of solving—that nobody else can even conceptualize. V1 needs you more than you realize. The GSA needs you. When Kelley talks about the Pinnacle of Human Achievement, he's mostly talking about you, Arik."

Arik watched her for a moment in the dark. "Priyanka told you all this?"

Cadie nodded. Arik looked down at the bed. He could feel his reality shifting as he began to grasp what Cadie was telling him. Everything she said made sense. In fact, on some level, he felt like he already knew most of it. If the Founders had tried to conceal their plans for Gen V, they had concealed them in plain sight. To see them, you only had to look at the big picture, to broaden your perspective, to stop looking at time in terms of weeks, months, or years, and to start thinking in terms of generations. To really understand your own place in history, you needed to be able to see yourself in the past tense.

Arik felt like he should be angry, but the clarity he was starting to experience felt positive and somehow empowering. He was starting to feel focused, and to realize a new and tangible sense of purpose. But there was also the sense that he was considered nothing more than a resource—that he would be allowed to reach his full potential only in areas that happened to align with V1's best interests. Arik knew there was more in what Cadie was telling him—more for them to discuss and explore—but all of that would have to wait. "Tell me about the baby."

Cadie took a deep breath and continued. "Priyanka brought me a DNA sample. He said if we could recover some part of you, nothing would have been lost but time."

"Priyanka?" Arik interjected. He recalled his discussion with Priyanka before he'd been allowed to leave the hospital, and specifically the way he'd brought up the baby.

"Arik, you have to understand that I didn't do it for him, or for V1, or for the GSA. I did it for me. You're all I have. If you died, I'd be completely alone for the rest of my life. Can you understand that?"

"But what did you do, Cadie?"

"I *created* our baby."

Arik stared at her across the bed. He was shaking his head. "What are you saying?"

"I used an infection," Cadie said. "A virus. I used your DNA to create our baby."

"How?"

"Listen," Cadie said. Arik could see that she was changing roles and starting to talk to him now as a biologist rather than his wife. She leaned toward him. "Most people think of viruses as parasites, but they aren't parasites at all. An organism has to be considered alive to be classified as a parasite. Viruses don't do any of the things living organisms do. They don't grow, they can't move on their own, and they don't metabolize. They don't even have cells. But the one thing a virus is very good at is reproducing. When it finds a suitable host cell, it attaches itself and injects its DNA through the cell's plasma wall. The virus's genes are transcribed into the host cell's DNA, and the host cell's genetic code is rewritten. Whatever its job was before, its new job is to do nothing but produce copies of the original virus, usually until it's created so many that the cell bursts open and spreads the infection."

"What does this have to do with the baby?"

"Everything," Cadie said. "Because the thing about viruses is that they're easily manipulated. The DNA they inject doesn't have to be destructive. It can be replaced with almost any kind of DNA you want, and it can be programmed to replace only certain parts of the host's genetic code. In other words, viruses are perfect vectors for genetic engineering."

Arik could see where she was going. "But you'd have to have an embryo first, wouldn't you?"

"Not an embryo," Cadie said. "By that time, it's too late. You need a zygote. A zygote gets half of its genetic material from the mother and the other half from the father. Before the zygote becomes an embryo, you have a short window of time in which you can make genetic modifications. And the best way to make those modifications is to let a genetically engineered virus make them for you. Do you understand?"

Arik nodded. He was following what Cadie was telling him, but still not entirely comprehending the implications.

"Arik," Cadie said, "the baby started out as Cam's, but it's as much yours now as if we conceived it ourselves."

She waited for Arik's reaction, but he was completely still. He didn't know what to feel. It occurred to him that human emotion had not evolved quickly enough to keep up with what mankind's scientific capabilities demanded of it. Sometimes the tiny components that made up an experience just didn't fit into existing emotional receptors, and the result was simply numbness.

"Arik," Cadie said, "the baby is *yours*. It's *ours*."

"Did you test the DNA Priyanka gave you?"

"No, because I didn't use it," Cadie said. "I used your DNA from ODSTAR instead. It was the only way I could be sure it was yours. I had to destroy the project, but it worked. She's a perfectly healthy baby girl. She's *our* baby girl."

Cadie's tearful smile was all Arik needed to tell him how to feel. For the first time, he reached out and touched his child. Cadie took his fingers away, pulled up her gown, and held his hand firmly against her flesh.

Arik looked up from Cadie's belly. "She's going to have that image of Earth inside her forever. Blue Marble. Like a genetic tattoo."

"I know," Cadie said. "I think it's beautiful. Wherever she ends up, whatever ends up happening to her, she'll always have something inside her that no one can take away."

CHAPTER FIFTEEN

OUTSIDE

SINCE THEIR LUNCH IN THE Wrench Pod, Cam had been bring-ing boxes of soil to Arik on his way home on a regular basis. Arik had just verified the results of the tests he'd run on the last sample, and needed to send Cam a message. He looked into his own eyes in his workspace and began recording.

"Connect to me as soon as you can," he said to himself. "I'll be here all day. And make sure you're alone."

Arik added the message to Cam's queue. Cam usually opened his workspace only a few times a day, so Arik wanted to get the message out to him as early as possible.

Cam responded sooner than Arik expected. Arik had just laser-sealed several chloroplast cultures inside borosilicate tubes and was about to go leave them in the dome when he heard the incoming connection request. He touched the wall and accepted the video stream.

"That was fast."

"What are you doing leaving me messages so early?" Cam said. "Don't you sleep?"

"I have to get in early to work on my side projects," Arik said. He noticed movement behind Cam. "You're not alone."

"You know what this place is like. There's no such thing as privacy here. No one can hear you, though." He tapped his ear indicating that he was using audio drops. The Infrastructure

Department preferred audio drops to mechanical transmitters and receivers since the drops freed them from having to worry about additional power supplies and maintenance. One or two drops allowed you to receive and transmit wireless audio for between three and six hours, depending on the size of your Eustachian tubes. The nanotubes in audio drops weren't sophisticated enough to encrypt or decrypt signals, however, which meant that technically, their conversation still wasn't secure. Arik took a moment to consider what the chances were of someone listening in at just the right time on just the right frequency, and decided they were negligible.

"I'll do all the talking, then," Arik said. "It turns out Venusian dirt isn't as sterile as I expected. Every sample you've given me so far contained organic molecules."

"Organic molecules?" Cam repeated. "You mean *life*?"

"No, not organic in that sense. I mean the building blocks of life. Carbon-based compounds. There's definitely nothing alive in the soil, but that doesn't mean it can't be made to support life. Or, more accurately, that life and the soil couldn't be made to support each other."

"That's good news, right? That's what you were hoping for?"

"That's significantly *more* than I was hoping for, though I still don't have any concrete results."

"What's stopping you?"

"Actually, that's what I need to talk to you about. I need more dirt."

Cam looked around him, then leaned in close to the polymeth. "Arik, I don't think I can get you any more."

"Why?"

"I can't explain now. Can you meet me tonight?"

"What time?"

"I'll let you know later."

"Is everything OK? Did I get you in trouble?"

"We'll talk tonight," Cam said. "I have to go."

Before Arik could respond, the video stream dropped.

That afternoon, Cam sent Arik a text message: "2100. The dock."

Arik sent Cam a confirmation and let Cadie know that he'd be working late.

● ● ●

Cam didn't meet Arik on the maglev platform this time. Arik thought about pinging him from outside the Wrench Pod but decided to go in on his own instead. He knew his way around by now. He'd been in enough times to pick up soil samples from Cam that he was almost always greeted by heavily gloved waves and deep nods of welding helmets as he walked through the shop on his way back to the dock.

But the shop was dark and almost empty tonight. Arik could hear a drill press on the far side and could see a single masked figure bent over a piece of steel in an isolated pool of light, but otherwise the Wrench Pod was as empty as Arik had ever seen it. He instinctively followed his normal unobtrusive route along the perimeter of the room.

Cam was alone in the dock. He was clamping down the rovers' power cords when he heard Arik step onto the hollow metal floor.

"Hey," Cam said. "Is there anyone left out there?"

"Just one person. I couldn't tell who it was."

"OK, good."

"What's with all the secrecy? What's going on?"

"The situation has changed," Cam said. He secured the last plug and sidestepped his way out from between the rovers. He spoke as he crossed the metal grate floor to the lockers. "I can't get you any more dirt, Arik. From now on"—he opened a locker and removed an environment suit—"you're going to have to get it yourself."

Arik stood still for a moment watching his friend, then smiled. "Are you serious?"

Cam was pleased with the drama he'd created. Although Arik had never actually said it, Cam knew how curious Arik was about the outside. When you grow up in a fully contained environment like V1, taking even a single step outside was the equivalent of crossing an ocean.

"Remember how I told you any idiot could operate an e-suit?" Cam said. "That includes you."

"Are we allowed to do this? Did you ask anyone?"

"Why would I do that? If I asked, they might say no. How does the saying go? It's easier to ask for forgiveness than permission?"

"Do you think anyone will find out?"

"People come in and out of here all day long," Cam said. "Nobody's going to notice, and even if they did, nobody would care. What's the worst that could happen?"

"I guess it's not like we can get fired."

"Exactly. And if we did, we could just play cricket and ping-pong all day."

"So show me how to use this thing."

"It's incredibly simple," Cam said. "The hardest part is the stirrups." Cam reached into a box in the locker and grabbed a fistful of short elastic straps with alligator clips at either end. "Sit down and take your shoes off."

Cam showed Arik how to attach the straps to keep his pant legs and shirtsleeves in place. Once you started sweating, he explained, it was possible for loose cuffs to bunch up and restrict blood flow to your arms and legs, increasing the risk of painful and debilitating muscle cramps. He then told Arik to tilt his head to the side and put two audio drops in each ear.

"And now to make you an official member of the Wrench Pod," Cam said. He stood behind Arik, reached over his head, and tied something tight against Arik's forehead. Arik turned to the mirror in the locker and saw that it was a clean white *hachimaki*, complete with the traditional rising sun on the forehead. "It shows that you're determined and focused," Cam told him, "and helps keep the sweat out of your eyes."

"This feels like a rite of passage."

"It is. You're one of us now." Cam held the dingy environment suit up against Arik to judge the size. "You're lucky. This should fit perfectly. I'm at least six centimeters too big for the biggest one. One day I'm just going to split it open and die of an embolism on the spot."

Arik started working his feet into the boots. "Let's not talk about dying right now."

"Seriously, this is all perfectly safe. You know I wouldn't let you do it if it wasn't, right? Zaire and I do this all the time."

"Well, I don't. The closest I've ever been to outside is the dome."

Cam was helping to shove one of the suit's boots onto Arik's foot, but he stopped. "Are you sure you're OK with this? I didn't mean what I said about the dirt. I can get you more."

"No way," Arik said. "I'm doing this. I just wasn't expecting it."

"Well, it wouldn't have been much of a surprise if you were, would it?"

"I just hope I don't turn out to be agoraphobic."

"Trust me, you won't have to worry about that. You can't see far enough out there to feel like you're in an open space. I'd be more concerned about being claustrophobic."

"Living here would have cured that a long time ago."

Arik put his arms through the suit's sleeves and Cam started sealing up the front.

"Once we get the cartridge in, the suit will finish sealing. It'll feel a little strange at first while it pressurizes, but you'll get used to it. I don't even notice it anymore."

Arik pulled on the gloves, and Cam threaded and latched them. Cam picked up Arik's helmet and stood in front of him.

"OK, here's what I want you to do," Cam said seriously. "Once you leave the outer airlock door, take a right and follow the edge of the building. In about forty meters, you'll come to a corner. Take a right and keep following the wall. In about another forty or fifty meters, you'll see a curved wall on your left. That's the Public Pod. You can do anything you want over there. The electromagnetic shields on the windows interfere with the rovers, and most of us are too lazy to walk all that way, so nobody ever goes over there."

The Venera Auditorium was the only structure in V1 besides the dome that had windows, but they were sealed up from the outside just a month after it was originally built. Apparently, the engineer who designed the twelve-centimeter-thick aluminum silicate glass panes didn't know enough about how the Venusian atmosphere filters sunlight, and requested the wrong coatings in the specification. The error was discovered after several of the Founders complained of irritated, bloodshot eyes and even partial but temporary blindness.

"What does the electromagnetism do to the rovers?"

"It screws up their navigation systems and cameras."

"Why didn't they just bolt the shields over the windows?"

"The structure wasn't designed to have holes drilled in it, and they didn't have enough spare welding material to weld the plates on back then. They tried an adhesive, but the atmosphere broke it down after about a week, and all the plates fell off. Finally they decided to run wires through the insulation in the walls between the panes and use good old-fashioned electromagnetism to make them stick."

"Clever solution, actually."

Cam held the helmet up close to Arik's head and judged the size. "Let's try a bigger one. You have an extra-large brain." He placed the helmet on top of a locker and started down the row looking for a more appropriate size. "By the way, that whole story about them using the wrong kinds of filters on the windows is all made up. You know that, right?"

"What do you mean?"

"You want to hear the Wrench Pod version of the story?"

"I don't know. Do I?"

Cam reached for a helmet. "What *really* happened was that the GSA never thought about how a three-thousand-hour day would affect people psychologically. Back then, the Venera Auditorium was the only structure in V1, so people couldn't get away from the light. Eventually it drove them all insane, and they ended up ripping each other to pieces with their bare hands. The GSA had to send in a new crew to clean up the mess and start over again."

"You guys seriously believe that?"

"Cañada claims to have used that trailer right there to haul the bodies out and bury them."

"Great. So now I have to worry about zombies out there in addition to everything else."

"That's right. He says if you take one of the rovers out into the magnetic field and switch on the com, you can hear the screams of the first wave of Founders being murdered in the static."

Arik waited for Cam to dismiss the anecdote with a grin, but he didn't. "You people are deranged."

"Now you're *really* an official Wrench Pod member," Cam said. "That story doesn't leave this room, by the way."

Cam looked surprisingly earnest. Apparently the Wrench Pod took their lore very seriously. "Don't worry. I can't really see myself retelling it."

"Here, try this on."

Arik slipped the helmet over his head. Cam put his hands on either side and moved it around to test the fit.

"OK, this one works. Feel OK?"

Arik gave Cam a thumbs-up, and Cam threaded and latched the helmet ring.

"All right. All you need now is your cartridge."

Cam pulled a hexagonal tube from the stack on the right side of the door.

"Turn around."

Arik turned his back to Cam, and a moment later, he felt a change in the suit. He could feel the glove and helmet joints stiffen and the seam down the front of the suit contract. The pressure changed inside the helmet, and a heads-up display in the visor showed him his air supply, battery life, suit pressure, and comm status.

When Arik turned back, Cam was standing in front of the wall using his workspace. He signaled for Arik to wait a second, then tilted his head and filled his own ears with audio drops.

"Comm check. Can you hear me?"

"Loud and clear."

"Good. One last thing."

Cam took a bucket down from the equipment rack and handed it to Arik. Arik had to hold it out from his body and bend at the waist to see the tools inside.

"The handle on the shovel telescopes if you get tired of bending down."

Arik nodded in his helmet. He was breathing hard enough that he was sure Cam could hear him.

"Don't worry. You're going to love it out there. This equipment is completely foolproof. Just remember: two rights, and the Public Pod will be on your left. When you're ready, come back the way you came. The entire perimeter is lined with white strobes, so as long as you stay where you can see them, you're fine. And there's a red strobe over the airlock so you can't miss it. Copy?"

"Copy."

"Stay out there as long as you want. I'm going to be in here rebuilding Clara's suspension, so I'm in no hurry. I'll be able to hear everything you say, and I'll keep an eye on your suit's status, so don't worry about your HUD. Now go have fun playing in the dirt."

Cam gave Arik an encouraging cuff on the side of the helmet. Arik nodded and turned toward the airlock. The suit didn't feel as heavy or as bulky as it looked, but it would take some getting used to—especially the helmet. Arik had never experienced such constrained vision before, and there was something disconcerting about listening to himself breathe. Being aware of every breath he took seemed to suggest that he had to consciously remember to take the next one. The feeling would pass, he told himself. He moved the bucket to his other hand and touched the pressure panel beside the inner airlock doors.

The huge slabs of steel slid apart noiselessly. There were no warning lights or alarms or automated instructions, presumably because nothing could go wrong. According to Cam, the system was foolproof. The inner and outer doors were physically linked, and the outer doors wouldn't open if the suit wasn't properly pressurized. The helmets were unbreakable, and the suits were a ballistic composite fiber material that couldn't be compromised by anything Arik would encounter out there. Cam wouldn't let him do this if it wasn't perfectly safe.

Cam's voice was in his ear. "Touch the panel on the inside of the inner door. When the panel next to the outer door turns green, you're good to go."

"Copy that."

Arik turned and touched the panel, and the inner doors closed. It was completely still in the airlock while the computer scanned and evaluated. Arik imagined what was happening all around him in the portion of the spectrum beyond human detection. The suit was communicating with the airlock, indicating its presence and reporting its status, but the airlock was necessarily skeptical. Since a suit could malfunction, the airlock had to run its own set of tests to determine the number of people inside it, probably using lasers that Arik wasn't able to see, or possibly radar. It used complex algorithms to determine that there was only one person standing there, to conclude that it was a bucket that Arik was holding rather than another human standing close by. The algorithms had to be smart enough to differentiate between a human and a rover, and to account for an infinite number of configurations of equipment, tools, and materials that might also be present. Once the airlock was confident in its evaluation, it would compare its number to the number of suits reporting in, and if and only if those two numbers were precisely equal would the panel beside the outer door turn green.

The airlock was not only relying on its own evaluation to be correct, but it was also relying on the software that Arik's environment suit used to evaluate itself. And both the airlock and the e-suit relied on the cartridge to accurately measure and report its status. And, of course, all of these systems relied on robust and functional hardware. It didn't matter how reliable your software was if the O-ring that maintained the seal between your cartridge and your suit had been allowed to deteriorate to the point where microscopic cracks formed that would expand under pressure and eventually cause the ring to rupture. Or if a helmet was inadvertently exposed to a chemical compound that weakened its molecular bonds over time just enough to allow them to break in a circumstance just beyond the limits of the helmet's own diagnostic tests.

Arik understood that even the digital world was fundamentally analog. Even in the seemingly unambiguous case of true versus false, there were billions of complex physical processes involved in determining that a one was actually a one and a zero was actually a zero. He knew that the word *foolproof* actually meant "good enough" and that once all the measurements were taken and all the variables defined and all the expressions evaluated—and once the physical world with its entropic underpinnings had its say—you could only hope that when it really counted, the results would fall mostly in your favor.

The panel turned green by the outer airlock door, and Arik reached down and touched it. The doors parted and the airlock was pierced by an expanding plane of hazy tangerine light. The brightness flooded Arik's helmet and burned away the sterile white glow of the diode tubes overhead. Arik stared out into the dense haze in front of him, then took his first steps out into a world that he knew was fundamentally beyond anyone's control.

CHAPTER SIXTEEN

DEAD AIR

ALTHOUGH ARIK WAS RECOVERING FASTER than expected, Darien still usually checked on him with a quick text or video message during lunch. When Arik checked his message queue, however, there was nothing current from his father. Darien's workspace hadn't been active for the last forty-two minutes and twenty-two seconds, and there was no status message. Arik knew it was unusual for his father not to make himself available in the middle of the day. He usually brought his boxed meal into his office and ate in front of his workspace, reviewing water sample results, checking pressure readings, and going through the queue of messages that had invariably accumulated since closing his workspace last.

But Darien was offline today. Arik sent out a ping and waited for a response. Somewhere in V1, a notification was being rendered on the closest piece of conductive polymeth to his father's last known location, and Darien's personal tone was being emitted from the surface of the plastic to help him locate it.

Arik didn't ping people very often. He preferred asynchronous communication. For issues that weren't urgent, it made much more sense to leave a message that could be responded to whenever it was convenient, and when the recipient had the time to devote to a thorough and appropriate response. Arik, along with most of Gen V, considered pings to be borderline rude, though there were plenty of people in V1 who felt differently. Certain people (namely those who didn't have jobs that required them to focus for long periods of time, and were therefore unfamiliar with the concept and merits of prolonged concentration) thought nothing of not only sending out dozens of pings a day, but even sending multiple pings to the same person. These were the user accounts that, sooner or later, found their way onto almost everyone's ping blacklist.

One of the original programmers of the ping system thought it would be a good idea to return the 3-D spatial coordinates of where a ping notification was rendered. It was probably done for debugging purposes and thought benign enough that it wasn't worth removing. Since ping notifications were rendered as close to an individual's last known location as possible (which was updated every ten milliseconds or so), someone eventually discovered that they could combine a ping's 3-D coordinates with a set of schematics to figure out exactly where anyone was in V1 at any particular moment just by sending a ping. And since almost all the inner walls in V1 were conductive polymeth, there was no place—literally *no place*—that a ping couldn't find you. Initially, the technique was too complicated for most people to figure out, but it was only a matter of time before the entire process was scripted and shared, and could be exploited by anyone, regardless of technical aptitude. After months of receiving daily complaints, the Technology Department finally took the time to remove the single line of offending code, thereby restoring a reasonable sense of privacy to V1.

Darien was an important enough man that he generally kept himself accessible, and even more so since Arik's accident. Even if his workspace wasn't open, he was almost always somewhere in the Water Treatment Department, which meant he was easily reached. And his and L'Ree's relationship wasn't such that Arik had to worry about his ping interrupting them in the midst of a midday tryst. But there was one activity in which Darien regularly partook that he would not allow to be interrupted. When Darien was playing cricket, nothing short of a catastrophic structural breach or flash oxygen fire could get him to lay down his bat.

• • •

Arik took the maglev to the Play Pod. The gym was usually moderately busy in the middle of the day as residents worked toward their weekly exercise quotas. Everyone in V1 was required to get a minimum of one hundred minutes of exercise per week (not to exceed four hundred and twenty minutes because of oxygen conservation ordinances). Since there was a limit on the rate at which oxygen could be consumed over a given period, you couldn't get away with cramming all your exercise in at the end of the week. Of course, nobody actually enforced exercise quotas, so only those who were incapable of disregarding the rules were actually bound by them. Most people in V1 simply had their favorite activities—cricket, martial arts, walking rather than taking the maglev—and it was pretty much left at that.

The Play Pod was divided into three main sections: the gym in the front, the pitches in the back, and the dojo off to the right. The gym contained several configurations of hydromills for low-impact cardiovascular training, two convertible resistance strength machines, and a low climbing belt that was seldom functional. There were polymeth slabs within reach of all exercise stations, usually dripping with water droplets from nearby hydromills.

The dojo was a separate room off to the right that ran the entire length of the Play Pod. The floor consisted of well over a dozen nylon and foam tatami mats, intricately arranged according to tradition so as not to visit misfortune upon V1 by the corners of too many mats intersecting at a single point. The dojo was used for yoga, tai chi, jujitsu, and, when Arik was a child, for various lessons and games that required an open space and a soft floor.

The four enclosed pitches were in the back: two on each side with an open carbon-rubber tiled area between. The walls dividing the front and back pitches could be removed to form two areas large enough for a full match of reduced cricket (five or six players per team).

Arik could see his father with Priyanka and Zorion in the front left pitch. He nodded to the occupants of the hydromills on his way back and stood on the mats between the pitches, watching through the polymeth barrier. Darien was batting. He was standing in front of the spring-mounted fiberglass wicket, eyeing Priyanka warily. Priyanka was considered the best bowler in V1, but Darien was a very competent batsman. In actual matches, they were considered to be ultimate rivals, but while practicing, they each focused on honing specific skills. Priyanka began his bowling action, and Arik saw that he was practicing his spin. The ball hit the mat and leapt away from Darien, who stepped toward it and popped it off toward the back wall. The ball was soft and designed to absorb the majority of the shock in order to limit its travel in confined spaces. Zorion caught it off the back wall and made a dramatic motion before tossing it gently back to Priyanka. Darien was adjusting his stance and Priyanka was just beginning another action when the walls of the pitch brightened with an intense red glow.

Activities in the pitches were limited to sessions that were defined by the amount of oxygen consumed during play. It would take fifteen minutes for the red to fade, at which point they could begin another session. The three men relaxed and moved toward the door.

Darien emerged first, but stopped when he saw his son waiting for him.

"Is everything OK?"

Arik nodded. "I need to talk to you when you have a minute."

"Sure."

"Hello, Arik," Priyanka said. "How are you feeling?"

Arik gave Priyanka the bare minimum acknowledgment. "Fine."

"Afternoon, Arik," Zorion said with the exaggerated civility that playing cricket often evoked.

"Hi, Zorion."

"What drags you away from the Life Pod in the middle of the day?"

"I just need to discuss something with my dad."

Priyanka once again inserted himself. "Anything we can help with?"

This time, Arik looked directly into Priyanka's eyes. "No."

Priyanka met Arik's stare. Darien looked back and forth between his son and his friend, clearly confused by the dynamic between them. It was Zorion who finally spoke in an attempt to dispel the tension.

"Well, we should probably be getting back, anyway," he said. He put his hand on Priyanka's shoulder. "As always, it was a pleasure, gentlemen."

Darien nodded. "Same time next week?"

"Absolutely."

Priyanka and Zorion left together through the gym. Darien watched them go, then started back through the door of the pitch.

"Give me a minute to gather my stuff."

Arik followed his father inside. You could stay inside a pitch between sessions as long as you weren't playing. If you began consuming oxygen faster than what was considered the standard rate, the walls would turn a deeper red rather than fading. If you persisted, an oxygen alarm would sound, which even the most devout cricketers couldn't possibly play through.

"I don't have very much time," Arik said. "I have to get back soon. Can we talk in here?"

"Of course," Darien said. His soft eyes could look every bit as concerned as kind. "What's going on?"

Arik touched the wall and the door of the pitch snapped shut. Everything emanated crimson as the red wall lights glowed. "Cadie and I had a long talk last night. She told me about the baby. And about her conversation with Priyanka."

"Good," Darien said. He picked up his bat and pitched himself against it. Arik thought he seemed surprisingly casual about the conversation they were about to have—perhaps even prepared. "I wanted it to come from her. I hope you don't feel like you've been misled. I think everyone's been as open and up front as they felt they could."

"Even about the baby?"

Darien lowered his eyebrows. "What do you mean?"

Arik leaned down and picked up the ball. "If the point of the baby was to replace me, why did Priyanka bring Cadie a DNA sample while I was still alive?"

"Arik," Darien said, "I don't know how much Cadie told you about your condition, but nobody expected you to recover. Priyanka was just acting on information from Dr. Nguyen."

"But Dr. Nguyen certainly knows that you can get a perfectly viable DNA sample from a cadaver. Or that DNA samples are easily preserved."

"I don't understand what you're getting at."

"What I'm getting at is that there was no reason for Cadie to get pregnant while I was still alive. Not if the goal was simply to replace a valuable resource."

"That's not exactly how I would have put it, but what else would the goal have been?"

Arik narrowed his eyes. "To try to force me into solving AP," he said. "To make the life of my unborn child depend on it."

Darien looked both surprised and skeptical, even a little annoyed. "Arik, you know that's not the way things are done here."

"How *are* things done here?"

"OK," Darien said. "I agree that it might not have been the best course of action, but it was an emotional decision, not a logical one. A lot of people were very upset about what happened. Your mother and I were devastated. Cadie was devastated. I think everyone just wanted to feel like they were doing something rather than just sitting around and waiting. Including Cadie."

"Let's not discuss Cadie's motivations," Arik said. There was a warning in his tone. "They were clearly very different than Priyanka's."

Darien watched Arik wring the ball in his hands before he responded. "I imagine so," he said finally. "But I'm honestly not in a position to debate Priyanka's motives."

"Fair enough," Arik said. "That's not what I came here to talk about, anyway. It really doesn't matter what anyone's motives were. The real question is what we do now."

"*Do*?"

"About the fact that we don't have enough oxygen to support another human life," Arik said plainly. He indicated the red walls around them. "We don't even have enough O_2 to play a full inning of cricket."

"How are things going at the Life Pod? Have you made any progress on AP?"

"Not enough to make a difference. Even if we figured out AP today, it would probably take months if not years to integrate the new processes into the life-support systems."

"So what do you propose? I know you well enough to know you didn't just come here to present a problem."

Arik bounced the foam cricket ball against the hard rubber tiles and caught it. He was clearly trying to steady himself. "I propose we build a second dome."

Darien looked confused. "A second dome? Out of what?"

"Whatever we have. And whatever we can get from Earth."

"Arik, we can't just add a second dome. V1 was designed to have a single centrally located oxygen supply. The entire life-support system would have to be modified to accommodate a second one. We'd need new fans, new ductwork, new sensors. The oxygen allocation, conservation, and distribution algorithms would have to be rewritten. The purification systems would have to be reconfigured if not entirely replaced—all without disrupting the existing system, and all using manpower and resources we don't have."

"What about expanding the existing dome?"

"The dome was always meant to become obsolete, not to be expanded. Increasing the diameter of a geodesic dome by even a few centimeters changes the dimensions of every single panel in the entire structure. We might as well start from scratch. Even if we had the material to rebuild it, how do you propose we breathe in the meantime?"

"OK," Arik conceded. "What about water electrolysis? We have enough steel to build electrodes large enough that we should be able to decompose water into plenty of oxygen."

"Fine, then what would we drink?"

"Obviously we would need more water from Earth."

"Where would we store it? And how would adding huge amounts of additional water affect our current storage and delivery and treatment processes? Could the existing pumps and valves handle the additional pressure, or would they all need to be upgraded? How would additional water and pressure affect corrosion rates? Where would we get the massive amounts of additional energy needed not just for the decomposition itself, but to manage the hydrogen byproduct that's created at twice the rate of oxygen? And what are the risks of storing compressed hydrogen—which is extremely flammable, as you know—anywhere near electrodes? Arik, you have to understand that V1 is an incredibly intricate and delicate ecosystem that was designed by thousands of engineers over the course of decades. We can't just modify it any way we want. V1 has to be expanded according to its original design. There's really no other practical way to do it."

Darien's reaction was exactly what Arik expected. His own simulations had already eliminated all of these possibilities, and easily half a dozen more. He wasn't proposing them with the expectation that his father would be receptive; rather, he was preparing Darien for the fact that what he was about to propose was the only possible solution remaining.

"You're right," Arik said. "We can't do anything that would significantly modify the course of V1, or put anyone at risk. The life of one child couldn't possibly be worth risking the lives of the entire colony, especially the life of a child meant to replace someone who now doesn't need replacing. That means there's only one thing left to do."

Darien could see now that Arik had been setting him up. "Which is what?"

"We have to send Cadie and the baby to Earth."

Darien watched his son for a long time before responding. "You're obviously well aware of the fact that we couldn't possibly build the Earth elevator in time to make a difference, so that can't be what you're proposing."

"We don't need a two-way system," Arik said. "I'm talking about sending a single person on a single one-way trip."

"How much thought have you given this?"

"Enough to know that it's the only logical solution. First of all, it doesn't require any new technology. The GSA has landed and returned dozens of people from Mars, and hundreds if not thousands of people from the moon. A single mission to carry a single person from Venus to Earth is entirely within the GSA's capabilities. And it poses no risk to V1 whatsoever."

"But there isn't enough time. She'd have the baby before she could get to Earth."

"She'd have the baby before the GSA could even approve the mission," Arik said. "That's why she'd have to be put into cryogenic hibernation within twenty-eight days from today, and she'd have to make the entire trip in hibernation."

"Doesn't that seem risky to you?"

"Hibernation has been used successfully during medical emergencies several times. There's no reason to assume it would pose any special risk to Cadie or the baby."

"Have you thought about the fact that you might never see her again?"

"Yes."

"And that, to be perfectly blunt, you would probably end up alone for the rest of your life?"

"There's plenty here to keep me busy."

"Have you talked this through with Cadie yet?"

"No."

"Good," Darien said. The walls had lost their tint and were almost fully transparent again. Darien looked out into the gym. All but one of the hydromills were in use, and two people were sparring in the dojo. Darien touched the wall, then tapped on the control pad that appeared beneath his finger. The door sealed, and the polymeth walls electronically fogged until they were completely opaque.

"What are you doing?"

"I'm going to tell you something that I need you to keep in the strictest confidence."

"OK."

"This is not something to be taken lightly, Arik. If you accept the responsibility of what I'm about to tell you, this will be a burden that you may have to live with for the rest of your life. You can never discuss this with anyone besides me. Do you understand?"

"Of course."

"I don't really know how to say this, so I'll just come right out with it. We haven't received anything but dead air from Earth since it emerged from the last radio eclipse."

"What do you mean *dead air*? We haven't been in contact with the GSA?"

"I mean we haven't picked up a single radio signal from any place on Earth."

Arik looked skeptical. "One of the communication satellites must have malfunctioned."

"We've tried them all. They couldn't have all malfunctioned."

"There could have been some sort of solar prominence that knocked them out. We wouldn't have detected it here because of the dense atmosphere. Or maybe the ERP antenna is down."

"All of our equipment is functioning fine, Arik. We can talk to Earth's communication satellites. They're all online, and according to their diagnostics reports, they're all functioning perfectly."

"What about the moon bases?"

"Same thing. We can communicate with the bases themselves, but there's nobody there."

Arik's gaze wandered along the floor for a moment. "Have we tried to get images?"

"We've pointed all the satellite cameras we have at Earth, but we don't have any telescopes up there, and we can't see anything significant under digital magnification."

"Well there's obviously *something* broken," Arik said. His voice was beginning to rise. "You just haven't found it yet."

"Nothing's broken, Arik. Earth has simply stopped broadcasting. I'm not just talking about the GSA. I'm talking about everything on the planet that produces a radio wave strong enough to leave Earth's atmosphere."

Arik was shaking his head slowly. "That's impossible. How could that happen?"

"We don't know. It could have been some sort of global natural disaster, or it's possible that the GSA hasn't been honest with us about the political situation on Earth, and there could have been some kind of massive war. Or it could turn out to be something trivial we haven't thought of yet, and the GSA could start broadcasting again tomorrow. But considering what it would take to wipe out an entire planet's radio communication infrastructure in such a short amount of time, we need to take very seriously the possibility that we may never hear from Earth again."

Arik watched his father. He waited for Darien to continue— to offer some further explanation, to outline the next steps, to at least reassure him that something was being done—but Darien was finished.

"So what the hell are we going to do?"

"The only thing we can do. We're going to keep listening and hope that we hear something. But in the meantime, we're going to assume that we're on our own from now on."

"On our *own*?" Arik was suddenly amused. "I hate to tell you this, Dad, but we can't survive on our own. If the GSA doesn't come back online—"

"Keep your voice down, Arik," Darien said. He spoke to his son with deliberate and forced calm. "It's not going to be easy, but we can do it. Remember, this is the whole reason for V1. This is why we've been working toward becoming self-sufficient. We already engineer all our own food, we recycle all our water, and we create our own atmosphere."

"For now we do, but what's going to happen the first time something goes wrong? What if our water tanks rupture? What if some sort of pathogen destroys the ferns? What if the main nuclear reactor melts down? There are hundreds of things that can go wrong. *Thousands.*"

"Probably hundreds of thousands," Darien said, "but how many of those things would kill us all anyway, with or without Earth?"

Arik didn't know what to say. The tenuousness of their existence was not something he had ever seriously contemplated. He was as familiar with emergency procedures as anyone, but he never actually expected to use them. On a rational level, Arik understood the precariousness of their lives, but having been born and raised on Venus, he couldn't help but ascribe to V1 the illogical and unconditional safety of home. But his father was right. Any number of things could wipe them all out at any given moment. The reality was that they were all alive due more to the merciful absence of a catastrophic event than to any real capability to prevent one.

Although something on the scale of total annihilation seemed far-fetched, the threat was certainly not without precedent. Millions of species had become extinct since life began on Earth—species much hardier than humans. After more than 160 million years of dominance, every dinosaur—no matter how powerful, intelligent, and well adapted—had been killed by a minuscule and insignificant cosmic coincidence. As recently as seventy thousand years ago, a simple volcanic eruption in Sumatra triggered an ice age that led to the extinction of most human species, leaving a mere one thousand reproductive pairs to give rise to modern man. Entire human cities had been destroyed by bombs, continents wiped out by plague, and ethnicities obliterated by genocide while the world stood by and watched, mouths agape, drinks in hand, dinner in the oven. Humans themselves were comprised of organic material manufactured in distant stars that had long since blown apart, destroying countless forms of life and alien civilizations in the process. V1 was built not because the destruction of Earth was possible; it was built because, given enough time, the destruction of Earth was inevitable, and from the perspective of the cosmos, today was really no different from a million or even a billion years from now. Arik began to understand that it wasn't confidence in our ability to keep ourselves safe that freed us from the constant fear of total annihilation—it was subconscious resignation born of our complete inability to prevent it.

"Arik," Darien continued, "I think there's a good chance that the GSA will eventually recover from whatever's happened on Earth. But in the meantime, we need to continue doing what we've always done, and what we always will do. We need to play the odds. We have to decrease our exposure. We need to constantly reduce the number of variables that our lives depend on. I know it sounds incredible, but we have to assume that nothing less than the future of the entire human race is at stake."

PART II

CHAPTER SEVENTEEN

THE WALL

CAM HAD PROMISED CADIE THAT he would be present in the airlock whenever Arik conducted an EVA. Realistically, they all knew there wasn't much he or anyone else would be able to do in the event of an emergency—and Cam trusted Arik and the environment suits implicitly—yet there was something about Cam being in close proximity to the airlock and in constant contact with Arik that made everyone feel better about the arrangement. If nothing else, Cam could make sure there was no one in the dock when Arik came back in who might report what was going on to the wrong person.

But when it became apparent that Arik was as experienced with EVAs as almost any of the new Wrench Pod members and that none of the other Wrench Pod members were even remotely concerned with what Arik was up to, Cam asked only that Arik let him know before going out, and send him a quick message when he got back. The only other rule was that Arik couldn't take out the last rover; nobody in the Wrench Pod seemed to mind Arik coming and going, and in fact he'd never even been asked what he was doing, but Cam knew that if Arik's activities started preventing actual wrenchers from getting their jobs done, there would be problems.

Arik had figured out exactly how close he could get a rover to the outside wall of the Public Pod before the magnetic field started significantly interfering with its operation. He learned to judge the distance by paying attention to the rover's steering and suspension. Since visibility was usually no more than a few meters, one of the components of the vehicle's navigation system was a short-range terrain-mapping device that used radar to scan the ground ahead, then fed the data into the main onboard computer. The computer then used the topographical model to dynamically adjust tire pressure and the rigidity of the rover's independent suspension in order to prepare and compensate for whatever was ahead. Since visibility was so poor, the main navigation system could also automatically steer the rover around protrusions or depressions that its algorithms deemed overly hazardous. When the navigation system was functioning optimally, the ride was as smooth as a maglev track. But when the rover encountered electromagnetic interference, the irregularities of the terrain began traveling up through the machine and into the driver's body. That's when Arik knew it was time to park. Of course, he could just as easily estimate his proximity to the Public Pod by flipping on the rover's radio and listening for the interference caused by the electromagnetism, but after hearing the Wrench Pod's myth about the static, he preferred to keep the radio silent.

Arik didn't wait to feel a change in the rover's steering and suspension this time. He was hauling the trailer, which meant that the rover had far less maneuverability than it normally had. The last thing you wanted while hauling the trailer was to get yourself into a situation where you had to back up. With the trailer attached, the rover's rear terrain-mapping system was useless, which meant not only did you have to worry about the awkwardness of maneuvering both the rover and the trailer, but you had to do it with no computer assistance. When hauling the trailer, the key was to make wide sweeping turns well before you reached your destination. Arik learned to stay just far enough away from the proximity strobes that he could make a full U-turn in either direction, but close enough not to entirely lose sight of them.

Arik swung the rover around so that it was pointing back toward the airlock, then applied the brake. He couldn't see the Public Pod itself through the dense fog from where he was, but he could just detect the curved pattern of asynchronous white strobes along the top of the structure. He would have liked to get closer since he had a fair amount of hauling to do, but he knew he would probably waste at least fifteen minutes maneuvering the rover and the trailer just to gain a meter or two.

He lowered the trailer's gate and began unloading a pressure washer that Cam had explained was intended for removing corrosion and other unwanted chemical coatings from metal surfaces. It consisted of two parts: one part contained the compressor, power source, and dissolvent reservoir, and the other contained a nozzle that was connected to the compressor by a long, looping black hose. Arik had noticed it on the equipment rack when he was trying to figure how out to conduct his next set of experiments, and after talking it over with Cam, they decided it could probably be used entirely without modification, provided anything toxic was flushed out first.

Arik needed a simple way to divide up the ground in front of the Public Pod into quadrants in order to separate and demarcate his experiments. He considered driving stakes into the ground and running string or wire between them, but he knew that any technique requiring significant physical labor meant that he would need at least two EVAs to get everything in place. Anyone who spent time outside on a regular basis was familiar with the concept of "the wall," which referred to the point at which the heat, dehydration, and the additional physical effort of wearing an environment suit all converged into exhaustion alarmingly fast. Arik had never hit his own personal wall, but he had gotten close enough to know that he needed to limit each EVA to only a single moderate task. The rule of thumb for new Wrench Pod members was to take the amount of work that you thought you could get done, and divide it in half. Anything beyond that, you were taking a serious risk.

The other problem with installing a grid was that anyone who happened to come across his work would almost certainly become ensnared and end up on the ground. Cam explained to Arik once that the reason environment suits felt so light was their remarkably efficient distribution of weight, and their microskeletal systems, which bore most of the burden. However, turn a "loaded" environment suit (one containing a fully charged cartridge) on its side, and those advantages were mostly lost, placing the full weight of the equipment on top of the person inside. Arik had been careful not to dig too deep in any one spot when collecting samples for fear of someone stepping in a hole and going down; therefore, he could hardly justify setting up what would basically amount to a system of tripwires.

So he decided to use markers that were already there to delineate his experiments: the shields covering the Public Pod's windows. There were sixteen shields spaced perfectly evenly, which meant Arik could keep track of sixteen different experiments planted in the ground in front of them. Although he assumed it would realistically take dozens if not hundreds of permutations to get results, four genetically engineered seeds combined with four crystal catalyst solutions to produce sixteen initial experiments was a reasonable start. Arik believed it was really just a numbers game at this point; if he could modify enough genes and combine them with enough different types of catalysts, he was confident he could get something to sprout. Of course, he could obviously conduct his experiments far more efficiently in his lab using borosilicate tubes, but hundreds of Venusian dirt samples lying around the dome would surely tip Subha off to the fact that Arik wasn't exactly giving artificial photosynthesis his full attention.

Arik mixed the first batch in the trailer and carried the pressure washer toward the strobes. When he was standing in front of the first shield, he estimated that he had walked a good fifty meters. He felt fine so far—even with the weight of the pressure washer's full reservoir—but he was already wondering if he would be able to get through all sixteen combinations in one day.

Arik made sure he was perfectly aligned with the shield, then opened the nozzle. The pressure drove the crystalline solution deep down into the loose Venusian soil, as Arik expected, but it also raised a surprisingly large cloud of dust and debris. The cloud was dense enough that until it settled, Arik completely lost sight of the Public Pod wall. Without a landmark, it occurred to him that he could easily get turned around and walk off in the wrong direction. Even after the mustard-yellow cloud had dissipated, enough of the solution had become airborne and adhered to his visor that his visibility was significantly diminished. He tried to wipe it away with his glove, but it had formed a thin crust against which his soft gloves were completely ineffective.

Arik walked back to the rover and mixed the second batch, which he then applied much more carefully. He held the nozzle as far away from his body as he could, and tried to keep himself rotated away from the cloud of dust. He had to maintain a wide stance in order to keep his balance, and since he wasn't able to watch exactly where he was spraying, he inadvertently clipped the heel of his boot with the pressurized stream. He knew that Cam had told him that it would take nothing short of a high-energy laser to penetrate an environment suit, but Arik also knew what high-pressure jets were capable of cutting through. Most of the saws in the shop were actually diamond-tipped high-pressure water jets which, when combined with even a relatively minor abrasive, could easily cut through twenty-five centimeters of solid steel without generating any significant heat.

He dropped the pressure washer and fell to one knee in order to inspect the back of his boot. There was a single clean spot in the location where Arik had felt the impact, but the microfiber didn't appear to be compromised, and the HUD inside his visor was reporting normal pressure. Arik told himself that there was no way the pressure washer could cut through an e-suit boot, even with the added abrasive properties of the crystals in the solution. If it were even remotely possible, Cam would have said something. He knew exactly what Arik was going to be doing. They had even agreed that Arik would probably need to use the highest setting in order to get the seeds and crystals deep enough into the ground and adequately combined with the soil. But Cam didn't anticipate the massive plumes of dust that the process produced, so if visibility issues hadn't occurred to him, what else might he have missed?

Arik decided there was no sense in overanalyzing the situation. It was actually very simple: if the pressurized stream had significantly punctured the suit, he would be dead already. And if the puncture was small enough that the suit could compensate for it, the HUD would report a breach. Assuming his suit's arrays of sensors—and the thousands of lines of software that gave them life—were all functioning and communicating normally, he was fine.

When Arik was back at the rover and the pressure washer was in the trailer, he wondered whether he should mix the third batch and keep going, or close up the gate and head back to the airlock. His EVA wasn't progressing as smoothly as he'd expected. He knew Cam's advice would be to scrub it, make some adjustments to the program, and try it again the next time he could get away from work. But when would that be? Arik knew he was already way too focused on terraforming, and that his time away from the Life Pod and his lack of progress on AP were not going unnoticed. It was difficult for him to accept that, for the first time in his life, he was not meeting or exceeding what was expected of him. He was completely confident that what he was working on was far more important than AP, and that the payoff of accomplishing something that everyone knew was impossible was worth whatever short-term price he had to pay, but he also knew that there were limits. He had to produce results soon, or get back to working on his actual assignments. He didn't have a good sense of how much more time he had, but certainly not enough that he could put off conducting his first batch of experiments by several days or even weeks. It was always possible that he could see results from his very first trials, but it was much more likely that he would be back out here dozens of times experimenting with dozens of combinations and techniques. There was simply no way to know, so he had to make the most of every opportunity he had.

Arik mixed the third batch and walked back to the Public Pod wall. He decided it was better to lose a little visibility than to risk clipping his suit again, so he stood directly in the plume of the debris as he applied the solution. He accumulated fewer crystals on his visor than he did the first time by backing away as soon as he was done rather than waiting for the cloud to dissipate, but he could still see that there were definitely more crystals absorbing and refracting the light from the strobes than there were before.

By the thirteenth batch, Arik had decided that he would finish. He was tired, but he was close enough to having all sixteen combinations applied that his determination to complete his EVA's objectives was suppressing his fatigue. His legs burned as he walked back to the rover, but they recovered sufficiently while he mixed the next batch. His arms were getting limp, though he found if he moved the compressor back and forth between his hands several times as he walked, he was able to keep up enough strength. His visor was so opaque and his eyes so irritated from sweat running down from his saturated *hachimaki* that he couldn't see the strobes around him anymore, but he could make the trip back and forth by memory. He knew he would have to drive the rover back very slowly, relying on its computerized navigation system to keep him on course, and he would probably have to go in and get a new helmet before he would be able to maneuver the vehicle into the airlock, but at least he would be finished, and his first set of experiments would finally be in progress.

Since the Public Pod's wall was curved, and his experiments followed the curvature of the structure, Arik had to mentally adjust the path he took back to the rover each time by a couple of degrees. He was thinking about the correct trajectory while on his way back from setting his final experiment when he moved the compressor from one hand to the other, then realized, while on his way down, that he had stepped through a loop in the twisted hose. Arik knew he was tired, but he had no idea how tired he was until he was lying on the ground without the strength to push himself back up. In a prone position, the suit's center of gravity was all wrong, and Arik felt himself anchored to the ground.

He decided to stay down and try to relax enough to regain some strength. The suit appeared to be fine since the HUD inside his visor reported nothing unusual. The cartridge hadn't been jostled loose, and he hadn't bent his glove or helmet threading. He had enough power and air that he could stay on the ground for at least thirty minutes recovering his strength if he needed to, and still make it back with resources to spare. If only he could reach his eyes. They stung so badly from the salt in his sweat that he instinctively bumped his glove against his visor trying to wipe them. His perspiration was becoming noticeably more potent, which Arik knew was a clear indication of dehydration.

Another symptom of dehydration is muscle cramps, and when Arik felt his calf constrict into a knot, he couldn't stop himself from screaming. The spasm triggered a cramp farther up in his hamstring, and as he writhed, the other leg seized up as well. Arik had experienced plenty of muscle cramps in his life while sitting in overly restrictive positions in front of his workspace or while sleeping, but he was always able to get up and walk them off, stretch them out, focus on relaxing enough that he could stop the worst of the pain. But locked in the environment suit, he couldn't even reach down and squeeze his legs to try to increase the blood flow. He had no choice but to lie on the ground and accept the pain unconditionally with his only solace being his screams and sobs.

When Arik opened his eyes again, the pain had subsided, but he was suddenly horrified by the realization that he'd fallen asleep. His oxygen and power indicators had gone from green to yellow, and his lower body was numb from lack of circulation. When he tried to move, the soreness in his leg muscles recalled the tight balls of pain from the cramps as they threatened to seize up again.

He tried to rub his legs, but the environment suit limited his reach. He finally succeeded in walking his glove down his leg and over his hamstring, but as he squeezed, the suit reacted to the pressure and pushed back. Arik lay back down and drew his legs up toward his chest, flexing and relaxing his muscles as much as he could to get the blood flowing again.

While he waited for his body to reoxygenate, he analyzed his situation. Most events that people referred to as tragedies happened suddenly and spectacularly: earthquakes shaking entire cities to the ground, spacecrafts breaking up in the heat of reentry, nuclear reactors melting down during routine tests. These were the things we worried about, guarded against, spent countless hours training for. But Arik was realizing now that disaster could be dissembled into small unidentifiable components and smuggled past even our best defenses. It could be allowed to gradually accumulate right in front of us without tripping an alarm or registering on a sensor. Misfortune knew how to use our egos and our pride against us to lure us into vulnerable and defenseless positions. The more obstacles you placed in death's path, the more it was compelled to slip in through the cracks.

Arik hoisted himself to his feet in a single fluid motion. His legs wanted to buckle beneath him, but he was prepared, and he pushed hard against the ground and forced them to support his weight. Gravity helped pull the blood back down into his muscles, and with the restoration of feeling came fresh pain and tingling with the intensity of a high-voltage electric current. But his legs were regaining strength. He was on his feet, and he knew he could walk. He just needed to make it to the rover. Even if he was unable to pilot it home, he could probably use the radio to contact someone in the Wrench Pod.

Arik slowly turned and tried to detect the faint light from the strobes in order to get his bearings. He rubbed at the rough coating of crystals on his visor, but they had only hardened and fused further in the heat. Since he couldn't see any lights, he knew he must be close to the rover. He could see the pressure washer on the ground with the nozzle and the compressor spread far apart. He remembered that he had just moved the compressor from his left hand to his right when he went down, which meant that if he stood with the compressor on his right side, he should be aligned with his original path.

By the time Arik had been walking long enough that he knew he should have reached the rover, he had already made a decision. He knew that this would be the moment when panic would set in and intensify to the point where he might not be able to think logically, so he wanted to be prepared to act without having to think at all.

Arik knew that if he had been wrong about the hand in which he was holding the compressor, he would have been walking in the opposite direction of the rover, and back toward the Public Pod, which he would have already reached. That left three possibilities. The most likely was that he had simply walked right past the rover and hadn't been able to see it, which meant he was continuing on toward the red strobe of the airlock. It was also possible that the pressure washer hadn't landed predictably, and that he was walking at an approximate right angle to his intended path. Ninety degrees in one direction would take him back to V1, roughly somewhere between the Wrench Pod and the Public Pod, which would enable him to easily follow the wall back to the airlock. Ninety degrees in the other direction, however, was the worst-case scenario. There was a chance that Arik was walking directly away from V1, out into the barren Venusian desert where nobody would even think to look for him until long after it was too late.

But even the worst-case scenario was manageable. If Arik turned around in time, he would be OK. If he was able to determine that he was walking in the wrong direction soon enough, he could turn back 180 degrees and correct his mistake. Given enough time, and assuming he could keep himself from panicking, he had a good chance of making it back no matter which direction he was walking in. The problem was that he had no idea what "enough time" meant. Although he was keeping a steady pace, he was extremely weak, and he was going through his remaining air and power alarmingly fast. Arik had never thought to ask Cam what would happen if he ran out of power while he still had air remaining. It was possible that the suit would depressurize, though it was also possible that it simply wouldn't be able to adjust to changes in pressure, which meant that he might be able to survive long enough to get inside. But the cartridge's battery life and remaining air pressure were roughly equal, so it really didn't matter if he could survive without power or not. There was nothing ambiguous about running out of air.

The answer to the question of when to turn around was obvious: once he had walked as far or slightly farther than the farthest landmark could possibly have been from the point where he fell, he needed to turn back. But the challenge was in accurately estimating his position. Arik's head was pounding from dehydration; although he was exerting a great deal of effort, he no longer had enough moisture left in his body to perspire, and the heat was affecting his ability to reason. He believed he had walked far enough that he should have reached the airlock, but there was no way to be sure. His oxygen was down to 18 percent, which meant he was probably getting very close to the point of no return, if he hadn't crossed it already. Very soon, it wouldn't matter whether he turned back or kept going. The outcome would be the same.

Arik was beginning to wonder if it might in some way be more dignified to just sit down and accept his situation. He envisioned himself using the remainder of his time to scratch out a final message in the Venusian terrain. He was trying to figure out if he would be able to fall into a deep enough sleep to avoid the unbearable panic and pain of suffocation when he noticed that he was walking directly next to a wall. He felt an intense wave of relief surge through him while simultaneously feeling ridiculous for almost resigning. He envisioned Cam finding his body with a terse apology to Cadie carved in the dirt only a few meters from the airlock. He imagined his friends and family trying to instill some sort of dignity into his mysterious and senseless death.

But there weren't any strobes. Arik was hoping to see the red strobe of the airlock, but there were no lights or beacons of any kind around him at all. The entire perimeter of V1 was lined with flashing diodes, and even through his encrusted visor, he should have easily been able to see them from this close. He stepped up to the wall and put his hand on the surface. Rather than the inert metal alloy shell of V1, the structure in front of him was concrete. He followed it for a few meters, looking for something familiar, but its face didn't change and no strobes came into view. He took a few steps back and tried to judge its height, but the top was lost in the haze. Arik felt a small piece of basalt under one boot, and although he was hesitant to expend the energy, he picked it up and lobbed it as high as he could toward the structure. A moment later, it hit the ground in front of him.

Arik was startled by his air indicator going from yellow to a flashing red as it dropped below 10 percent. Whatever he had found, it wasn't V1, and he knew he wasn't anywhere near the airlock or anything else he could identify. His best guess was that he had been walking in the opposite direction of V1 and had hit a wall that somehow defined its boundary. He'd never heard of a wall enclosing V1, and he couldn't imagine what it was designed to keep out, but right now that wasn't important. If the wall was indeed the perimeter of V1, walking in a line perfectly perpendicular to any point along it should take him back to V1.

Arik began walking with the wall at his back. Whatever happened, he would walk as far as he could and not deviate from his path.

CHAPTER EIGHTEEN

A HOLE IN THE WALL

THE SORENESS IN ARIK'S LEG muscles made him feel like he'd been beaten from the waist down. He had no idea that skeletal muscle cramps and spasms could be so intensely painful and could leave such lingering tenderness. But he began to realize that there was something about the sensation that he enjoyed— something about the remnants and repercussions of something arduous and dangerous and stupid that made him feel alive. He didn't sit in front of his workstation where he could keep the strain off his legs; he stood and moved around and let himself feel the pain.

He brought up the most detailed schematic of V1 that he could find. The view defaulted to his current location (his home lab), but he re-centered the 3-D image on the dome—the very center of V1—and began zooming out. He expected to be able to retreat infinitely, but the perspective froze precisely at the moment when all of V1 filled the frame. He tried to pan, but the model wouldn't move in any direction. He zoomed in on the main airlock and found he was able to pan at that level, but once again the image froze at exactly two hundred meters from the outer airlock doors—right around where Arik believed he had encountered the wall.

The schematic was a vector-based three-dimensional representation, which meant that it was essentially a collection of mathematical formulas describing V1 in great detail. Vector-based schematics allowed the viewer to inspect the model from any altitude and from any angle; the computer simply needed to use the vector's equations to recalculate and render the requested perspective, which it could do, for all intents and purposes, instantaneously. Even the most complex vector-based graphics with the most detailed textures requiring millions of calculations per microsecond were trivial for modern computers to render. The only limitations were the amount of data represented in the vector's formulas, and any arbitrary constraints intentionally injected into the model itself.

Decompiling the schematic and looking for the block of instructions that prevented it from being viewed past a certain set of coordinates would not have been practical. Schematics were far too complicated to be authored by hand; the tools used to compose them generated equations that were designed to be evaluated by computers rather than read by human beings. But the vector viewer—the program that interpreted and rendered vector-based models—was much simpler. While removing the limitations from the model itself would have been prohibitively complex, removing the code from the viewer that observed and enforced those limitations was much more feasible.

Just as Arik brought up the source code for the vector viewer, he got a video connection request from Cam. He had hoped to know more about the wall before they spoke, and for a moment, he considered ignoring the request. But Cam would know that Arik's workspace was active, and Arik knew that he owed Cam an explanation. He took a moment to prepare himself, then accepted the connection. Cam did not wait for a greeting.

"What the bloody hell happened out there?"

"I know," Arik said. "I screwed up."

"That's a bit of an understatement. What did you do to your helmet? I had to use hydrochloric vapor to get it clean."

"It was the crystalline catalyst. It reacted with the heat and fused to the visor. I couldn't see well enough to get the rover inside."

"Arik, you probably couldn't see well enough to get the rover inside because you were half dead. Did you know your cartridge got scrapped because they thought it was defective? It registered as completely empty. Nobody has ever seen that before. They figured it had to be broken because nobody thought anyone could survive on so little air."

"Did I break any Wrench Pod records?"

"This isn't a joke. Do you have any idea how close you were to not coming back? You were literally no more than a breath or two away."

"Believe me, I know."

"And do you know what would've happened if you'd run out of power?"

"I was wondering about that."

"The suit holds a residual charge for about five minutes, then after that, all your equipment, with you inside it, would've been crushed down to about the size of your helmet in less than a second."

"Fortunately I would have probably already suffocated."

"Trust me, the implosion would have been much more merciful."

"I'll keep that in mind for next time."

"There isn't going to *be* a next time. You know that, right? You know you can't go back out there."

"Can we talk about this in person?"

"It's OK, I'm alone." Cam moved to the side so Arik could see the room behind him. "There's an all-hands drill going on right now."

"That's not what I mean. There's something else I need to talk to you about."

"Something more important than you almost killing yourself?"

"I found something out there."

Cam squinted at Arik in the polymeth. "What do you mean?"

"I'll explain when you get here."

Cam's eyes flicked up to the top right of his workspace as he checked the time. Arik could see he was contemplating his schedule. "Where are you?"

"At home."

"Are you sure you weren't hallucinating? Seriously. I'm not saying you didn't see anything, but it wouldn't be the first time someone thought they saw something out there that didn't exist. Especially with as little oxygen as you were probably getting."

"I should have proof by the time you get here."

Arik could see that Cam's vexation was starting to yield to curiosity. "I'll be on the next maglev. This better be good."

The video stream closed. Arik opened his vector authoring tool and created the simplest model possible—a single micropixel point—then added zoom and pan constraints to it. He ran the vector model viewer inside another program that showed him in real time the lines of codes that were being executed, then loaded his test model. He zoomed out until the model froze, then switched to his code editor.

The vector viewer wasn't as easy to modify as Arik had hoped. He was expecting to simply remove a few statements that checked to see if any zoom or pan constraints were specified in the model, but the logic turned out to be inherent in the camera control algorithms themselves. Fortunately they were well isolated and easy enough to reverse engineer that Arik had revised versions working against his test model by the time Cam arrived. He opened the front door from his workspace, and a moment later, Cam was standing behind him.

"There's something I forgot to tell you," Cam said.

"What's that?"

"I'm glad you're alive."

"So am I," Arik said. "And I fully realize that I'm an idiot."

"I'm the idiot for letting you go out there without more training. How did you let your air get so low? You didn't notice the big red blinking alert right in front of your face?"

"I committed the ultimate EVA sin. I got lost."

"How can you get lost when you're surrounded by over two hundred ten-thousand-lumen diode strobes?"

"It turns out they're useful only if you can see them."

Cam gave Arik a look of exaggerated disbelief. "Um, should I have mentioned that? I assumed it was self-explanatory."

Arik checked his watch. "How much time do you have?"

"Not much," Cam said. "Tell me what you found out there."

"Hopefully I can do better than that. Hopefully I can show you."

Arik loaded the V1 schematic into his modified version of the vector model viewer. He zoomed in on the dock.

"OK, this is the dock, and here's the airlock." He zoomed out a few levels and began to pan. "Here's the outside wall of the Public Pod, and this is right about where I left the rover, right?"

"Looks right."

"I got turned around and started walking in this direction…" He panned away from V1, and this time, the model did not freeze.

Cam leaned forward. "What the hell is that?"

About two hundred meters from the public pod, there was a thick red line segment.

"I was hoping you could tell me."

"I have no idea."

"It's some kind of a wall."

Arik zoomed out until they could see all of V1. The wall formed a meandering perimeter around the main structure and the ERP.

Cam looked from the schematic to Arik. "Wait a minute. You walked all the way out there?"

"Apparently."

"And you actually saw this thing?"

"I was standing right in front of it."

"Could you tell what it was for?"

"No."

"How tall is it?"

Arik tilted the view and zoomed in on the section opposite the airlock.

"Twenty-five meters. Jesus."

"That can't be right. What's it made out of?"

"It looked like it was mostly concrete."

Cam shook his head. "No, that's impossible. If it was concrete, it would require regular maintenance. Who's maintaining it if we aren't?"

"That's a good question. Maybe we didn't build it."

Cam sat in the plastic chair that Arik wasn't using. "If we didn't build it, then who did?"

"I don't know, but think about it: it's far enough away that nobody would ever find it unless they were either looking for it, or they were lost. You spend fourteen hours a day in the Wrench Pod, and you've never heard anything about it. Yet someone obviously put a huge amount of work into building that thing, and someone seems to be maintaining it."

"Are you suggesting there's someone—or some*thing*—on Venus that we don't know about?"

"No," Arik said. "Whatever's out there, the Founders know about it. And they know about the wall too. Otherwise, it wouldn't be in the schematic. But it's being kept secret. I had to modify the vector viewer to be able to see it."

Cam stood up again and pointed. "What's that right there?"

Arik panned a few meters, recentered, then zoomed in. "It looks like a door. I must have been right next to it."

"Two and half meters wide. That's big enough to get a rover through."

"So what's your theory?"

Cam shrugged. "I don't have one. I agree it's strange, but maybe it's just a wall. Maybe the Founders built it to prevent wind erosion or something."

"It's big enough to keep out a lot more than wind," Arik said. "And it doesn't make sense that you didn't know about it."

"There's a lot about the Wrench Pod I don't know yet. Maybe it just hasn't come up."

"Maybe. Or maybe nobody else in the Wrench Pod knows about it, either. How much concrete do you have in the warehouse?"

"Not enough to maintain something like that. We hardly use any concrete anymore. It deteriorates too rapidly."

"Well, it looked well maintained to me. I didn't see any cracks in it, or any rubble or debris on the ground. Is there anyone in the Wrench Pod you trust enough to talk to about this?"

"No way," Cam said. "At least not yet. I think we should keep this quiet."

"I agree."

"And whatever you do, don't go back out there."

"I have to check on my experiments."

"*I'll* check on them," Cam said. "You have to promise me, Arik. I can't be responsible for something happening to you. We'll figure something out, but for now, you *cannot* go back out there."

Arik hesitated. There was much more to do than just observe. There were dozens of additional experiments that needed to be performed, possibly even hundreds before he started seeing results. They needed a new technique for mixing and delivering the seeds and crystal catalyst solutions, and they needed to find new areas where they could work without being discovered. There was no way Cam could take on a project like this in addition to his other responsibilities. Arik knew that the pace at which he could work through Cam would be far too slow to yield results before he had to give up and get back to AP. But he also knew his friend well enough to know that there was no way Cam was going to concede.

"OK," Arik finally said. "You have my word."

CHAPTER NINETEEN

THE OTHER SIDE
OF THE WALL

ONLY NEW WRENCHERS WERE ASSIGNED inventory duty. Cam
had managed to avoid it, but with every week that he wasn't chosen or managed to talk his way out of it, his odds deteriorated.
Arik knew that sometime in the next six weeks, Cam would be
asked to spend his days roaming the warehouse with a polymeth
tablet and a mass scanner, lost among the towering racks, pallets,
and stacks of material. For seven straight days, as long as none of
the rovers broke down, he would have no reason to be anywhere
near the dock.

Arik never told Cadie about getting lost outside V1, but he
did tell her he was taking a break from his terraforming research
to try to make progress on AP again. She assumed, therefore,
that whatever it was he was building pertained to his work in
the Life Pod—an assumption Arik made no attempt to correct.
When she asked him what the device was for, Arik told her he
would explain it to her when and if he ever got it to work; the idea
was a long shot, and he wasn't ready to discuss details yet.

He could think of no better name for his device other than
a "plug gun." The barrel was a long, transparent piece of pneumatic tubing that he salvaged from a scrap heap. It had a plastic
stock and rubber recoil pad that fit against his shoulder, and a
large, empty wire-and-steel frame on the top that was designed

to accept an environment suit cartridge in order to provide the gun with power and air pressure. There was a small loading port in the bottom for inserting shells, and an ejection port in the side for dispatching them once they were spent.

The plug gun was designed to be held against the shoulder with the muzzle pressed firmly into the ground. It was a double action design: the first sucked a plug of dirt up into a chamber where it was mixed with seeds and a crystalline catalyst solution from a borosilicate shell loaded through the bottom port, and the second action simultaneously drove the mixture back down into the hole from which the plug came and ejected the glass shell through the port on the side.

The plug gun had several advantages over the pressure washer. It was designed to operate without raising dust or debris so as not to affect visibility, and since the crystals were loaded through glass shells, everything could be premixed in the lab and applied much more efficiently. It was small enough that it could be placed in the back of a rover rather than requiring the trailer, and because the plug gun was so precise, Arik could apply his experiments in a clean, simple, and dense grid.

In theory, the plug gun would allow him to set up just about as many experiments as he wanted. An environment suit cartridge had plenty of air and juice, and since all the solutions were premixed and the process required so little physical effort, it seemed perfectly feasible that he could set at least a hundred plugs in the course of a single EVA. Since this could very well be his last shot at getting outside for the foreseeable future, and his final opportunity to prove the viability of terraforming, Arik knew he had to maximize his chances of happening upon just the right combination of genetic engineering and catalytic compounds.

But increasing his numbers also meant increasing the amount of space he required. Since he didn't want to disturb his experiments by the Public Pod, he would need a new site—one where he could use as much land as he needed, and where he was certain nobody would come across his work. Arik knew of only one place within range that guaranteed him the space and seclusion he required: the other side of the wall.

It turned out that getting through the door wouldn't pose much of a problem. Arik was able to locate four doors in the security manifest that did not appear on any schematic. He assumed one was the door in the section of the wall almost directly opposite the airlock, and the remaining three were evenly distributed along the rest of the wall. They were all locked, but Arik was able to fix that without being prompted for so much as a password or biometric verification. Whoever engineered the system had relied on the woefully inadequate principle of "security through obscurity," which held that a system was secure as long as no one knew it existed. The flaws were obvious.

Arik was initially planning on trying to talk Cam into letting him go back outside one last time, but he eventually concluded that it was actually better for Cam to remain staunchly opposed. Despite the amount of time Arik had spent outside, he had clearly proven that plenty could still go wrong, and that there was no way to prepare for every possible scenario. Arik had already accepted that he might not come back, but he obviously couldn't expect Cam to accept that as well. By Cam prohibiting Arik from going outside, Arik hoped that he would feel that he had done everything in his power to prevent an accident. By blatantly disregarding Cam's instructions, Arik was taking responsibility for his own actions and, should something go wrong, claiming all the blame for himself.

Arik learned through Cadie that Cam had finally been assigned inventory duty. Cadie told Arik that she wouldn't be able to eat with him that day because she and Zaire were having lunch with a mutual friend in the Code Pod.

"Maybe I'll meet up with Cam then," Arik said. "I need to get out of this place."

"He can't," Cadie told him. "Cam's in the warehouse for the week. That's why Zaire's free. You want to come with us?"

"Actually," Arik said with a pensive frown, "you know what I feel like doing? Playing some cricket."

"Good," Cadie said. "You work too much."

He set an automated away message, closed his workspace, grabbed his cricket bag (which he had started storing at work), and left for the Play Pod. If all went well, he told Cadie, he would be back in a few hours, hot and sweaty from a midday pickup game. It was unusual for Arik to show Cadie any affection at work, so she was caught off guard when he paused on his way out to kiss her and tell her how much he loved her.

Cadie looked surprised, but not displeased. "Is everything OK?"

"Everything's great," Arik told her. "I'll see you this afternoon."

No one tried to stop Arik as he walked through the shop to the dock. Since it was never explicitly acknowledged that Cam had given Arik EVA training, there was no way Cam could effectively ban Arik from the Wrench Pod, so Arik got all the same nods and waves from the wrenchers that he always got. His routine was slightly different this time, however; today Arik was carrying his cricket bag over his shoulder, and rather than taking his usual path, which brought him right past the warehouse entrance, he took the long way around.

There were other subtle differences in Arik's behavior. Rather than leaving his watch in a locker, he extended the strap and put it on over his environment suit, and instead of hanging up his cricket bag, he laid it gently in Betty's trunk. And in addition to the cartridge he loaded into his e-suit, he propped a second one up against the rover's passenger seat and strapped it down.

Arik considered stopping by the Public Pod to check on his experiments on his way out to the wall, but decided not to for two reasons. The first was that he knew the door he was looking for was almost precisely opposite the airlock, so the safest way to locate it was to come out of the airlock and continue on a perfectly straight path. Although it seemed simple enough to stop by the Public Pod first, then head out to the wall from there, Arik had learned the hard way the virtues of reducing all possible variables during an EVA. Even the most innocuous deviations from one's itinerary could provide disaster with just the sort of opportunity for which it relentlessly and tirelessly waited.

The second reason Arik wanted to get out to the wall as soon as he could was that the door's lock was on a timer. The automated away message that he left before closing his workspace triggered a timer that would unlock all four doors around V1's perimeter one hour after it was activated, then lock them all again two hours after that. Arik had ceaselessly debated with himself the logic behind automatically relocking the doors; it made much more sense to leave them all unlocked and to simply lock them manually once he was safely inside again. However, he ultimately decided that he had a responsibility to automate the process. Although the prospect of missing the window and getting locked out of V1 was horrifying, he felt he had to leave the colony as well secured as he found it in the event that, for whatever reason, he wasn't able to make it back. Although there didn't seem to be any danger of letting anything harmful out of V1, Arik had no idea what he might be letting in. Even leaving the doors unlocked for just two hours could be putting V1 at risk.

Arik found the wall easily, and the door was exactly where the schematic placed it. It was a massive slab of metal that had somehow gotten slightly dented near the center. There were columns of bolts through the steel, presumably securing it to further layers of steel beneath with alternating grains in order to strengthen it against warping, and it hung inside a metal frame by four bulky hinges. Beside the door, protruding from the concrete wall, was a tremendous wheel that Arik assumed provided leverage against a set of screws and gears in order to move the mass of steel. But not yet. He checked his watch and saw that he still had a little more than thirteen minutes before his script removed the locks—just enough time to assemble and test the plug gun.

He walked around to the back of the rover and opened his cricket bag. The components inside interlocked and snapped together easily, and the spare environment suit cartridge slid perfectly into place where it activated inside its frame. He took an empty borosilicate glass cylinder from his bag and loaded it through the bottom port, then placed the muzzle carefully against the dirt and leaned into the stock. When he felt that his leverage and balance were right, he pulled back on the action bar. There was a jolt as the pneumatic chamber instantly filled with dirt. When he pushed the action bar forward again, there was a slight kick as the chamber abruptly emptied and the shell ejected from the side with a high-pitched and melodious *ping*.

Arik had built a lot of things in his life, but nothing that made him grin precisely like this.

He laid the plug gun across the back of the rover, checked the time, then pressed both gloved palms against the surface of the door. He hadn't calibrated his watch perfectly with the beginning of the timer, but within a few seconds of his expectation, he felt the vibration of the massive steel bars as they withdrew into the wall. Arik stepped back and used the tip of his glove to gently press a button on his watch and start the two-hour countdown. He would have liked to have waited a few minutes to see if anything happened now that the door was unlocked (had he tripped an alarm? Would the door automatically lock again? Would someone or something open it from the other side?), but he was already beginning to feel the pressure of the countdown. He stepped to the side and began applying his weight to the massive metal wheel. With every half turn, he could see the giant slab of steel pivot.

When the door was open about half a meter, it occurred to Arik that he should probably have some sense of what was on the other side before opening it the rest of the way. He left the wheel and peered through the gap. As far as he could tell, the other side of the wall was indistinguishable from the side he was on. There was nothing to see but a few meters of rocky ground gradually swallowed up by the thick mustard-yellow atmosphere. If there was anything out there, it wasn't coming forward to meet him, but waiting for Arik to come to it.

He went back to work on the wheel. The gears weren't difficult to turn, though when the door was open wide enough that he judged he could get the rover through the gap, he found he was slightly winded and already damp with perspiration. He wondered if he should change his plan and leave the door open since closing it behind him would not only consume additional energy and air, but it would also require him to reserve enough strength to open and close it again on his way back. But he knew he wouldn't have much walking to do since he had the rover, and even if he injected all one hundred solutions into the ground, the plug gun was an efficient enough tool that it required very little effort to use. It was better to stick to the plan.

Arik maneuvered the rover carefully through the gap, and as he expected, there was another wheel protruding from the wall directly opposite the one on the inside. For some reason, closing the door was easier than opening it had been, though with every half turn and every few centimeters that the gap narrowed, he found himself increasingly reluctant to cut himself off entirely from V1. He checked behind him several times to look for some hint of what the wall was intended to defend against, but all he could see was the thick yellow haze. Leaving the door open, even slightly, would have made him feel better, but he was committed to following his EVA's program as closely as possible. He had planned it logically and objectively precisely to avoid making spontaneous and emotional decisions that he knew could later reveal themselves to be tragically erroneous.

Before getting back in the rover, Arik removed a small steel canister from an outside pocket in his bag. He unscrewed the top, depressed the nozzle, and applied the supercooled isotopic iodine inside to the surface of the door from as high up as he could reach all the way down to the ground. The liquid would evaporate rapidly in the Venusian heat, but not without leaving behind enough residue to emit a clear radioactive beacon while it decayed over its half-life of eight days. Arik had initially planned to use a simple radio transmitter to help him find his way back, but even the smallest one he could find or build in a reasonable amount of time would have been noticeable to anyone or anything that might happen by the door. The isotopic iodine, on the other hand, was completely invisible without the right equipment, and couldn't be removed or deactivated.

Arik calculated that he would need between forty and sixty minutes to get all one hundred solutions injected into the ground, which gave him about thirty minutes to locate an ideal spot. He really didn't know what constituted "ideal" except that it should receive all the remaining sunlight of the Venusian day, and should be inconspicuous but still easy enough for him to locate again sometime in the future. He knew he would probably end up using a piece of ground a few meters down from the door just outside the shadow of the wall, but locating a suitable plot of land was only part of the objective of this portion of the EVA. The secondary objective was exploration.

Although his instincts were telling him to lay down his experiments and get back inside as quickly as possible, another part of him was compelled to continue driving slowly away from the wall. Arik was used to being outside by now, but this was something else entirely. He had left V1 in every relevant sense. There were no strobes around him to help him maintain his bearings, and no one standing by in the airlock in the event of an emergency. He was on the other side of a massive wall that neither he nor Cam could even begin to explain, and with every meter he traveled, he burned another second off the timer that could cut him off from everyone and everything he had ever known. Receding behind him was the safety and familiarity of V1, and in front of him, concealed in the hazy yellow smog, was both the fear and exhilaration of the unknown.

The rover's suspension and tire pressure had stopped adjusting itself, and Arik suddenly realized that he was driving on a road. He stopped and raised the trajectory of the radar mapping device. On the screen between the hand controls, he could see the well-packed terrain stretch out before him with the rocky Venusian desert on either side. He raised the radar farther, ignoring the warning from the navigation system that the trajectory was now out of range, and watched in astonishment as the small screen rendered something he could not understand: massive round structures concealed in the haze ahead, each one several times taller than the tallest section of V1. There were plenty of hills and mountains on Ishtar Terra, but what Arik was seeing was far too perfectly formed to have occurred naturally. He advanced slowly, his eyes flicking back and forth between the rover's screen and the dense yellow atmosphere in front of him until he was close enough that one of the enormous structures began to emerge. At first he thought it was a perfect cylinder, but as it revealed more of itself, it took on the unmistakable hyperbolic shape of a nuclear reactor cooling tower.

As the rover continued forward, additional towers emerged beside flat rectangular structures that Arik assumed housed the nuclear reactors themselves. He knew that none of this could be related to V1's power grid; their entire fusion generator was no bigger than Arik's bedroom, and certainly had no use for a cooling tower. This was clearly a remnant of more primitive nuclear technology when fission reactors generated indirect energy by creating steam that drove turbines, and required massive cooling towers to transfer heat waste to the atmosphere. Arik recalled Cam's story about the original Founders, about an initial colony of unsuccessful settlers. It wasn't a perfect fit, but even the most far-fetched folklore sometimes had long, tenuous roots that tapped into a distant reality. It was obvious that V1 was not the first settlement on Venus; at least one entire human civilization had come before them, and apparently gone.

Arik continued forward past various dilapidated structures. The last cooling tower he saw was partially destroyed, its black carbon scoring telling of a quick but violent explosion. In some ways, the settlement had actually been more successful than V1—at least temporarily. Expansion had clearly been a priority, though they seemed to have struggled to meet their own energy demands. Arik wondered how they supplied themselves with oxygen and food. Most likely, they had been entirely dependent on Earth—so much so that even the smallest disruption in communication or launch delay could have been catastrophic. To these people, the GSA would have been God.

Or maybe this settlement even predated the GSA. If Arik rummaged through the debris, perhaps he'd find the insignia of the European Space Agency, or even logos from long-defunct NASA. Considering the age of nuclear fission technology, this could very well have been built before the last worldwide economic and environmental cataclysm. Arik tried to imagine what living here would have been like. There was no way they could have had the technology to get home if the settlement had proven unsustainable. While the people on Earth were witnessing economic collapse, global power shortages, and one environmental catastrophe after another, to the Venusian colonists, the entire process would have manifested itself as nothing more than a perfectly good radio signal from Earth one day, and inexplicable dead air the next.

Arik was about to turn the rover around when he noticed the road surface changing and his visibility dramatically improving. He lowered the radar again to safeguard the rover's axles, then checked his watch. If he still wanted to set up his experiments, he would need to get back very soon; however, his original EVA objectives now seemed distant and misplaced. Arik had inadvertently discovered an entirely new world—the only world he had ever witnessed outside V1—and its secrets and stories were mesmerizing. With the atmosphere clearing, he was starting to be able to see farther than he thought possible on Venus, and he wanted to see more.

The rover's tires began slipping, and Arik could see that the terrain had become much finer, almost gritty. He had no idea how the rover's navigation and traction systems would adapt, so he parked and decided to continue a few more meters on foot. He could see as much as a hundred meters ahead of him now, so there was no chance of getting lost, and the dark terrain was almost perfectly flat with only occasional gentle outcroppings. The soil was different here, and Arik pulled the plug gun from the back to help him get a better look at what was below the surface.

The ground became increasingly soft as he walked, and his boots began to sink with every step. He approached one of the outcroppings around him—about a six-meter-long cone-shaped mound that he assumed was basalt or some other type of volcanic rock—but before he reached it, he stopped. He watched the black ground around him carefully and was almost positive that he detected movement. He used the end of the plug gun to prod the surface in front of him to make sure it was secure, and just beside the mound, the muzzle sank below the surface. When he withdrew it, a thick tar-like substance clung to the tube in long viscous threads like black mucus. Arik assumed he was on the edge of an impact crater where the surface was still partially molten, but when he squatted down and inspected the mound next to him, he realized he could not be next to a lava pool.

What he had thought was some sort of a rock was in fact a tremendous skull several times larger than the length of his entire body.

CHAPTER TWENTY

THE HOMELESS

ARIK KNEW THAT HE WAS experiencing some form of shock. He was perfectly aware that he should be monitoring his suit, checking his watch, getting the rover turned around and pointed in the direction of the radiation beacon, but none of those things seemed important anymore. He was fixated on the colossal skull in front of him, and his mind reeled from trying to comprehend its implications.

No evidence of life had ever been discovered on Venus—even simple microbial life. There was no way something of this magnitude could have evolved and gone unnoticed for this long. A creature with a skull that size would have to be between thirty and forty meters long, weigh hundreds of metric tons, and would have to be the largest terrestrial or aquatic animal in the history of life on Earth.

He experienced short moments of clarity—even moments when everything made perfect sense—but he found that they were impossible to retain. While the brain was perfectly capable of adapting to the gradual changes that invariably accompany the passage of time, it was perfectly incapable of accepting an entirely new reality all at once. Arik logically understood what he had just discovered, but he was unable to accept it.

The same world that fascinated him only moments ago now sickened him, and Arik began to worry about vomiting in his helmet. The nausea and disorientation convinced him that he needed to get back to the rover, but just as he started to turn, he found himself careening forward from a massive blow to the back of his helmet. His legs were unprepared for the sudden forward momentum, and after a few feeble steps, they fell behind and he went down into the sand and sludge in front of him. He scrambled backward and turned himself over, instinctively raising the plug gun to defend himself, and the moment he felt pressure on the muzzle, he jerked the action bar back. His visor was almost entirely coated with a combination of grit and the thick black mire he had fallen into, but he could see far enough in front of him to witness the pneumatic chamber turn crimson, then yellowish as his attacker's intestines filled it and pressed against the plastic tubing. The shrill scream from above penetrated his helmet and pierced his eardrums. He reversed the action of the plug gun and the weight that was on top of him was gone.

Whatever knocked him down had not been wearing an environment suit.

He was trying wildly to get to his feet when he had his legs jerked violently out from under him, then he felt himself being dragged by his boots away from where he had fallen. Just as he regained the presence of mind to try to kick and fight, he felt himself pinned to the ground at the arms and legs. A tremendous weight was applied to his chest, and a moment later, a green spark appeared through the grime on his helmet and gradually grew into a long, blurry emerald flame. A heavy fleshy appendage landed on his visor and slowly and deliberately wiped aside enough of the film that he could see what was on top of him.

It was a human form, though grotesquely disfigured. It was completely exposed except for a primitive plastic respirator through which Arik could see a nose of only a few protruding shards of cartilage, and exposed gums and jaws in which were set short metallic teeth filed into points. It was bald, and its head and face were covered in wide black lesions. Its eyes were hard and dry and misaligned, and they looked at Arik more with curiosity than savagery. In its webbed stump of a hand, it grasped a green laser cutter, which it lowered slowly toward Arik's visor.

Then a hole appeared just below the creature's eye, directly through its sinus cavity, and for a moment, Arik could see deep into its head before it burst apart, coating his visor and turning his vision red. A fraction of a second later, he heard the shot.

The weights on his arms and legs were gone. There were two more shots in close succession, then a third, and then it was silent. Arik wondered if he'd been shot, but the HUD inside his helmet reported that his suit was intact. He tried to see what was around him, but his vision was almost completely obscured by the red and black fragments dripping from his visor.

He felt his heel being kicked, and a moment later, his helmet rocked back and forth as his visor was wiped down. There were two environment suits above him: one kneeling over his head, and the other standing at his feet. He could see mouths moving through the visors, but he wasn't receiving their audio.

They each grabbed one of Arik's arms and hoisted him up. Arik watched them talk to each other as they looked at his eyes and inspected his suit. Their environment suits were an entirely different design than Arik's—some sort of flexible metallic material—and their visors encompassed more of their helmets, affording them greater peripheral vision. Both the faces inside were bearded, gaunt, and clearly exhausted.

They guided Arik gently, each holding an arm, moving at his pace. Arik looked up and saw that they were approaching a vehicle. He tried to find the rover but couldn't see where he'd left it. Both of the men had long rifles on their shoulders with fat, illuminated digital scopes, and the taller one was holding Arik's plug gun.

A pressure door emerged from the side of the truck, then divided into two. One of the men used a running board to step up into the opening, then turned and took Arik's hand. Arik stepped up and was simultaneously pulled and pushed inside. He sat down on a bench and watched the doors close and seal them in.

It was dark inside the truck, but there were enough instruments with diodes and brightly lit screens that Arik was able to see. There were two more rifles mounted on the wall, four pistols with trigger guards wide enough to accommodate gloves, and what appeared to be machetes, but with handles designed to be gripped with both hands. A green diode above the door illuminated, and both the men removed their helmets. One of them picked up a small wireless device and sat in front of a wide monitor in the back of the vehicle. His long, unkempt black hair was wet and flat with perspiration.

A picture appeared on the screen, and Arik could see that it was coming from a camera mounted on the top of the vehicle. As it panned, he noticed crosshairs in the center of the image, and a muzzle protruding from either side.

The other man removed Arik's helmet and stowed it under the bench. He had thin blond hair but a fierce and full red beard. His mustache grew down over his mouth like red stalactites, and he was chewing something vigorously.

"You're all right now, boy," the man said in an accent that Arik didn't recognize. And then to the other man: "Do a thermal scan before we go."

The screen went dark and began panning. It centered on a small pink mound on the ground with another slightly darker mound nearby.

"It looks like three down," the man controlling the camera said. "One thanks to this kid. Nothing moving now."

The man with the red beard pounded on the wall next to him and the vehicle started moving. It gained speed rapidly and they all bounced and swayed with the rough terrain. The men sitting on either side of Arik seemed more concerned with their equipment than with him.

"What's happening?" Arik finally asked. He wasn't sure what the right question was. "Who are you?"

The man with the black hair snapped his rifle into an empty rack on the wall. "Right now, we're your very best friends in the world. Do you have any idea what would have happened to you if we hadn't found you?" He picked up Arik's plug gun and inspected the stained muzzle. "This is a damned interesting contraption. It did a hell of a job on that poor bastard back there."

"Who were they?"

The man removed the cartridge from Arik's plug gun and casually stowed it in a cabinet with other cartridges of various sizes and shapes. "They're the homeless," he said.

"Here you go, boy." The other man was offering Arik a plastic bottle. "Drink this. Are you hurt?"

"I don't know. I don't think so. Where are we going?"

"We're taking you home."

Arik could feel that the vehicle was moving quickly. He knew he hadn't traveled more than two kilometers away from V1, which meant he didn't have much time to ask questions.

"Where are we?"

The two men looked at each other. The man with the black beard put his head back and squeezed two clear drops into one eye.

"Should we tell him?"

"Fuck it. That place is demented. He deserves to know."

"It may be demented, but it pays well. You sure you want to bite the hand that feeds us?" He passed the eye drops to the other man.

"I'm sure he's figured most of it out by now, anyway. Haven't you, Arik? Where do you think we are?"

"I'll give you a hint," the man with black hair said. He blinked his watery eyes. "It ain't Ishtar Terra."

Arik looked at each of the men and wondered if it was a mistake to admit how much he had figured out. But he knew this could be his last opportunity to talk to anyone willing to give him the truth.

"Somewhere on the continent of Antarctica," Arik said. "Judging by the length of the day."

The man with the red hair smiled. "So it's true what they say about you! You *are* a fucking genius!"

"All the more brains for the homeless," the other man said flatly.

CHAPTER TWENTY-ONE

DECONTAMINATION

WHEN THE INNER AIRLOCK DOORS opened, Arik found the dock aglow in red emergency lighting. Two men wearing full isolation suits and masks waited in the center of the room beside a large plastic bin. There was a female voice calmly reciting instructions, but they were too muffled by his helmet for him to understand. The scene brought a fresh wave of panic over Arik as he tried to draw a correlation between his actions and what appeared to be an actual level-zero emergency. He shouldn't have left the doors in the wall unlocked. All of V1 had been vulnerable for well over an hour. He imagined what the man in the van had called "the homeless" cranking open the steel barriers, running in coordinated packs toward V1, using the airlock's emergency ingress lever to get inside. He envisioned the grotesquely deformed figures sweeping through the halls and pods of V1, closing their trap-like jaws around the flesh of the people he loved, tearing it off in red and black chunks. He saw fleshy appendages using laser cutters to dismember bodies and divide human remains, to open the tops of heads to get at the fatty proteins inside.

Something was very wrong.

Arik took a step back as the two men approached, though he knew he had nowhere to go. When they were close enough, he recognized them as his father and Dr. Nguyen. Darien's gloved hands broke the seal of Arik's helmet and began unthreading the collar. Dr. Nguyen stepped behind Arik, and Arik could feel him doing something to the back of the suit. As his helmet was removed, Arik listened to the eerily sedate voice emanating from the polymeth around them:

"—emergency level zero. This is a full oxygen lockdown. Report to your nearest oxygen station and await further instructions. Attention. We are currently at emergency level zero. This is a full oxygen lockdown—"

"What's going on?" Arik asked his father. He had bigger questions that he knew would be the catalyst for hours of discussion, argument, and debate—perhaps even the end of V1—but his immediate concern was for the safety of Cadie.

Darien leaned in close. "You are to say absolutely nothing until we are alone." Most of his face was covered by his mask, but all Arik needed to see were his eyes. "Do you understand?"

"Where's Cadie?"

"She's safe. I promise."

"I want to see her."

"You will," Darien said, "but you have to trust me when I tell you that the best thing for everyone right now is for you to follow my instructions exactly. Do you understand?"

Arik watched his father. He knew that his current situation put him at a tremendous disadvantage—that the Founders had no doubt planned for exactly this contingency and had anticipated everything he was likely to do. Arik needed more information before he could act rationally. He needed leverage. He knew that the best thing to do right now was probably nothing at all. Darien was still looking for acknowledgment from Arik that he wasn't going to attempt something impulsive or reckless. Arik nodded.

Darien dropped the helmet to the bottom of the plastic bin. This was not how Arik imagined his reentry into V1—the beginnings of a new and entirely different life for himself and his generation—but the level-zero emergency put him on the defensive. It forced him right back into the subservient and obsequious role he had sworn only minutes before to never recognize again. But even without the chaos, Arik was realizing that he would probably never be able to challenge his father, to demand anything from him, to address Darien as a true peer. The foundation of Arik's relationship with his father would always be deference, not equality.

"How does it look?" Darien said. He was working on the latch inside the suit's metal collar.

"It's reporting full integrity," Dr. Nguyen said from behind Arik, "but I want to do a field decontamination just to be sure."

The two men helped Arik out of his suit. Everything they removed went into the plastic bin: gloves, Arik's watch, cuff and sleeve straps, the sweat-soaked *hachimaki*, and finally the entire suit itself.

"Your clothes too, Arik," Dr. Nguyen said. "Everything goes in the bin."

Arik hesitated, but he didn't protest. There was no one else in the dock, and from what he could see of the shop from where he was standing, the entire Wrench Pod was empty. By now, everyone in V1 would be sealed inside pressurized oxygen chambers or zipped into temporary tents. Arik peeled off his clothing and dropped it into the bin. His body was wet with perspiration and he stood shivering in the center of the dock, his bare feet pressing into the metal grate floor.

The two men stood back, and Dr. Nguyen opened a portable decontamination kit. He removed a small canister, shook it vigorously, and punched a hole in the top with a tool that was embedded in the cap. A fine vapor was ejected from the nozzle

that Dr. Nguyen directed up and down Arik's body while cir-
cling him. The vapor was drawn to Arik's bare skin, where it
adhered and quickly dried into a fine white powder. Dr. Nguyen
then removed a wand from the kit, twisted the handle, and began
moving it slowly just above the surface of Arik's skin. It emitted a
deep ultraviolet light that Arik could tell was interacting with the
dried vapor. He could also tell from the clicking sound it made
that it was searching for dangerous levels of radiation. When Dr.
Nguyen was satisfied, he tore the top off a foil bag and removed a
light-blue robe and a pair of slippers.

"Put these on, please, Arik."

The material felt waxy and it clung to his skin, crinkling as
he moved. The last item in the kit was a carton of powder with a
small, stiff plastic brush fastened to the side. Dr. Nguyen removed
his gown and gloves and dropped them into the bin.

"Darien, if you'll finish up here, I'll escort Arik to his room."

Darien nodded, then leveled a serious look at his son. "We'll
talk soon."

Arik could tell they were on their way to the Doc Pod. Aside
from Dr. Nguyen giving Arik curt instructions along the way,
the two did not speak, though the oxygen lockdown instructions
effectively filled the silence. The maglev tubes glowed red like
giant arteries.

When they got to the room, Dr. Nguyen directed Arik to the
shower. He gave Arik a plastic hazardous waste bag that was for
his robe, slippers, brush, and the empty detergent carton when
he was finished. Arik was told to use the powder all over his body
but to avoid getting it into his mouth, eyes, and nostrils.

By the time Arik got out of the shower, the lighting had
returned to normal and the recording had stopped. There was a
set of new clothes on the bed, still wrapped in crisp cellophane,

and a bottle of water on the bedside table. Arik's skin was irritated and swollen from the detergent and the stiff plastic bristles.

Arik had figured out back in the dock that the level-zero emergency was probably just a drill, but it wasn't until he was in the shower that he realized its purpose. With everyone in V1 sealed inside oxygen chambers and tents, there was nobody for Arik to come into contact with while being escorted to the Doc Pod. Other than Dr. Nguyen and Darien, the last time anyone saw Arik was when he was prepping for his EVA. With all of his equipment and clothing collected and presumably incinerated, there was no evidence that he had ever returned. As far as the rest of V1 was concerned, Arik was still outside.

Arik touched the fogged polymeth wall beside the door, and was not surprised when it didn't open.

CHAPTER TWENTY-TWO

QUARANTINE

WHEN ARIK WOKE UP, THE small hospital room was dim, and he couldn't tell whether it was late in the evening, or if he'd slept all night. He instinctively checked his wrist, but it was bare. He started to feel around in the bed for his watch when he recalled his father dropping it into the plastic bin along with the rest of his equipment and clothing. It all felt like a dream to him at first, but unlike dreams that tended to fade the more you went over them in your mind, everything was streaming back, filling in, pushing away the numbness of sleep and replacing it with the mounting dread of reality.

When Arik sat up, he realized that someone had been in the room. His workspace filled the wall with a video message cued up, the frozen first frame of his father's grim face casting a somber glow. There was a hard compact case on the chair in the corner, and a boxed meal had been placed on the table by the bed.

The sight of the food made Arik realize how hungry he was. He picked up the plastic box, broke the vacuum seal, then set it back down while he waited for the chemical reaction to heat the stemstock inside. Darien's huge blue eyes were looking just past Arik, seemingly transfixed by something on the other side of the room. Arik thought about how sensitive our perception of eye alignment was, how we can always tell when someone is looking directly into our eyes, and how obvious it is when eye contact is intentionally being avoided. He thought about what his father had said to him back in the dock and still couldn't resolve the ambiguity: had Darien been looking out for Arik, or was his primary concern maintaining the secrets of the Founders? He stood up in front of his workspace and activated the message.

Darien's face became animated. His eyes wandered around the room as he gathered his thoughts and tried to settle on where to start. Arik backed away and sat down on the edge of the bed. He could hear the hot gasses escaping from the boxed meal, and the smell of the stemstock filled the room.

His father took a deep breath and looked up.

"Arik, I can't imagine what you must be thinking right now. I'm sorry I couldn't be there in person when you woke up, but there's just too much going on. I brought you something to eat, and there's a case with a few of your things on the chair. Dr. Nguyen recommended a short quarantine period, just to be certain everything is OK, so I'm afraid you won't be able to leave just yet. I'm sure he'll be in shortly to explain.

"I don't quite know where to start. I know you must have a lot of questions, and I'll answer them all as soon as I can, but there are a few things I want you to know right away.

"First of all, I need you to understand that V1 was the best life your mother and I could give you. It may not seem like it right now, but you have no idea how lucky we are to live here. We have air, food, water, shelter, protection. You've seen what it's like out there for people who don't have the things that we have, and believe me when I tell you that you haven't seen the worst of it.

"Arik, the human race has failed spectacularly. I don't know how else to say it. There are no governments left, no laws, no economies. There's so much waste and poison and destruction out there that it's easier to contain ourselves than to contain it.

Humanity's greatest achievement has turned out to be finally overcoming the forces that, for hundreds of thousands of years, prevented us from destroying ourselves.

"I don't know that anyone fully understands how it happened—how mankind was intelligent enough to defeat the natural system of checks and balances, but somehow not intelligent enough ensure its own survival. The easy answer is that there were simply too many variables. While one part of the world was perfecting cost-effective solar technology, another part of the world was pumping so many pollutants and particles into the air that sunlight couldn't penetrate the atmosphere anymore. Just when wind turbine technology reached its peak, weather patterns became too unpredictable to know where to build them. Nuclear technology was supposed to be the big savior, but it ended up being the most destructive form of energy in history; the proliferation of reactors also meant the proliferation of weapons-grade enriched uranium and plutonium. The equations were just too complex, and there were just too many competing and chaotic and neutralizing forces for anyone to fully comprehend.

"But the biggest problem was that people had completely lost control of their lives, and when people lose control, they lose hope. And when that happens on a massive scale, Arik, the hopelessness becomes a ravaging and consuming and dehumanizing pestilence far more destructive than any nuclear detonation.

"V1 isn't a lie, son. It's hope. It's a reason to live. It gives us a purpose. It's our mission. It's the only pod system on the planet that's been successful and that's actually growing. It's the only place left where there are families, culture, medicine, celebrations, scientific advancements. For better or for worse, Arik, it really is the pinnacle of human achievement.

"I want you to know that your mother and I have no regrets. I don't expect you to understand this until you have children of your own, but there's nothing a parent wouldn't do for his or her own child, including lying when necessary. Whatever you're feeling right now, I want you to understand that all of this is for you. Everything your mother and I have done has been to give you and Cadie and Gen V and your children and your children's children a chance at not just survival, but *happiness*. Arik, if humanity has a future at all, V1 is it."

Darien paused, closed his eyes, took a breath. He shifted in his chair before continuing.

"There's something else I have to tell you. An employee of mine, your former teacher, Rosemary Grace, attempted suicide last night by overdosing on serotonin inhibitors. She's in a coma right now with very little brain activity, and we have no idea if she's going to recover. I'm so sorry to have to tell you this—I know how fond of her you were—but I want you to understand how difficult the truth about V1 can be to live with. She was a very strong woman, but even for her, the enormity of what V1 represents was too much."

Arik shook his head in defiance of what his father was telling him. Rosemary was one of the most influential role models in Arik's life. She was his teacher, his mentor, and his friend. She had occasionally even taken on the maternal role that L'Ree had never been able to fully embrace. The thought of someone he loved so much feeling so hopeless and defeated as to attempt suicide made Arik feel sick.

"This is exactly what your mother and I have been trying to protect you from. As much as we hated having to lie to you, we hate even more that you know the truth. Of course we would have told you eventually, but not yet. You're in your prime right now. You're on the verge of technology that will provide humanity with limitless air. You just got married, and you and Cadie will be starting a family of your own soon. The last thing we want is for you to be distracted and derailed by all this.

"I want you to know that if you decide you want things to go back to the way they were, we can do that for you. I know you're not the kind of person to walk away from a challenge, but don't think of this as giving up. In fact, it's exactly the opposite. Forgetting would mean that you could focus on more important challenges, things that you really do have the power to change. It would let you get back to the life that all of humanity needs you to live right now. I want you to think about that."

Darien looked beside him, then back at Arik. "I have to go now, son. I'll be there as soon as I can. Let Dr. Nguyen know if there's anything you need. I'll see you soon. And remember that your mother and I love you very much."

Darien reached up and touched the polymeth. The recording froze, flickered, faded. Arik stood up and touched the wall to start the message over again, but it had already been erased.

CHAPTER TWENTY-THREE
GENETIC FINGERPRINT

ARIK PACED THE LOCKED HOSPITAL room, darkly amused by the irony of his confinement. The space he was in was really no different from his entire world—it was simply a little smaller, slightly more cramped. Yet somehow, it never occurred to him to feel trapped until now. His entire life, he had accepted his containment without ever seriously questioning it. True imprisonment, Arik now realized, was not the inability to move about or go where one wished; it was the realization, acknowledgment, and ultimately the acceptance of that inability. Imprisonment was more powerful as an idea than it was as a physical condition. He thought about how many people who considered themselves free were simply oblivious to their restraints.

To Arik, freedom was not something to be realized physically, but virtually through his workspace. He understood now that he compensated for his life of containment by immersing himself in the infinite and boundless potential of software and science. But that didn't mean he wasn't invested in the physical world. In fact, he was beginning to realize just how dependent on Cadie he was—how always having her nearby had made him take her for granted. Arik could recall only a few days in his entire life when he and Cadie hadn't been together. Their relationship was as fundamental to their existence as the food they ate or the air they breathed.

Arik wondered how Cadie was making sense of everything that was happening—wondered what information she was being given. Even if she'd been assured that Arik was fine and would be returning home soon, he knew that not being able to see him—not even receiving a message from him—would be traumatic for her. And the reality was that she almost certainly had not been given any such assurances. The reality was that Cadie probably had no idea whether Arik was even alive or dead. He needed to figure out a way to contact her.

Arik was surprised by how much of his workspace was functional. He had assumed that Fai would have revoked everything but his ability to receive incoming messages from his father and maybe read-only access to his own personal files. As he explored, however, he found that his account was almost entirely intact. He could even see that Cadie's workspace was currently active, though every attempt to communicate with her failed.

The interface allowed him to request various types of communication connections, but each attempt resulted in an unexpected protocol error. Rather than restricting Arik's access to the messaging program (which he could have easily found a way around), Fai had taken the much more thorough and low-level approach of blocking Arik's access at the network level to the underlying communication protocols. The result was that even if Arik were to write his own messaging software, the network would reject any and all packets originating from him (and probably to him, as well, unless originating from his father). Of course, he could always write his own protocol that the network knew nothing about, but Cadie's communication client would have no idea how to interpret it.

Arik was behind an incredibly simple but incredibly effective firewall.

The fear was obviously that he would communicate the truth about V1 to Cadie or Cam and put the entire pod system at risk. He knew his quarantine had nothing to do with the possibility of latent radiation sickness or an undetected injury. It was a psychological quarantine, a containment of information. But he understood the Founders' concerns. They were right to take precautions; even if the truth didn't destroy V1, it would profoundly alter its path and almost certainly prevent it from reaching its full potential. Eventually it would have to come out, but not until V1 was ready. Once certain milestones had been reached, the Founders would complete Gen V's initiation, and a new generation would be born and raised under whatever pretenses were necessary to ensure its survival.

But he still needed to send Cadie a message. By now, she would have been told something to explain his disappearance. Whatever it was, it would have to account for why she wasn't able to see him, or even talk to him, or send him a message. Arik had no intention of transferring the burden of what he knew to anyone else—least of all his wife—but he needed for Cadie to know that he was OK.

Arik had never tried to hack into anyone's workspace before, but as an exercise, he had considered various attack vectors. Compromising an arbitrary workspace was a nontrivial task, but there were two workspaces that he suspected were particularly vulnerable to an attack originating specifically from him: L'Ree's and Darien's.

Everyone in V1 knew that the V1 Computing Cloud used biometrics to authenticate user accounts, and since workspaces were typically invoked by placing your hand on a piece of interactive polymeth, most people assumed V1CC was doing a palm and fingerprint analysis. But Arik knew you could just as easily press an elbow or your knee or even your tongue against an interactive polymeth surface to bring up your workspace since user accounts were actually associated with genetic profiles. Even though humans share 99.9 percent of our genetic encoding, guessing the remaining 0.1 percent was impractical. But since half of Arik's DNA came from his mother and the other half came from his father, half the genetic puzzle was already in place. To get into one of their workspaces, all he needed to do was figure out the other half. With a 50 percent head start, enough CPU cycles, and with the experience he gained working with digital DNA while building ODSTAR, Arik hypothesized that in six to twelve hours, he would be sending Cadie a message through either his mother's or his father's workspace.

Since Arik didn't have his BCI, he needed to figure out an efficient way of interacting with his workspace. For relatively simple tasks, on-screen controls and voice commands were sufficient, but Arik knew he was going to need to review a great deal of source code and write hundreds if not thousands of lines of code himself. Without a more efficient input method, it would probably take him longer to assemble the program than the program itself would need to run.

Arik moved everything on the small bedside table over to the bed and pulled the chair out from the wall. The table slid easily into the corner, and the three pieces of polymeth engaged. He moved his workspace over and divided it among the three surfaces. Arik usually preferred to stand and move around while he worked, but since he would need to use his hands on the table, he pulled up the chair and sat down. It took him about thirty minutes to get the eye tracking and gesture systems properly calibrated and to create a suitable command pallet on the table for his fingers to work with. The configuration wouldn't even come close to matching the efficiency of his BCI, but with a little practice, he would still probably be able to work far faster than anyone else in V1.

There was obviously no way for Arik to spoof the genetic medium itself—to fake an actual cell with actual genetic material inside it. Therefore, he would need to focus on the layer of software that sat between the physical interpreter and the account authentication layer. His program would need to make the authentication code think that billions of slightly different hands were being pressed against the polymeth in impossibly rapid succession.

It occurred to Arik as he worked that given any form of DNA sample—a toenail clipping, a hair from a brush, a flake of skin— he and Cadie together could probably compromise anyone's account. Cadie would extract and digitize the genetic fingerprint, and Arik would insert it into the right place in the security software stack. In fact, he could probably even do it himself with enough time to write some custom software around the shell program's physical interpretation modules. At its heart, V1's entire security model was effectively obsolete. It relied on areas of expertise being disparate and disconnected, and computers being too slow to make "brute force" attacks practical. From the perspective of its original designers, it must have seemed impossibly complex, but to a generation that was completely comfortable crossing scientific boundaries, and to people who interacted with machines and technology as naturally as with one another, it was nothing if not full of possibilities.

It was becoming increasingly clear to Arik how much V1 depended on the ignorance and predictability of its inhabitants. He thought about the ease with which he was able to get outside and even discover and unlock the doors that kept V1 isolated from the rest of the world. If he had really thought about it, he could have probably figured out their true location in the solar system just from the pinch of dirt perched on the grate floor of the dock. How many other clues were there all around them just waiting for the right combination of critical thinking, inspiration, and serendipity? How long would it take for someone else to figure out the secret of V1? Arik's generation, he realized, would become increasingly difficult to control. The foundation of ignorance on top of which V1 was built was already beginning to crumble. It was suddenly clear that eventually it would all need to be torn down and rebuilt if it was going to survive at all. The time remaining before Ishtar Terra Station One would need to be reinvented, reengineered, and entirely reconceptualized—as all complex systems must eventually be—was exponentially dwindling. The only question was whether those in control would figure it out and admit it to themselves in time to dismantle and reconstruct the colony in a controlled and orderly way, or whether it would be allowed to collapse into chaos and barbarism like the world that gave rise to it.

When the program was finished, Arik wrote a series of software tests to verify its functionality. The tests uncovered a couple of potential bugs, which he fixed, then he ran the tests again. They all passed the second time, so he kicked off the final process and obscured the active console in case someone came in.

Arik slept while the program ran. It was designed to wake him up in one of two circumstances: either when it encountered a successful authentication, or when it exited after trying every possible genetic combination without finding a match.

The alarm sounded after only two hours. Arik had been in a deep sleep, and it took him several minutes to figure out that it was a false positive. The program had guessed his genetic fingerprint and successfully logged back into his own workspace. Arik had intentionally omitted the step of comparing newly generated genetic sequences against his own since, over the course of billions of iterations, it would have slowed down the entire process. It also served as what software engineers liked to call a "sanity check"—if the program finished without having guessed at least one known genetic sequence (his), he would know that there was a fatal flaw in its logic.

He didn't feel like he was tired anymore, but when the alarm sounded a second time a little over six hours later, he was again in a deep sleep. This time it wasn't a false alarm. When Arik sat down in front of his workspace, he found that the program had exited after exhausting every possible genetic combination. Arik wondered if someone from the Code Pod had been alerted to the attack during the night and hardened the system against it, or whether the authentication mechanism itself might have even detected the billions of unsuccessful attempts and locked itself down, but when he tested his program using his own genetic profile again, it worked as expected.

V1CC was clearly still vulnerable to the attack, and the program passed all of Arik's tests and sanity checks. The fact that it had failed to derive either of his parents' genetic codes from his own left only one reasonable possibility: Arik wasn't directly related to either Darien or L'Ree—or anyone else in V1, for that matter.

CHAPTER TWENTY-FOUR

TIME CAPSULE

EVERY ARGUMENT HAS ONE OR more premises from which a conclusion can be drawn. Premises are the underpinnings of an argument, providing it with a solid foundation on top of which the conclusion sprawls, imposing and presumably unshakable. The vulnerability of an argument, therefore, lies in its premises rather than its conclusion. Attack a well-formulated argument's conclusion and your advances should be easily deflected and rebuffed. Chip away at enough of its premises, however, and the entire argument will eventually implode, collapsing under its own weight into an unsalvageable pile of nonsense and falsehoods.

Darien's argument had seemed sound to Arik. Parents will do anything to ensure the well-being of their children, and knowing the truth about V1 could have endangered Gen V, therefore the Founders were justified in concealing the truth from Arik and his peers. It was a simple argument that, distasteful as it was, Arik had actually managed to accept surprisingly easily. But now the argument's primary premise had been shown to be false. Darien and L'Ree were not Arik's parents, which implied that lying to him and the rest of Gen V was, in fact, *not* justified. With his primary premise disproved, nothing Darien said could be trusted.

Arik felt like he was slipping down the side of a mountain that he knew he would eventually have to climb all the way back up. Every time he believed he had regained his footing and could start making progress, the ground beneath him gave way once again, and he found that he still had further to fall. But he had to be close to the bottom now. There was not much more about his reality that could be challenged and exposed as a lie. He already felt almost entirely disconnected from everything and everyone he had ever known. He was mentally and emotionally isolated every bit as much as physically. All that was left was to discover that Cadie and Cam had been somehow using him, as well. On his way down the mountain, Arik had gone over an edge, and his relationships with his wife and his best friend were the final over-hangs to which he clung. Should they give way, there was nothing left below him but an endless and unrecoverable free fall.

As he paced the tiny room, he began making connections. He was almost positive that Cadie and Cam, along with the rest of Gen V, were victims as well. Arik now believed that they were all adopted. He had taken the remains of Darien's argument and started piecing together one of his own. If it's difficult to lie to your own children for anything less than their own well-being, it stands to reason that far more trivial lies could only be told to those you felt almost no connection to whatsoever. In order for all of V1's secrets to be kept for all these years, no one in Gen V could be biologically related to the people who raised them. One hundred sets of parents could not do to their own children what had apparently been done to Gen V.

The argument was sound. The pieces were starting to fit.

Arik's theory was that Gen V was deliberately and carefully assembled. He believed they were selected from pod systems all over the world specifically for their genetic potential, perhaps even before they were born. It was even possible that they were bred or had been genetically conditioned. Once they arrived at

V1, they were distributed among the most capable members of the population and raised to perform specialized tasks, to excel in areas where V1 was lacking, to solve problems that nobody else was able to solve. They were resources, raw materials to be cast and converted as necessary, thinking machines enslaved by false inspiration.

For all the questions that the collapse of Darien's argument raised, it also managed to answer at least one: Darien had claimed that there was no economy, yet the dark-haired man who helped rescue Arik from the homeless mentioned that V1 paid well and warned the other man against biting the hand that fed them. However much of the earth had been destroyed, and however many wars had raged and governments collapsed, some sort of economy still thrived, and V1 was clearly a major component.

It followed that V1's economic interests were connected to its investment in Gen V. Arik had assumed that the man in the van who confiscated the cartridge from the plug gun was simply using the opportunity to appropriate some salvage, but now his motives were much clearer. On a planet that was no longer capable of providing even the most basic of human needs, what could be more precious and valuable than air? And in an economy where air was the most highly valued commodity, what could be more important than figuring out how to produce it as quickly and cheaply and in the largest quantities possible? Artificial photosynthesis, Arik now saw, was modern-day alchemy. But it represented much more than money. Oxygen was power.

It seemed like an extreme conclusion, but it made too much sense to dismiss. If AP was the ultimate way to increase the supply of air, it stood to reason that terraforming was the ultimate way to destroy demand. There was no doubt in Arik's mind at this point that it was far more practical to engineer ferns, vines, trees, and perhaps even algae that could survive the harsh and toxic conditions of Earth than it was to focus on artificial photosynthesis, yet terraforming had been categorically dismissed, ridiculed, and even forbidden. Terraforming had the potential to ruin everything the Founders had worked for.

In some ways, the Earth had been thrust back billions of years to the carbon-rich age that first gave rise to life. It had been ripped apart, torn down, allowed to dilapidate and decay, and now it was ready for a fresh genesis. But this time, it could be shaped, directed, expedited. Rather than requiring billions of years of evolution through more or less random mutation, it could be done with precision and efficiency through engineering and technology. Arik had no doubt that were it not in direct opposition to the economic interests of V1, his grandchildren could know what it was like to exist outside containment.

Arik was suddenly sickened by the recollection of what Darien had told him about Rosemary. At the time, it seemed perfectly feasible to him that a woman with Rosemary's passion for learning and admiration for innovative and creative thinking could feel impossibly trapped and suffocated by her life in V1. But now the idea that she would even consider taking her own life was unfathomable. Arik realized that Rosemary hadn't given up on V1; she had been silenced, and Arik believed he knew why.

He brought up the proposed V2 schematics and the water pressure data that Rosemary had copied into his workspace the morning they met in her office. He had been so consumed by his responsibilities at the Life Pod and his terraforming experiments that he hadn't had a chance to review her work as she requested, but he now knew exactly what the problem was. Both the physical and the computer models were using elevated water towers rather than pumps to pressurize the V2 water supply, but the tiny sensors embedded in the physical model were showing more relative pressure than what the computer model was simulating. Arik exposed the computer model's hydrostatic pressure formula and made a single modification to it: he recalculated the value of g—the variable representing local gravitational acceleration—using the gravitational constant of Earth rather than Venus. The results immediately updated, and every number was in perfect agreement with those from the physical model.

Rosemary obviously knew exactly what the problem had been. In fact, Arik believed that she had created the error intentionally, then passed it along to him in order to communicate with him in a way that he could understand and that would hopefully go undetected. She knew that the truth about V1 was something he would have to discover for himself—a conclusion he would need to reach gradually, proving it little by little along the way. She also understood the type of thinking he would need to use in order to reach a conclusion that was almost beyond comprehension. Arik now realized that everything Rosemary had ever taught him about problem solving and how to think both critically and creatively was in preparation for solving this one puzzle. He wondered how long it would have taken him to figure out that something that was supposed to be a constant—an immutable, invariable, unquestionable fact—was flat-out wrong. When would he have remembered that the only way to solve some problems was to *question everything*?

Arik knew that all these new premises he was forming led to one unavoidable, unyielding, and very simple conclusion: he would never be allowed to leave the room he was in with the knowledge he now possessed. Even before he had figured out the truth about his parents and Rosemary, it was clear that he'd seen and figured out way too much to ever be allowed to communicate with anyone in Gen V again.

Darien had promised to be there in an hour. He sent Arik a short video message apologizing again for not being able to get there sooner. Once again he committed to answering all of Arik's questions, promised to explain and to stay for as long as Arik needed him to. And then, Darien added, they would discuss options, figure out what was next, determine the best course of action for everyone. But Arik knew that this was no different from any other decision he had ever been presented with. In the end, it would not be his to make. His remaining time and energy were better spent preparing rather than trying to resist.

His top priority was to protect his terraforming research. He knew it would not be safe in the central quantum storage grid, no matter how well he obscured, encrypted, or obfuscated it. He thought about trying to transcribe it to silicon paper, but an hour wasn't nearly enough time, and he knew that a request for a notebook would be met with suspicion and that its contents would be reviewed. Even if he used a cipher, and even if nobody managed to break it, his work would never find its way back to him or anyone else who could successfully interpret it. There was only one place Arik could think of where the data could be safely concealed and that no one would think to look for it: the ODSTAR device that he and Cadie had built.

Fai had blocked Arik's access to all known communication protocols at the network level, correctly assuming that even if Arik were to write a new protocol that the network routers were not able to detect, no other nodes on V1CC's network would know how to interpret it. What Fai had not taken into account, however, were communication protocols that Arik had already written and that other nodes on the network already understood.

Arik had decided to write a custom protocol for transferring data to and from ODSTAR in order to increase its efficiency and simplify the hardware. The process of encoding and decoding data to and from strands of DNA was time-consuming, so Arik wrote a protocol that buffered the data and fed it to ODSTAR as the device was able to process it. Fai had been too proud to ask Arik for any details about how ODSTAR worked, which meant he had no idea that the protocol existed and therefore couldn't have blocked it. Arik searched for the ODSTAR node on the network and found that it was available, ready to read or write data to or from any network node that knew the proper protocol. As a test, Arik queried it for available space, and ODSTAR reported that there was over six hundred megabytes of storage capacity remaining in the specialized twenty-forth chromosome that Cadie engineered. During the process, no communication packets had been blocked or dropped.

It took several minutes to compress and transfer all the data and for it to be successfully encoded. Once Arik was certain it had all been copied and had verified its integrity, he removed the ODSTAR node from the network, then deleted the protocol library he had written to communicate with it. Without the library, and without a specification describing how the protocol worked, it would be nearly impossible for anyone but Arik to read or write data from ODSTAR again.

The last thing Arik needed was a time capsule. He needed something he could bury deep inside V1CC's code base with the truth about V1 encoded in it so abstractly and obtusely that it would be meaningless to everyone else in V1 but him. Since he had to assume that his workspace would be compromised, he needed something he could hide in plain sight, something that would find its way back to him without him needing to go looking for it, something that Fai himself would deliver right to Arik at precisely the right time.

One thing the Code Pod loved to delegate to Arik were incoherent and unrecognizable error codes in the shell program. They claimed they didn't have the time to spend on such trivial tasks, but Arik knew that most of them simply didn't understand the shell program's code base well enough to debug it themselves. Somehow Arik needed to express the truth about V1 in the span of a single error code—condense everything he had learned into one line of alphanumeric characters that would baffle everyone in the Code Pod but speak as clearly to him as a prophetic voice from the past.

By the time Darien arrived, the table was next to the bed again, and the chair was back in the corner. Arik's workspace was closed, and he was lying on the bed with his back to the door. He didn't react when the panels snapped open and the man who raised him stepped in.

Darien stood just inside the room and silently watched Arik for several seconds before he spoke.

"You must have quite a few questions for me," Darien finally said.

"No," Arik said without rolling over or opening his eyes. "I don't want to know anything else. I just want to forget."

Darien nodded at Arik's back. "I think that's best," he said sympathetically. "I really think that's the right decision. I'll go get Dr. Nguyen."

Darien left and the door snapped shut. Several minutes later, Arik felt the air circulation in the room change very slightly, and then he fell asleep. The next time he woke up, his brain was exposed, and he felt tingling in his head.

PART III
A NEW WORLD

CHAPTER TWENTY-FIVE

THE CIRCUMFERENCE
OF THE EARTH

ACCESS TO V1'S MAIN FREQUENCY scanner and receiver wasn't restricted. Instead, access to specific frequencies themselves was controlled. But there were several frequencies used during the day-to-day operations of V1 that anyone was free to scan and listen in on. At least, such frequencies used to be open; since the accident, Arik noticed that V1 had been locked down in several new ways, presumably in attempt to prevent more accidents as the integration of Gen V continued to displace personnel that were far more experienced and disrupt processes and procedures that probably hadn't changed significantly in well over a decade.

Arik wondered if he might get only one shot at this—if his use of the scanner might be detected and called into question. He certainly wasn't doing anything wrong or potentially dangerous; however, he had probably thought the same thing initially about researching terraforming, and later about going outside. He would need to work quickly and to record everything in case someone tried to stop him before he could find whatever it was he was looking for.

Arik used the receiver's software interface to lock in 882.758 MHz—the difference between the two frequencies specified in the message he had sent himself across time. The scanner accepted the input, which meant the frequency wasn't being blocked, and the fact that all he heard was static told him that the frequency also wasn't being used for any type of encrypted chatter. Arik piped the audio stream into his workspace so he could record it. It was five minutes before noon.

Cadie was at work. Arik was supposed to be working as well, but he sent Subha a message that morning letting her know that he had a headache and wouldn't be in until after lunch. Like everyone in V1, Subha gave him a lot of leeway since the accident. Arik had never taken advantage of it until now.

He was in his home office with the door closed. Since Cadie wasn't home, he wasn't using headphones; if it turned out that the message was so faint that he couldn't hear it emanating from the polymeth, he could replay it and amplify it as necessary. The static was low and constant, and he increased the volume enough that he would be able to hear anything below it. Since he didn't entirely trust his ears to be able to detect the message, he was also using a sound visualization program that converted even the smallest audio anomalies into graphical waves and movements. It drew a three-dimensional green line through black space, which Arik could rotate and zoom to get different perspectives on any sound waves it interpreted. The line was slightly jittery from tiny amounts of ambient noise.

Arik checked the time on both his watch and his workspace. They were identical. It was thirty-three seconds past noon, and still all Arik could hear was static.

After a full minute had passed, Arik began to worry that he had made a mistake. He wondered if the code should have been interpreted more literally. Perhaps the message was being broadcast on the original two frequencies, 922.76 and 40.002, and the word *DELTA* was intended as a clue on how to postprocess the data. At a full three minutes after noon, Arik configured the scanner to check the two encrypted frequencies but found that they were quiet, as well. Dead air, just as his father had told him. And even if for some reason there had been chatter, Arik knew that he would probably not have been able to decipher it.

At fifteen minutes past noon, Arik decided to replay the recorded static while continuing to record in the background. He increased the sensitivity of the visual effect and expanded its threshold beyond the range of human hearing. At these levels, the green line was reacting dramatically to any electromagnetic radiation that happened by the frequency. Arik put a pair of headphones on over his ears, turned up the volume, and fixated on the agitated green line.

He listened to almost thirty minutes of static, jumping back occasionally when he thought he heard or saw something significant, but whatever it was, it was never there the second time. It was now almost one o'clock, and when the recording software reported nothing out of the ordinary in the additional twenty-three minutes of static he hadn't listened to yet, Arik took off his headphones and shut off the audio. He sat in the dark with the visualization software giving the room a jittery green glow.

Arik hadn't realized how badly he needed some kind of message to be there until he knew that it wasn't. Even though the chances of detecting something were small, the disappointment was far more intense than he anticipated. He looked down at his hands and saw that they were shaking, and he could feel perspiration forming on his face and neck. He wanted to hurl his headphones against his workspace and watch them shatter, ram his fist into the polymeth, smash the bones in his hand and snap his wrist.

The message was far more than just a mystery he had been trying to solve for the last three days. He had no idea what he expected to hear, but some part of him believed it was much more than just an explanation for Earth's sudden radio silence. Whatever it was, it would give him some purpose beyond his current work in V1—something more profound to devote himself to than scientific distractions and pathetic attempts to please Subha and Kelley. The message, Arik now realized, somehow represented a life beyond the containment and sterility of V1.

Most of Arik's life had been a search for this message in one form or another. He had searched for it in science, in mathematics, in computers, and even in Cadie. Over the course of the last few days, Arik had come to believe that rather than finding the message, the message had finally found him, and at a time in his life when he needed it most. Arik knew that the idea of a mysterious voice embedded in the static of radio waves delivering truth and somehow giving him purpose was absurd, but he wanted to believe that it was possible. He wanted to believe that the message represented more than just an archetypal need for meaning—a form of faith which, in most humans, manifested itself as religion, but in a godless and engineered society like V1, could take the form of hidden messages in radio noise.

Arik should have been on his way to work, but he had already made the decision that he would not go back. He wasn't ready to move on. It would be easy to return to the Life Pod, to eventually figure out AP, to stand up onstage in front of all of V1 while Kelley once again declared him a savior. But even the image of his baby daughter confined to an oxygen tent was not enough to make him give up on the message yet. In fact, his refusal to give up was somehow as much for her as it was for him. He wanted to change V1 before she was born. There was something about this world that made him reluctant to bring another life into it.

But life could not be stopped; it was the world that would have to change.

He brought up the original output from the shell program and tried to see it from a fresh perspective.

2519658000000 922.76 40.002 DELTA

As far as he could tell, there was no other reasonable interpretation of the numbers: the first one had to be a date, and the second two had to be radio frequencies. But if nothing had been broadcast on either of the frequencies—or the delta frequency—on the specified date, the meaning had to be hidden elsewhere.

Arik began looking for patterns. Why these two specific radio frequencies? Why not random frequencies? Why not the frequencies the Wrench Pod used to communicate with the remote maintenance rovers? Why not the frequencies used by the backup communication system? Why not one of the frequencies reserved for distress beacons? The two things the antennas had in common were that they were both used for communicating with Earth, and they were identical models of identical design. They were ten meters high with visual diagnostic systems built into them, and they both were installed on rooftops.

The visual diagnostic systems consisted of tiny cameras built into the tips of the antennas aimed down at their bases. If the antennas ever malfunctioned, the Infrastructure Department could bring up their video streams to make sure they were physically intact before sending someone out in an environment suit to inspect them. Arik couldn't imagine that the antennas themselves could be significant in any way, but he did know that he had probably been outside several times prior to the accident, and could have come into contact with one or both of them. He brought the two cameras' video streams up and placed them side by side.

If it hadn't been for the labels in the top left-hand corners of the images—*ERP (922.76)* and *V1 (40.002)*—the two views would have been entirely indistinguishable from each other. The cameras' fields were just wide enough to capture the bases of the two antennas, but nothing beyond them that would have betrayed the fact that they were positioned a kilometer apart on entirely different rooftops. Arik reconsidered the various meanings of the word *delta*. The fourth letter in the Greek alphabet. The fourth-brightest star in a constellation. The sediment-rich mouth of a river. The only definition that had any meaning to him was the variation in a variable or function, and since the message had originated from him, that had to be the correct interpretation.

Arik took a snapshot of each video stream and ran them through a bitmap comparison algorithm to see what the differences were between them. The cameras weren't capable of being optically zoomed, but Arik could digitally zoom in and enhance specific regions if they stood out for any reason. The first difference the algorithm reported was in the two labels in the corners. Arik applied a mask to the two regions and ran the algorithm again. The computer still uncovered several thousand differences, most of which Arik couldn't see himself, so he adjusted the threshold of the algorithm and ran it a third time. This time the highest percentage of variation occurred around the shadows cast by the two antennas.

The sun was far enough away from Venus that the shadows cast by the two antennas should not have been significantly different, but after a moment of reflection, Arik realized that the discrepancy was probably because of the curvature of the surface of the planet and the fact that the two structures were a kilometer apart. This was easily explained and would not have seemed significant to Arik except for the fact that the shadows were unusually strong. Shadows on Venus were usually little more than faint blurs because of the incredibly dense and refractive atmosphere, but today they had an unusual amount of definition. Today was the exact middle of the Venusian 3,024-hour solar day, and the sun was as strong and as close to being directly overhead as it ever got. Since it was never perfectly overhead, because of their distance from the equatorial region, both antennas always cast shadows of some length, but they were probably as prominent right now as they ever got.

Arik piped the output from the bitmap comparison algorithm into another algorithm to calculate the exact difference between the lengths of the two shadows, which turned out to be .0015708 meters, or 1.5708 millimeters. Now that Arik was accumulating data, he needed to start thinking about how to interpret it. He wondered if the number represented another radio frequency, but if so, the decimal point was probably not in the right place. Although it would be easy to scan all the frequencies that could be associated with the number, Arik's intuition was leading him in another direction. Since he knew that the height of both antennas was exactly ten meters, and he knew that the antennas were exactly one kilometer apart, knowing the difference in the length of the shadows cast by the antennas because of the curvature of the planet's surface would actually allow Arik to calculate the planet's circumference. This experiment was first performed by a Greek mathematician named Eratosthenes over two hundred years before the birth of Christ in order to calculate the circumference of the earth for the first time. The relevance of the circumference of Venus, which Arik already knew to be roughly 38,000 kilometers, was not at all obvious, but the calculation was easy enough that the path seemed worth pursuing. If nothing else, he might uncover additional sets of radio frequencies to scan, or reveal another lead worth investigating.

The antennas and the difference between the lengths of the shadows that they cast formed a theoretical triangle that Arik needed to finish solving before he could go any further. He used a visual triangle calculator to figure out the values he didn't have yet. The most important value was the angle between the antenna and the 1.57-millimeter shadow, which turned out to be .009 degrees. Arik needed to figure out what fraction of the planet's circumference the distance between the two antennas represented, which he knew could be expressed as 360 over .009, or 40,000 kilometers.

The answer was wrong. The difference between his results and the actual circumference of Venus was 5 percent—a margin of error worse than that achieved by Eratosthenes, who used nothing more than a deep well, a stick, and a man he hired to pace out the 800 kilometers between the two landmarks. Arik began the experiment over again, starting with two new screenshots of the video feeds, and allowed the computer to calculate down to as many decimal places as it needed. Once again, Arik found that even though he was 250 million kilometers away, he had somehow calculated, with great precision, the circumference of the earth.

CHAPTER TWENTY-SIX
REDUNDANCY

ARIK DIDN'T KNOW MUCH ABOUT the human brain beyond its regions, their basic functions, and generally how neurons, axons, and dendrites operated. Therefore, as he tended to do with so many other things, he made sense of it through software analogies.

Arik thought of the human brain as a critical software system that could never be fully taken offline and therefore had to be continuously patched over the millennia, extended and expanded through new layers of code written on top of the old, updated in real time so as to never drop a single instruction. Eventually such software systems took on a life of their own, growing far too complex for any one person to comprehend holistically. Software engineers were inevitably forced to specialize in specific paths and features and functions, and the best any single developer could hope to do across the entire system was "tinker." Modifying such systems was an exercise in trial and error—or, in evolutionary terms, natural selection.

Arik understood now that his brain had been altered—not by Dr. Nguyen, but more likely by a team of the best neurosurgeons V1 could afford, probably smuggled in and out beneath the cover of level-zero emergency drills. But as good as they were, and as powerful and sophisticated as the computers and robotics that assisted them, they were still using trial and error. The human brain was the most complex structure in the known universe other than the universe itself, and the best even the smartest of us could hope to do with it was tinker.

To help him understand what was happening to his mind, Arik needed a new metaphor. In his History of Computation and Computing class, Arik had learned about a data storage technique called RAID, or Redundant Array of Independent Disks. When magnetic and early solid-state media were still used for data storage, the world's most critical data was sometimes stored across multiple hard disks, or a redundant hard disk array, so if any one drive failed, no data would be lost. Some RAID levels could even protect against multiple drive failures simultaneously. As an additional precaution, data used to be backed up on a regular basis. It was compressed, encrypted, copied, burned onto various types of permanent physical media, locked away in two or more geographical locations thousands of kilometers apart to guard against natural disasters, hackers, war, terrorist attacks, and, most dangerous of all, simple human error.

Although Arik had no idea how memories were stored, he now understood them to be stored in a fantastically complex and redundant fashion. They were copied, broken down into individual components, distributed among different parts of the brain, associated with as many other memories and given as many paths to and from them as possible. Perhaps over time, some memories even migrated out of the brain and were distributed across our entire nervous system where they sat in our stomachs, our hearts, our legs, our fingers, and our eyes, ears, and noses. Perhaps some lessons learned were even selectively encoded into our DNA and passed down to our children in order to save them from having to make some of the same mistakes we did. Wherever and however experiential memories were stored, Arik now believed that you could not destroy them without destroying the entire organism; the best you could do was make the brain forget where to find them and how to piece them together.

But even that information was redundant. Every piece of lost information contained the address of every other lost piece, so all you had to do was stumble upon one and the rest could be restored and remapped and eventually fully reconstituted. As soon as Arik understood the meaning of the message he had left for himself, he began to understand everything. He remembered the first time he pinched and rubbed the little pyramid of sulfur-yellow earth between his fingers; the fear and exhilaration of stepping outside for the first time; the morning he nearly knocked the outer airlock door out of its track when Cam was teaching him how to pilot a rover; the ill-conceived plan to use a pressure washer to deploy experiments outside the Public Pod; the seizing and spasm of the dehydrated muscles in his legs; the burning of his lungs as he tried to suck a breath out of an empty environment suit cartridge, and the rush he got from the deep, cold, oxygen-rich gasp after stumbling into the airlock and ripping off his helmet.

Arik remembered the wall, the thick steel door, the ruins of the nuclear reactors and cooling towers. He remembered the black viscous ooze that had once been a lapping, breezy blue ocean, but was now almost indistinguishable from the burnt shores that contained it. He remembered the massive hollow eye sockets of the whale skull, the blow from behind, and the red and yellow guts in the muzzle of his plug gun, sucked through the abdomen of his attacker. The inhuman face looking down at him curiously just before bursting apart and painting his visor red and black. The men who retrieved him: one whom Arik had liked and felt safe with, the other who seemed unpredictable and dangerous. The red glow of the oxygen lockdown and the calm and detached voice reciting instructions. The masked faces of his father and Dr. Nguyen. The stained and contaminated environment suit and all his equipment and clothing going into the bin. Standing in the dock naked, arms raised, shivering, the metal grate pressing into his feet. The field decontamination. The powder that scoured his pale, dry skin. The stillness and isolation of quarantine. Rosemary's staged suicide. And finally the time capsule that proved to be the catalyst that reignited all the pain and amazement of his discoveries.

Something else about the human brain was becoming apparent to Arik. Unlike computers, not all data was alike. There was a fundamental difference between the way the brain preserved memories and the way it stored information. Although Arik was able to remember conducting terraforming research, he wasn't able to recall the research itself. Although he remembered transferring the data to ODSTAR, he had no recollection of what he had transferred.

Arik looked behind him at the shelf on which the ODSTAR device once sat. He knew that Cadie had destroyed it along with all the DNA inside it, and that he himself had deleted the only copy of the protocol library that could be used to communicate with it. But he also knew that the data it held was not lost. He knew that his unborn daughter's genetic tattoo was much more than just a stunning image of a near-extinct planet. She also had within her the power to recreate it. It was encoded in her DNA, contained in her very composition, locked up where no one would ever know to look for it, and where no one could ever take it away.

CHAPTER TWENTY-SEVEN

DECISION-MAKING PROCESSES

THE QUESTION ARIK WAS PRESENTED with was this: how do you fool a foolproof system? The answer was obvious: you don't.

But Arik suspected that Cam's claim that the airlock was foolproof actually implied qualifications. Given a, b, and c, you can always expect x, y, and z. To remove those qualifications was to essentially declare the system perfect, to hold it to an impossibly high standard, to invite a relentless barrage of randomly shifting conditions until just the right combination unlocked events that might have seemed completely inconceivable one moment, but were tragically obvious the very next.

Arik knew well the story of the first spacemen to die in the line of duty. Three Apollo astronauts asphyxiated when a spark from faulty wiring ignited their pure oxygen environment and a hatch without explosive bolts prevented their escape. A situation that should have given a first-year chemistry student pause somehow escaped the notice of a thousand of the best engineers in the western world. Arik knew that every situation and environment had buried somewhere within it the components to cause it to ignite. It was mostly luck that kept reactive elements apart from one second to the next. As he'd learned from history books and videos, millions of people had smoked at petrol stations, ridden roller coasters with microscopic stress fractures, flown in planes with leaky hydraulic lines, all without even knowing that the mysterious laws of the cosmos had put them on trial and, for whatever reason, decided in their favor. A great deal of effort went into the systems that tried to keep entropy contained, but sometimes there were just too many variables to keep track of.

Of course, sometimes chaos was intentionally unleashed and used to one's advantage.

Arik needed to get outside one last time, and he needed to do it in a way that was supposed to be impossible. All the environment suits and helmets were now secured inside lockers with independent biometric electromagnetic bolts. Since the locks didn't interface with the V1 Computing Cloud in any way, they couldn't be hacked, and since they contained their own shielded power source, it wasn't possible to easily disrupt the current. Other than providing it with an approved genetic fingerprint, the only way to get one open was to destroy it. Shattering or cutting one open would have probably been relatively easy if not for the fact that the necessary tools (liquid nitrogen, hydrologic snips, power hammer, laser cutter, etc.) were now likewise secured.

Going to Cam wasn't an option. Cam had presumably been kept away from Arik in the Doc Pod for the same reasons Cadie had, but Arik and Cam never reconnected after the so-called accident. Arik didn't know exactly what was keeping them apart, but between Arik's empty promise not to go back outside, emotions surrounding the baby, and the trouble Cam must have gotten into once it was discovered that he was the one who had given Arik EVA training, there was certainly no shortage of material.

In the same way that Arik's ability to communicate had been taken away while he was in quarantine by blocking his access to network protocols, he was now being kept inside V1 by his inability to access an environment suit. But as far as Arik could tell, that was the only precaution that had been put into place. He was still able to access the Wrench Pod, even in the middle of the night when nobody was around, and he couldn't see any physical modifications to the airlock itself. But every environment suit in V1—even the emergency suits stored in the dome next to the nutrient tank—were now biometrically secured, and even if Arik could figure out how to break open one of the bolts, it would be extremely difficult to do it in a way that wouldn't be detected very soon after he did it. It wasn't enough just to get outside; he needed to do it without anyone knowing.

Arik was surprised that the Founders hadn't taken more drastic measures to ensure that he would never be able to get back outside. They could have stationed a guard inside the dock at all times; Fai's team could have modified the airlock's evaluation routine to report certain biometric signatures; the Wrench Pod could have required every EVA to be documented and submitted in advance, approved, and even supervised. But the genius of V1 was in its ability to imprison through subtlety and inference rather than brute intimidation. Arik believed that one of the most fundamental laws of human psychology was that force caused resistance. Make people feel trapped, and they will never stop attempting to escape. But obscure the trap itself well enough, and it was possible to stop the idea of escape from even forming in your prisoners' minds. Arik's neurosurgery proved that the Founders believed it was more important to remove the will to escape than the means.

The one thing Arik had going for him was that he knew even foolproof systems could only guard against known vulnerabilities. By its very definition, there was no way for the unknown to be anticipated and accounted for. Just as Fai couldn't have taken into consideration communication protocols that he knew nothing about, those in charge of the Wrench Pod could not account for the one piece of key information they didn't know Arik had: technically, you did not need an environment suit to survive outside.

Arik didn't know how long it was possible to endure exposure to the radiation and poisonous gasses in the atmosphere, but he had witnessed it himself. None of his attackers on the beach had been using any form of life support more sophisticated than a respirator, and although prolonged exposure had obviously taken its toll on them, Arik assumed that he could recover from a single exposure of limited duration. It was always possible that the homeless spent only a few minutes, or maybe even just a few seconds, outside at any one time, but the visibility was good enough on the beach that day that Arik would probably have seen any nearby vehicles or structures from which they could have emerged. They had almost certainly traveled at least a few kilometers on foot before reaching him, which meant it was probably possible for Arik to survive the one-kilometer walk between V1 and the Earth Radio Pod—even completely exposed.

Obtaining a respirator was easy. Several hundred of them were strategically placed for emergency use throughout V1. However, in order to minimize the possibility of detection, Arik decided to build his own out of items in his lab and from the Life Pod supply closets. He used shatter-resistant borosilicate glass that was easily moldable at 822 degrees Celsius, plastic tubing, rubber sealant, a microfiber filter, and miniature perchlorate "birthday" candles that, once ignited, produced enough oxygen for one person for about one hour. He fashioned a hood out of a shirt to cover his head and face, and selected a pair of tight-fitting goggles which, although useless against radiation, would keep any caustic particles in the air out of his eyes.

But even though Arik was willing to leave V1 without an environment suit, he knew that the airlock wouldn't permit it— at least not knowingly. The airlock walls were equipped with sophisticated spatial analysis technology that was used to create an extremely detailed three-dimensional model of all the objects inside. Before the outer airlock doors were allowed to open, the number of functional environment suits had to be exactly equal to the number of human entities it detected. Arik's first thought was simply to make himself appear as something other than a human entity. What if he crouched down and made himself the size of one of the small robotic rovers? What if he lay down in the trailer and covered himself with a tarp? As he read through the airlock's specifications, schematics, and repair manual, how- ever, he realized that the system would not be fooled so easily. In addition to using radar and visible spectrum scanning, the airlock's sensors also scanned in the infrared range, allowing it to detect temperature variations down to a millionth of a degree. It used ultrasensitive electrodes to detect the electric field gen- erated by the human body's central nervous system, and it was equipped with microphones sensitive enough to pick up indi- vidual breathing patterns and heartbeats, even through environ- ment suits. After every object in the airlock was analyzed and identified, its total weight was measured and compared to a cal- culated estimate. Finally, all this data was fed into an extremely sophisticated algorithm that was designed to answer one simple question: was it safe to open the outer airlock doors?

Arik wasn't prepared to call the system foolproof, but he was willing to admit that fooling it probably wasn't practical.

In Arik's experience, whenever a great deal of attention was paid to one part of a system, it was often to the detriment of another. As sophisticated as the early Apollo training capsule was, under the right circumstance, it was reduced to little more than a crude and extremely expensive incinerator. In order to fool a foolproof system, you simply had to take a step back and look for the one thing that nobody else thought of. It was always there—you just had to know how to find it.

While reading through the airlock's specification, Arik discovered that there was one way to override the computer's decision-making process and force the outer doors to open. Outside the airlock, just to the left of the doors and flush with the wall, was a lever that could be pulled to mechanically force the two doors apart about one centimeter at a time. The designers of the airlock had no doubt weighed the risks of a mechanical override against the possible advantages; it was obviously designed for emergency use only, and since it could be operated only from outside, there was no way anyone inside the airlock could use it to force the doors apart. Additionally, since the inner and outer doors were physically linked, there was no way both the inner and outer doors could be open at the same time, potentially contaminating the entire dock and Wrench Pod, if not all of V1. It therefore seemed perfectly reasonable and safe to provide a means of reentry in the event of a complete power failure. From the perspective of the designers and engineers, it must have seemed entirely impossible for someone to intentionally use the emergency ingress mechanism to subvert the airlock's safety procedures in order to get out rather than in. It couldn't be done, and even if it could, why in the world would anyone try?

The emergency ingress lever was exactly the mechanism for bypassing the airlock's decision-making process that Arik was looking for, but there was one significant obstacle: since it was located outside the airlock, he would need a partner. As there was no one in V1 whom Arik could enlist to assist him in an apparent suicide mission, his only option was to turn to the unfeeling, unassuming, and indiscriminate nature of technology.

As he began learning the programming language of the robotic rovers, Arik reflected on how perfectly complementary humans and computers were. Tasks that were simple for humans were still surprisingly complex for computers to perform, but even the most basic of computers could instantly perform tasks that no human in history could ever hope to achieve. For instance, it would be impossible for any human to manage all the variables that went into maintaining V1's life-support system, and even the most brilliant of human savants could never hope to perform so much as a tiny fraction of the simultaneous calculations that even the most outmoded computers were capable of. Yet even a three-year-old child could probably complete the task of locating and pulling a lever with nothing more than the most basic of verbal instructions.

It would have been much easier for Arik to control the rover remotely, but there was no way for him to access his workspace from inside the airlock. You could take a polymeth tablet into the airlock with you, but in order to avoid possible interference with the spatial analysis systems, the airlock automatically shut them down as soon as the inner doors closed. The only way the robotic rover could operate the emergency ingress lever was if it were programmed to work entirely autonomously.

The instructions that Arik prepared for Malyshka (the rover that seemed to be in the best repair) were written in a language called SEMAL, or Spatial and Environmental Manipulation Language, and took Arik nearly two days to learn. SEMAL had constructs for dealing with three-dimensional objects and their movements through space, as well as built-in algorithms for visual interpretation and error correction. There were libraries that made writing code for the rovers much easier since they contained all the logic for manipulating things like the camera boom and other appendages. Arik also found he was able to import 3-D models from the dock and airlock schematics into his program, which meant rather than spending time recreating a digital representation of the physical environment, he was able to focus on teaching Malyshka how he wanted her to manipulate it.

When Arik transferred the program from his workspace to Malyshka, she immediately came to life. She switched on her work lights, raised her camera boom to get a better perspective on the room, began sending out radar pulses, and waited for the verbal command that would commence the execution of her mission. The whine of Malyshka's servomechanisms, the pings and ticks of her self-diagnostics, and the grinding of her thermoplastic resin treads on the metal grate floor panels were louder than Arik was expecting in the absence of the typical ambient construction noise, but he figured he still had at least three hours before anyone would even be near the Wrench Pod for their morning shift. Just in case, he was prepared with a story about debugging the airlock software for Fai—a procedure that had to be done in the middle in the night so as not to disrupt any scheduled EVAs.

Assuming the program worked, Malyshka would find her way into the airlock, activate the pressure pad beside the outer doors, wait patiently while the airlock evaluated its contents and reached the decision that it was safe to proceed, then slowly advance through the outer airlock doors as they parted. She would then give Arik exactly three hundred thousand milliseconds to finish drinking his water, get his equipment in place, and stand inside the airlock with the inner doors closed behind him. Malyshka was programmed to then locate the emergency ingress lever, grasp it with a sufficient amount of pressure, exert down-ward force on it until its resistance reached a certain threshold, then repeat the operation exactly forty-nine more times. If the doors didn't open within about twenty minutes or so, Arik would assume that Malyshka had somehow gotten confused and was unable to complete the mission. He would exit the airlock and take manual control of the rover from his workspace in order to guide her back inside where he would watch the footage she had captured, examine her logs, and make the necessary adjustments to her instructions in preparation for a second attempt.

All she needed was the command from Arik to begin execu-tion. Arik had already gone over his equipment checklist—res-pirator, two perchlorate candles, goggles, compass, hood, gloves, decontamination kit, change of clothes—but there was one more process he needed to complete: he needed to convince himself one last time that he was making the right decision.

Arik liked absolutes. Although he understood that the world was fundamentally analog, he preferred digital representations of it. True and false were easy to work with, and he liked how they simplified the decision-making process. But he knew that an exclusively Boolean approach wasn't realistic. The world didn't easily reduce to yes or no, on or off, a one or a zero. No one could ever be entirely sure that they were making the right decision—no matter how apparently clear-cut it was—until they looked back on it later and evaluated it with the advantage of per-spective. Arik knew that the world wasn't powered by the simple diametric opposition of right and wrong; rather, it was the much more complex dynamic of cause and effect that drove the steady unraveling of time and space. The relevant question was never whether something was the *right* thing to do; all that mattered was whether a particular action yielded a desirable reaction.

He accepted that direct exposure to the outside could kill him in any number of ways. His brain could swell uncontrollably from the heat, or the corrosive compounds in the air could cause his respirator to fail. His lungs could react negatively to being filled with pure oxygen and the tiny gas exchange sacs at the end of his respiratory system could collapse. He could get disoriented again, or somehow injure himself severely enough that he wouldn't be able to make it back to the airlock. Arik knew better than anyone how dangerous and unpredictable EVAs were, even with all the proper equipment and a carefully planned program. To attempt one with so many unknowns and without so much as an environment suit was to knowingly put himself at a level of risk that he could not even begin to calculate, much less fully prepare for.

It was also very possible that he could simply fail to meet his mission objectives. Although he believed he had unlocked the ERP's doors, he could make it all the way out there only to find that he wasn't able to get inside. Or he could discover that he was unable to operate the radio equipment, or that other pod systems wouldn't respond to him. Even if he executed perfectly, there were any number of ways that he could either fail or give himself away and get caught. And this time, he expected that he would have to sacrifice much more than just his memories.

Arik thought about how he was taking risks far beyond anything he had ever imagined. He couldn't tell anymore how far he was willing to go, or even what he might be capable of. The alternative was to suppress what he knew, distract himself with things like AP and whatever other projects Kelley hoped V1 could profit from. He could focus on raising and teaching his daughter, finding joy in his family and work, living a long and relatively safe and possibly even somewhat fulfilling life with his family and friends. He could reconcile with Cam, play the occasional cricket match, get together with other couples after work to watch video feeds, or immerse in massive and exotic 3-D worlds, or play four-handed chess. He could convince himself that he was looking for just the right opportunity to act, patiently waiting for an opening that he secretly hoped would never come.

None of his options evaluated to a distinct true or false. There were simply too many variables left undefined for him to reach a definitive conclusion. He might not even know if he had made the right decision until looking back on it from the perspective of weeks, months, or years. Since none of his options were inherently right or wrong, he knew to focus on cause and effect, to reverse engineer the problem, to envision an end result and work backward from there. He thought about the world he wanted his daughter to inherit, and about the kind of person he wanted to be, not just in her eyes, but in his own. He thought about what he wanted to be to Cadie, to Cam, to the rest of Gen V, to all of V1 and the world beyond, whatever that was. There was only one thing he could do to become the man he wanted to be, and it didn't matter anymore what it might cost him.

He spoke aloud the name that he and Cadie had decided on for their unborn daughter, *Haná*, and the rover advanced. A little more than five minutes later, Arik began his final EVA.

CHAPTER TWENTY-EIGHT

EARTH RADIO POD

As soon as Arik's eyes detected the light from the ERP's strobes through the dense smog, he realized he was going to make it. Less than twenty minutes before, he had been sure he was going to die.

His mistake had become clear to him the moment the airlock doors were wrenched apart; he should have programmed the rover to accept a verbal abort command. As the heat blasted in through the crack and pressed in on him, Arik realized with surprising objectivity that it would be impossible for him to survive. Just because the homeless could function outside didn't mean that he could. There was something about them that had escaped Arik's attention—some physical mechanism for resisting the heat that he hadn't noticed, some genetic disposition earned over dozens of generations that wasn't part of him. It was clear to Arik now that for him to step outside V1 without an environment suit was much worse than ignorant and misguided—it was suicide.

But when the rover completed its routine, Arik was still alive. He could have aborted by hitting the pressure pad beside the outer doors, but he didn't. Instead, he slipped through the opening and stood just outside the airlock, bracing himself against the scalding wind, deliberately drawing oxygen from his respirator, trying to decide whether he should continue or go back inside. He had made it this far. He was standing outside

V1 almost completely exposed, experiencing the harshness and rawness of the planet more directly than probably anyone else in V1 ever had, and he was alive. Rather than the clean, cool, perfectly humidified breeze of the air circulation system, he was feeling hot, dry, gritty wind; rather than an environment suit maintaining a perfect barometric pressure of one ATM, he could feel the heavy air pressing against his eardrums. Although he could already feel the onset of a headache and his breathing was noticeably labored, he was also experiencing an intense feeling of liberation. He surprised himself with the decision to continue, and the vaguely philosophical notion that this was as good a way to die as any, and probably better than most.

Although it was impossible to become fully acclimated to such extreme temperatures, he found that he was able to function well enough to maintain a steady pace and to navigate effectively. Twenty minutes after leaving the airlock, the ERP's strobes hung in the haze before him, and as he changed course toward the red one, he knew that he was going to live.

• • •

The ERP's airlock was designed for a single person and very little equipment. It was similar to the air exchange chamber between the Dome and the rest of the Life Pod, but it was obviously much older and not as well maintained. The pressure pads beside the doors were stiff and cracked, but functional.

The ERP was big enough to hold only two people. There were two transparent plastic chairs that had been left askew from the last people to use them, and a shallow counter that met the wide polymeth wall. There was a squat nitrogen cooling chamber in the far corner, inside of which Arik found an opened boxed meal and three vacuum flasks of water. He hadn't brought his own bottle because he didn't know how contaminated it might become along the way, so he helped himself to one of the cold silver flasks, keeping it raised until it was empty.

Arik had never fully understood the logic behind the Earth Radio Pod. Because communication with Earth was considered almost as important to survival as air and water, the ERP had supposedly been built a kilometer away from V1 so that it might be spared in the event of a catastrophic accident. Other than its security system, it operated completely independently from the rest of the colony. It had its own computer and life-support systems, and a small fusion reactor housed in a steel box outside provided it with power. None of these precautions really made all that much sense to Arik. The ERP was every bit as susceptible to an accident as V1 itself—perhaps even more so, considering its proximity to its nuclear power supply—and any incident from within V1 that would have been prominent enough to take out the entire communication system probably wouldn't have left anyone behind to use the ERP anyway. But since Arik now believed that the actual function of the ERP was to communicate with other pod systems, he understood why it was imperative that it be kept completely isolated, and why all radio signals to and from it were heavily encrypted.

Arik left his respirator, goggles, and mask on the counter beside the door and sat down in front of the polymeth wall. Since the ERP had its own isolated computer system, workspaces from the main V1 Computing Cloud couldn't be accessed, so all the equipment was operated through a single shared workspace. The scanning software was identical to the software used in V1, and it was already open and active. Arik turned up the volume and began scanning.

All of the signals strong enough for the scanner to stop on were encrypted, and each time he came across one, he was prompted by the tuning software for a pass phrase, access code, or some other form of credential. If he had access to his own workspace, he might have had a chance at cracking at least a few of the less cryptographically secure streams, but without the necessary software and CPU cycles, he wasn't even able to sniff out the types of encryption being used. He thought about broadcasting a hail on frequencies just above and below the frequencies with encrypted chatter hoping that whoever was broadcasting might also monitor adjacent channels for unexpected incoming broadcasts, but he decided that sending out hundreds of arbitrary hails was unnecessarily risky. The safest thing to do was to program the scanner to skip encrypted signals, and to hope for the best.

After reconfiguring the scanner's filtering criteria, he got a hit almost immediately. Beneath the static, he could pick out a distant but articulate female voice with an elegant and melodious accent:

"—minor symptoms including a temporary decrease in red blood cell count. Fifty to one hundred rems: decreased immunity, temporary sterility in males, and mild to severe headaches. One hundred to two hundred rems: nausea and vomiting for a twenty-four-hour period followed by ten to fourteen days of fatigue. Women experience spontaneously terminated pregnancies or stillbirths. Fatality rate of ten percent if untreated. Two hundred to three hundred rems—"

Arik recognized the broadcast as a table of radiation exposure levels and symptoms. He had been preparing to broadcast a hail in response when he realized from the rhythm of the voice that it was a recording.

"—latency period followed by bleeding of the gums and nose, hair loss, fatigue, nausea, and the breakdown of intestinal tissue. Untreated, death is imminent. Most levels of chronic and acute radiation sickness *can be treated*, and many genetic mutations can be reversed. We have an onboard hospital, food, clean water, and a nineteen percent oxygen atmosphere. We can provide safe and free passage to Sakha, South Station Nord, New Elizabeth, and the Hammerfest pod systems. If you register one thousand rems or less, *please* hail us immediately on the following frequency: two-five-nine-point-seven megahertz. If you can hear this broadcast, we can reach you. This message will repeat."

There was a long pause, but Arik didn't wait. The scanner had been working in the background, searching for other frequencies with unencrypted chatter, but it had already finished cycling and there were no other hits. Arik changed the tuner's frequency by hand and transmitted a hail.

CHAPTER TWENTY-NINE

CREEPING DOSE

WHEN HE GOT BACK TO the dock, Arik sealed all his clothing and equipment inside red hazardous waste pouches and dropped them down the disposal chute. He performed a field decontamination on himself as thoroughly as he could, and put on the change of clothes that he'd left for himself in the dock. Malyshka was back in line with her two sister rovers, but her work lights were still on and she was still alert. Arik wasn't done with her yet.

Malyshka hadn't been idle while Arik was in the ERP. Assuming her instructions were correct, after operating the emergency ingress lever exactly fifty times, Malyshka should have turned around and very slowly approached the outer wall of the Public Pod. The electromagnetic field would have prevented Arik from manually guiding her, and her cameras would have been useless, but acting completely autonomously, she should have been able to measure atmospheric conditions at frequent intervals right up to within a few meters of the window shields. If any of Arik's experiments had been successful—if anything at all had sprouted—there was a small possibility that the rover might be able to detect it.

Arik transferred the data from Malyshka to his workspace, then shut her down and clipped her back in to charge. He closed his workspace, picked up the carton of powder and the plastic brush from the decontamination kit, and left the dock. This late at night, the maglev operated only on request, and since nobody else needed it, it was waiting for Arik outside the Wrench Pod where he had left it.

As soon as Arik reached his home pod, he swallowed two pain pills. He had felt OK in the dock, but now the pounding in his head was becoming much less bearable. This wasn't one of his usual headaches that tended to concentrate itself around the site of his incision; this time, the pain filled his entire skull, radiating in short sharp bursts up from the base of his neck all the way through the frontal lobes of his brain. Arik believed he was suffering from what was casually referred to around V1—and especially the Juice Pod—as a "creeping dose." The more scientific name for it was *acute radiation poisoning.*

This wasn't a complete surprise, and not as serious as it sounded. Arik knew that he was exposing himself to radiation, which is why he had taken the precaution of a field decontamination. He knew that even a minor and ultimately harmless dose could cause symptoms, especially when coupled with severe dehydration. What Arik didn't know was how much radiation he'd actually been exposed to.

He would have liked to have worn one of the yellow hexagonal radiation badges that everyone in the Juice Pod kept pinned to their shirts. In the event of an accident, radiation badges could report exactly how many rems an individual was exposed to, and over what period of time. But the badges were kept in a sealed storage locker that Arik didn't have access to, and he couldn't think of a good way of casually asking for one that wouldn't have raised too many questions. He considered building his own, but he didn't have a good way of testing it, and Arik firmly believed that the only thing worse than no data at all was data you couldn't trust.

It was a calculated risk. He knew he was taking a chance, and now all he could do was wait. Arik finished his bottle of water, then took the carton of powder and the plastic brush into the shower.

As he stood under the driers, he began to experience almost debilitating fatigue. The pain medication was starting to neutralize his headache, but he'd been awake for almost twenty-four hours and had endured tremendous physical stress. Arik partially dressed himself and went into his office. It was obvious that he wasn't going to be able to get up for work, so he added a text message to Cadie's queue asking her to let Subha know that he wouldn't be in until after lunch. Cadie would be awake in about two hours, and Arik knew that the first thing she would do is open her workspace—probably even before getting out of bed. He wanted to wake Cadie up—to talk to her and be with her, even if he didn't tell her about going back outside—but he didn't trust himself not to reveal too much. He needed time to think about what he was going to say, and about what his next move was going to be.

There was one more thing Arik wanted to do before he slept. He felt like he needed to review the environmental and atmospheric measurements that Malyshka had collected. He could save a detailed analysis for after he'd gotten some rest, but he wanted to see if his eyes could detect anything prominent in the data—any sort of anomaly salient enough to grab his attention at first glance.

But before Arik could bring up the data, something made him pause. He was conscious of his heart beating in a way that he'd never experienced before, escalating into a violent pounding that he could hear as well as feel, and although the medication had dulled the pain in his head, he was aware of an unsettling accumulation of pressure inside his skull. His breathing grew shallow and rapid. He began to sweat from every pore in his body, and when he looked down, he could see that beads of perspiration had already formed on his chest and arms. His throat opened involuntarily, and his stomach convulsed.

Arik instinctively ran to the bathroom and vomited for the first time in his life.

CHAPTER THIRTY

MOVING PARTS

ARIK DIDN'T GO INTO WORK at all the next day, or the day after that. He'd spent the last two nights on a futon on the floor of his home office. Before Cadie left on the morning of the third day, she knelt at the foot of the cushion and rubbed his leg.

"You really need to go see Dr. Nguyen. This has gone on long enough."

Arik shook his head without lifting it from the pillow. "It's just a virus. There's nothing he can do."

"He can give you an antiviral."

"By the time it had any effect, I'd be feeling better anyway."

"You don't know that for sure."

Arik pushed himself up and leaned against the polymeth wall. His shirt was damp with perspiration. "If I'm not feeling better by the end of the day, I'll go tomorrow."

"Do you promise?"

"I promise. In the meantime, stay away. This would be a lot worse for you and the baby than it is for me."

Before Cadie left, she brought him a boxed meal, two canisters of water, and an extra blanket. When she came home at lunch to check on him, she found he was up and working, and by the next morning, he had almost fully recovered. But Arik knew that his condition hadn't actually changed. He had entered the deceptive and almost cruel latency period of radiation sickness—the incandescent honeymoon, as it was sometimes called. Arik knew that he would get sick again, but what he didn't know was when, or how bad the symptoms would get. The next several days would be critical.

He and Cadie went to work together that day. As soon as they got in, Arik sent Cam and Zaire a short and cryptic text message: "Work late tonight. Leave at exactly 2100. Take the maglev home." Arik and Cadie had lunch together in front of their workstations, and by 1900, Cadie was tired and ready to go home. Arik told her that he couldn't stop—that he might be close to a breakthrough and just needed two more hours. He brought her a boxed meal and a canister of tea, and after they ate, Cadie napped on the futon on the floor of her office. Just before 2100, Arik woke her up by stroking her hair.

"It's time," he told her.

She blinked at him and smiled. "Do you have something to show me?"

"No," Arik told her, "but I have something to tell you. I'll explain on the way home."

• • •

The maglev cut a circular path through V1 with the Life Pod and Dome at the center, and most of the other pods positioned at intervals along the outside of the track. The train consisted of sections that were magnetically levitated fifteen millimeters off a single wide rail in the center. The magnetic cushion almost entirely eliminated friction and allowed the train to be conveyed completely silently in either direction simply by applying electromagnetic currents. Aside from the emergency calipers, there wasn't a single moving part anywhere in the train or the rail system, which meant that it was extremely reliable and almost entirely maintenance-free.

Eliminating moving parts from machinery was the best way to improve reliability. Since the subatomic laws of the universe dictate that it's physically impossible for any moving part to move in precisely the same way every single time, each and every moving part in a system represents some measure of unpredictability and unaccounted-for variability. A vulnerability, you might even say. What if one critical part didn't move quite enough? What if it moved too much, or too quickly, or with slightly more or less velocity than the last time it moved? What if it didn't move at all? How many times can it move before it wears out? How will friction change the way it moves over time? How long will it take to break down the lubricant designed to reduce that friction? How does temperature affect the properties of that lubricant? And if (or when) one moving part fails, how will it affect all the other moving parts downstream of it? The amount of unpredictability in any given moving part wasn't usually the problem; it was when all the tiny swirls combined into one massive vortex—when they accumulated and compounded and cascaded into a chain reaction that was far too complicated to be fully understood even after the fact, much less beforehand when there was still time to prevent it.

By 2100, almost everyone in V1 had found where they wanted or needed to be for the next eight to twelve hours, which made the maglev an ideal place to have a private conversation. Not only was it a good place to be alone, but the maglev sections had no roof and only very low walls, which meant that it generated a fair amount of wind noise while piercing the tunnels between pods. And there were no conductive polymeth surfaces to covertly gather sound waves.

When the maglev stopped in front of the Wrench Pod, Cam and Zaire were standing on the platform. Arik knew that things would be awkward between him and Cam, but as he watched them step into the last section and seat themselves opposite himself and Cadie, it occurred to him that things could also be very awkward between Cadie and Zaire. He wondered how much Zaire knew about the baby. Had she encouraged Cam to do what he did, or was it possible that she didn't even know that the baby had once been her husband's? How would her feelings toward Cadie affect her feelings toward Arik, and how would all their emotions influence their ability to listen objectively to what Arik had to tell them?

Arik realized that the moving parts that drove human emotion and interaction were far more intricate and delicate and explosive than anything found inside man-made machinery. He knew that in order to change all of their lives, he needed to tear down everything that had been built up between them, compact it all down into a clean and solid foundation on top of which he could start building something completely new, something with no moving parts, something so towering and imposing that none of them could dismiss it.

He took a moment to look at each one of them—to be sure he had everyone's attention as he considered how to start. His expression was more determined than hesitant or anxious.

"The first thing I want to do is apologize to all of you for everything I've done, and for the way I've been acting. Cam, I know I got you in a lot of trouble. Cadie, I know I've been distant and withdrawn. Zaire, I know none of this has been easy on you, and I know it's put a strain on your and Cam's relationship. But right now, all of us need to put aside everything that's happened between us. Everything. Anger, guilt, hard feelings, jealousy—whatever it is. Agreed?"

There had been a certain amount of trepidation and even defiance in their expressions, but Arik could see that he had successfully changed the mood. The significance of the meeting had been elevated beyond the possibility of mere argument and squabbling. Everyone was nodding, presumably in agreement that their friendship was more important than dwelling on the past.

"There are things about this place that all of you need to know, but that I can't tell you." Arik looked at each of them in turn and let his words take effect. "You're going to need to see them for yourselves, which is why I'm going to ask you do something that none of you are going to want to do, but that I promise you will be the most important thing you've ever done in your entire lives. You're all going to have to trust me unconditionally."

Cadie was visibly concerned by what she was hearing. Her hands were folded over the bump under her dress. "Arik, please. What are you talking about?"

"In ten days, I want all three of you to leave V1."

"*What?*" Cadie blurted out. Zaire didn't react, but Cam was slowly shaking his head.

"Just listen to me," Arik said. "Two hundred meters out from the airlock, there's a wall, and in that wall is a metal door. Cam, you know what I'm talking about. All I'm asking you to do is in ten days from now, suit up and take a rover out to that door. Everything you need to know will be waiting for you there."

"Arik, I'm sorry," Cam said, "but I can't be a part of this. I should have never let you go outside. I don't know what happened to you out there, and I don't know what's happening to you now, but I can't be a part of this anymore. This has to stop."

"Then *I'll* do it," Zaire said. Everyone looked at her. She tried to conceal her discomfort and apprehension behind her resolve.

"No you won't," Cam told her. "I won't let you get involved in this. None of us are doing this, not unless we know *exactly* what we're getting into."

"I don't need to know," Zaire said. "All I need to know is that Arik is asking us to trust him, and I do. I think we owe him that much. You don't have to do this if you don't want to, but I'm going."

"No," Arik said to the group, "all of you have to go. It's absolutely imperative that all three of you go out there together. I can't stress that enough. It has to be all of you, and it has to be at exactly the right time."

"Then we'll *all* do it," Zaire said. She looked at Cam. He was looking back at her defiantly.

"Listen carefully," Arik said. "At exactly eleven hundred hours in exactly ten days from now, the three of you are going to suit up and take a rover out to the wall. You're going to leave a locker open for me, and twenty minutes later, I'll meet you out there. We're not going to talk about this again between now and then. We're not going to debate it, and I'm not going to remind you. You just have to do it. All of you. You have to swear to me."

"Even if I wanted to help," Cam said, "there's no way all of us can get out of V1. Zaire and I can get the suits, but there's no way we can get Cadie through the Wrench Pod and into the airlock, and there's no way you'll be able to follow. Things have changed since your accident, Arik. People will stop us."

"There won't be anyone around to stop you," Arik said. "I'll take care of that."

"How?" Cam said.

"By doing the only thing that's guaranteed to bring every single person in V1 together into one place," Arik told them. "I'm going to solve AP."

The maglev was back at the Life Pod platform and it decelerated to a smooth stop.

"Don't let me down," Arik said. He stepped off the train, but Cadie did not follow. "I can promise you that we will never get another shot at this."

CHAPTER THIRTY-ONE
RED HERRING

THE TERM *RED HERRING* ORIGINATED from the practice of distracting hunting dogs from the scent of a fox or a badger with the pungent odor of a cured fish. It later came to be used in the areas of literature, science, and politics to refer to anything that lured attention away from the issue at hand.

Arik had come to believe that the term *artificial photosynthesis* was an innate red herring. Instead of describing a problem, it inherently suggested a solution. The issue at hand wasn't actually how to reverse engineer a photosynthetic plant's metabolic pathways—the real problem was how to generate large amounts of oxygen using readily available elements as quickly, cheaply, and efficiently as possible. But at some defining moment in V1's history, someone had been unable to escape the confines of their own experiences and imagination, and had confused inspiration with implementation. Emulating photosynthesis in an attempt to generate oxygen was like trying to achieve flight by copying birds, and so far, the exercise had yielded just about the same level of results.

To solve AP (clearly a misnomer, but the phrase had become a convention), Arik knew that he had to play by a different set of rules. Plants' ability to produce their own food and expel oxygen as a by-product had evolved over the course of more than a billion years, starting with the simplest forms of algal scum. Their technique had been judged and refined by what has always been the single constant and only valid measure of success: survival. Millions of years of minute and almost imperceptible genetic mutations had steered hundreds of thousands of species of plants down paths that had proven to be evolutionary dead ends, yet some small percentage of mutations had proven beneficial, compounding and accumulating into unimaginable complexity, specialization, and elegance. To reverse engineer photosynthesis in less than ten days was about as practical as trying to understand the principles of flight by taking apart a heavy Sagan rocket with a screwdriver. But using an electron-core computing cloud to model and dramatically accelerate the processes that gave rise to photosynthesis in the first place might just be possible.

Arik's previous attempts to crack AP had consisted of building software models of the tulsi ferns that were cultivated in the dome along with their aeroponic life-support systems, but even with the help of a team of extremely competent chemists and biologists, Arik felt like he would never be able to do better than what he perceived as a rough approximation. Computer models had always been rough approximations, and rough approximations had never been good enough. Weather had never been consistently and successfully predicted beyond a percentage of certainty, and models of the universe could suggest only general theories regarding both its origin and its eventual demise. Beyond a certain point in the development of computer processor technology, the problem was no longer a shortage of CPU cycles, but instead reflected humanity's inability to ask their binary counterparts the right questions. For years, electron computers had been sitting relatively idle waiting for their creators to finally pose a challenge worthy of their unimaginable faculties.

Arik understood that the effective use of an electron computer required a realistic and practical division of labor between computer and human. Humans were good at intuiting possibilities, while computers excelled at testing those possibilities by the trillions. Therefore, rather than starting with something incredibly complex like modern-day photosynthesis and trying to distill it down to something that could be modeled and programmed, Arik decided to start with a small number of simple elements and use the computer to see how they might evolve into more complex results. Rather than reverse engineering photosynthesis, Arik believed that he could *arrive* at photosynthesis—or perhaps something even better—through a process he liked to call *evolutionary engineering*.

Assembling the virtual environment for Arik's experiment was fairly straightforward since he already had most of the software models he needed. Years ago, he had built precise software abstractions of protons, neutrons, and electrons, and written algorithms to model gravitation, electromagnetism, and strong and weak nuclear forces. (Of course, this software had already existed for decades, but Arik trusted only code that he himself had authored.) He then used his low-level nuclear models to assemble higher-level models of all the elements in the periodic table, and then used those models to assemble molecular models even more complex. Since he began working in the Life Pod, Arik had also added to his software library several routines for simulating things like temperature, atmospheric pressure, and all wavelengths of light energy.

Arik had all the software models and most of the algorithms he needed; what he didn't have was an efficient way to combine and test trillions of permutations.

Random mixing and matching wasn't good enough. Arbitrarily combining models of the physical world in a virtual environment might eventually yield some interesting results, but even an electron computer could easily spend months or years playing such a complex and unconstrained guessing game. Arik needed a much more intelligent approach. He needed an algorithm that knew how to pursue paths that were promising and swiftly abandon those that were obvious dead ends. It had to understand how to build on success, learn from failure, branch out, and pursue multiple possibilities simultaneously, and it needed to understand how to build increasingly complex systems out of proven simpler ones. Arik needed an algorithm intelligent enough to condense over a billion years of evolution into just a few days.

He wondered what it would be like to be able to actually witness and perceive evolution. He imagined entire species coming and going at the speed of soap bubbles forming and popping; ice caps expanding and receding at the rate of a rapid heartbeat; continents drifting apart and dispersing like sea foam. Even watching a simple vine grow at as little as ten times its normal speed makes what we perceive as a dumb and static tendril look like the long, thin appendage of an intelligent primate skillfully searching out better light and more secure anchorage.

As Arik worked, he gradually began to repartition his life. He no longer thought in terms of day and night, and he stopped trying to keep track of mealtimes. He slept when he was exhausted and ate when he was weak. He responded to connection requests from Darien with a line or two of text, and completely ignored all other messages. The only schedules he observed were the cycles imposed by pain pills and stimulants. Cadie stopped asking him when or if he would be home, and started bringing him changes of clothes and boxed meals instead.

In place of his own circadian rhythm, Arik adopted the rhythm of the computer. For reasons he didn't fully understand, his program seemed to reach milestones at predictable intervals. A milestone was defined as the completion of a simulation that yielded no less than a tenth of a percent more oxygen than a previous milestone. Every time a milestone was reached, Arik assembled an experiment in a borosilicate tube and brought it down to the dome to physically validate the results.

Between experiments, Arik tried to understand the formulas that his program was producing. With Cadie's help, he had been able to make sense of the first few milestones, but the output had rapidly grown too complex for either of them to really comprehend. With every milestone, the computer was getting closer to solving AP, and Arik and Cadie were getting further from understanding how.

The definition of when AP was technically solved was somewhat subjective. Subha had suggested that nothing less than the production of one dioxygen molecule for every molecule of carbon dioxide that went into the process constituted a viable solution. She called it the "One-to-One Rule." Arik and Cadie had verified a one-to-one ratio milestone over forty-eight hours ago, and with time to spare, Arik allowed the computer to continue. If increasing photosynthetic oxygen production by a factor of two didn't guarantee him an audience with everyone in V1, nothing would.

When the computer predictably and unceremoniously achieved the two-to-one milestone, Arik assembled two verification experiments. He and Cadie each carried one down the corridor and into the dome. Both of the absorption disks turned blue within moments of being exposed to sunlight, and the oximeters sealed inside the tubes verified the results of the process. Cadie touched Arik's pale and gaunt face. His pupils were artificially dilated from his regimen of stimulants, and he squinted in the bright natural light. Neither of them spoke, but they shared a weary and almost unbelieving smile as acknowledgment of what they had accomplished.

Arik prepared four more borosilicate tubes. He sent three of them home with Cadie and kept one for himself. The baby was only about a month away, and Subha had begun watching Arik and Cadie closely. She was aware that they had been putting in long hours, and she had started extending her workdays as well. On more than one occasion, she had tapped the crystal of her watch while raising her eyebrows at Cadie's belly. When Arik sent her a connection request, she accepted almost instantly, and he could hear the anticipation in her voice when she agreed to meet him in the dome.

Before he left his lab, Arik stopped the computer simulation, deleted the program, and permanently erased every piece of data it had produced and recorded.

CHAPTER THIRTY-TWO

SLOPES

CADIE AND ARIK HAD AN early dinner, and probably for the first time since the day they were married, went to bed at the same time and without opening their workspaces. Arik told Cadie that everything had gone well with Subha, and that the assembly would happen on schedule. He knew that Cadie wanted to ask him about the things he'd said on the maglev, but she didn't. They dimmed the wall lights and talked about Haná instead, about what projects they might work on in the future, about really needing to reconnect with Cam and Zaire, and frankly with each other. And then they just lay beside each other in the warm glow of the walls and didn't talk at all.

Before they turned the lights all the way down, Cadie brought Arik a sedative.

"You really need to get back on regular sleep schedule," she told him.

"I know," Arik said. He took the pill from her palm and swallowed it with a sip of water.

"I'm concerned about how much weight you've lost. Are you getting sick again?"

"I don't know," Arik said. "I might be."

"You can't go on like this," she told him. "You have to ease up on yourself."

"Don't worry," Arik told her. "Everything is going to be different soon. I promise." Cadie lay down beside him and tapped out the wall lights. Arik started to say something about his lips and nose feeling numb, but was asleep before he could finish the thought.

He was awakened by a feeling of pressure in his abdomen, which turned into a severe, stabbing pain when he moved. He'd been asleep for almost eleven hours, and Cadie was gone. He put his feet on the floor and pushed himself up, clutching his stomach with one hand and steadying himself against the bed with the other. His clothes were damp with perspiration and he was shivering. He wiped his nose and saw blood on the back of his hand, and when he got to the bathroom, he found he was bleeding from the inside as well.

The latency period was over. The cells of his digestive tract were dying and he was shedding dead intestinal tissue. He knew he wouldn't be able to eat again until he was treated, and that the biggest risk over the next forty-eight hours was dehydration and shock from a water-electrolyte imbalance. Since his body was gradually losing its ability to absorb nutrients, he knew he would eventually need to take in fluids intravenously, but for the next two days, he needed to find ways to keep himself alive with whatever he had.

If he could figure out how much radiation he'd been exposed to, he would have a better idea of what to expect and how he might be able to treat himself, but since he hadn't worn a radiation badge, there was no way to know. At least there was no obvious way. In Arik's experience, there was almost always a way to recover lost information, to calculate a missing piece of data, to derive whatever you didn't know from whatever it was that you did. One of Arik's core beliefs was that the inability to solve most problems was ultimately because of a failure of the imagination.

He could have tested his clothing or a piece of his equipment, but he had sealed everything up in lead-lined pouches and dropped them down the hazardous waste chute in the Wrench Pod. If he could get a sensor outside now, he might be able to estimate what his exposure had been, but going back to the Wrench Pod before ensuring it was empty was far too risky. He thought about trying to get a reading off the robotic rover, but it would have been fully decontaminated in the airlock before being allowed back inside. With Cadie's help, it would probably be possible to estimate his exposure based on the rate at which his cells were dying, but he doubted they had the time to gather enough data to identify a meaningful trend. And the less she knew about his condition at this point, the better.

Searching for a way to extrapolate a missing piece of data was sometimes like searching for your glasses. It often took the exercise of retracing your steps before finally reaching up and finding that they had been perched on your head all along. It suddenly occurred to Arik that Malyshka would have picked up radiation levels as part of her atmospheric analysis during the second part of her mission. Arik had downloaded the data after getting back from the ERP, but before he had a chance to examine the results, he began to experience the onset of radiation sickness. The information he needed had been right in front of him all along.

Arik sat in his office and brought up his workspace. He had messages from Subha and Cadie, but he ignored them. All of Malyshka's data was in a raw binary format that Arik would need to process into some sort of visualization before he could make any sense of it. He opened up his code editor and began working on a simple script to parse the file and plot the results.

The charts were rendered in a virtual stack on his work-space, and Arik began flipping through them. Although he was looking for detailed radiation data, the slopes of the lines in the atmospheric composition overview made him pause. The chart plotted parts per million by volume against distance using the outer airlock door as one reference point and a point a few meters out from the Public Pod wall as the other. The carbon dioxide, methane, nitrogen, and oxygen lines were flat for most of the rover's journey. Carbon dioxide was at the top showing about 780,000 ppm, or about 78 percent of the atmosphere, with only trace levels of oxygen at the bottom of the chart. But about twelve meters out from the Public Pod wall, the lines suddenly crossed as CO_2 and methane fell while nitrogen and oxygen rose. Since Arik had programmed the rover to stop several meters out from the Public Pod wall, the chart wasn't complete, but the visualization software was able to extrapolate the missing data points by finding trends in the data it did have. At zero meters from the wall, the computer estimated the atmospheric composition to be about 70 percent nitrogen, 20 percent oxygen, 10 percent carbon dioxide, and the remainder divided up among methane, argon, helium, and hydrogen. If the computer was right, there was an area of a few square meters outside V1 where the air was theoretically breathable. Radiation was obviously still a problem, but radioactive material decayed over time, and with the proper motivation, could easily be contained.

The same environment that was now gradually killing Arik was also giving life to his work far beyond anything he had hoped for.

He felt like he needed visual confirmation. On a rational level, he already knew what was out there, but he needed to witness it for himself, to touch it, to maybe even remove his helmet and breathe it in. Just the visualization of the data was stunning—the thin lines running stubbornly parallel, then abruptly crossing, leaping and plummeting and trending toward unmistakable signs of life—but he needed to see the miracle of what was out there with his own eyes, to attend what only Malyshka had witnessed, to know for certain that everyone who had ever told him that something was impossible was wrong.

But he could feel himself getting sicker, dying one cell at a time, and he knew that if he still intended to make the rendezvous, he needed to better understand his condition. He scrolled forward through the charts until he got to one plotting radiation levels against time. The single line on the graph had a constant positive slope indicating, as he expected, a steady increase in radiation levels the longer Malyshka was outside. Arik converted the units on the y axis from millirems to rems, and was startled to see that Malyshka had been exposed to a dose of radiation sufficient to kill, within about a day, any human being who didn't have the equipment or genetic disposition to resist it. But Malyshka had been outside for almost two hours while Arik had been exposed for only approximately forty minutes. He zoomed in on the forty-minute hash mark on the x axis and plotted a point directly above it on the line. The y coordinate showed exactly 1,200 rems—at least 200 rems above what was considered fatal.

Arik checked his work, re-extracted the radiation numbers from the raw binary data, then re-rendered the chart. The results were the same. From the research he had done, for exposure above 1,000 rems, death was considered imminent. The only treatment was pain therapy. There was nothing anyone could do but make the patient as comfortable as possible while his cells mutated and died, while he waited and prayed for the relief and peace of a coma, while he gradually disintegrated and bled to death from the inside out.

But there was one piece of data that still had to be factored in: *dose fractionation*. Although Arik had been exposed for forty minutes total, it wasn't forty consecutive minutes. He'd spent close to an hour inside the ERP, and had probably been at least partially decontaminated in the ERP's airlock. Since his dose had been fractionated, his cells would have had time to repair some of the damage to their DNA. Although he didn't have exact figures, with reasonably close estimates he believed he could use a fractionation formula to determine whether or not he really was a walking ghost.

Arik found a formula and composed the correct equation, but he stopped before evaluating it. He looked at the string of variables and constants, his mind automatically solving and reducing, but he looked away before it was done. Even though he could calculate a concrete number, he knew it wouldn't be any better than a guess. There was no practical way for him to know exactly how long he had been outside, exactly how much time he spent in the ERP, exactly how complete the airlock's decontamination process had been, exactly the rate at which his cells were capable of repairing themselves. He didn't even know for sure if he had been exposed to the same levels of radiation as Malyshka, since they had been close to a kilometer apart. If the numbers were on the high side, he knew he could find a way to adjust the inputs to yield more favorable results. If they were on the low side, he would be left wondering if any of his estimates were overly optimistic. The data was bad. Regardless of where the numbers fell, he would not be able to trust them.

But that's not what ultimately stopped him from doing the calculation. Arik decided to leave the problem unsolved not because the answer might be wrong, but because he now knew that it didn't matter anymore. The plan had already changed. Arik knew that what he had to do now was bigger than himself, and more important than his own life. In forty-eight hours, it wouldn't matter anymore whether he lived or died. His influence would instantly diverge from the confines of his own limited existence, and the future would no longer be up to him.

CHAPTER THIRTY-THREE

THE IMPOSSIBLE

SUBHA WORE A LONG PURPLE and gold sari that covered one shoulder and sparkled in the sunlight. Arik was helping her get set up to broadcast from inside the dome. She was holding one of Arik's sealed and shrouded borosilicate tubes, and there was another down by the nutrient tank as a backup. Subha put her hand on Arik's arm and he stopped. She asked him if he was OK. She said they could postpone, that everyone would understand. Arik told her that he looked much worse than he felt, and that there was nothing he wanted more than to see this through. It was just the remnants of a virus. He had already seen Dr. Nguyen, and there was nothing to worry about. She looked at him carefully through his tinted goggles. The blood vessels in his eyes had started to burst, staining the white parts bright red, and his pupils were fully dilated from stimulants. He badly needed to vomit, but the antinausea medication was holding it back.

They wished each other luck, and Arik left the dome. He took off his goggles and stopped by his office briefly on the way out. Outside the Life Pod, the maglev was waiting to take him to the Public Pod, but he took it in the opposite direction instead.

The Wrench Pod was deserted, as Arik expected. The lighting was minimal, and it was so quiet that Arik could hear the air circulation system above him as he walked through the shop toward the dock. He didn't see anyone through the archway in the back of the room, and it seemed too quiet. There were no footsteps ringing out against the metal grate, no tiny ticks and pings from equipment being locked into place. It occurred to him for the first time that Cadie, Cam, and Zaire might not be there. Arik believed that he had made an impression on them on the maglev ten days ago, but there was really no way for him to know if they had taken him seriously or not. Cam might have talked Zaire out of blindly trusting Arik, and of course there was no way Cadie could get outside V1 without their help. Since Arik had made it clear that all of them were to go together, just one of them having second thoughts would have been enough to end it all.

But when he stepped through the archway, he saw three figures in environment suits standing in front of the row of lockers. Cadie was fully suited up, and Cam and Zaire were missing only their helmets and gloves. Zaire was behind Cadie, inspecting her cartridge port, and Cam was making sure her helmet was properly threaded and locked. Cadie's suit was much too big for her, completely swallowing the bulge in the middle.

"What are you doing here?" Cam said. He looked at his watch, which he'd strapped on over his environment suit. "Shouldn't you be presenting?"

Arik could tell from Cam's tone and expression that he was still skeptical, that there was no way he would be there if Zaire and possibly Cadie hadn't insisted, that some part of him resented Arik for abusing their friendship and forcing him into this.

"I'm on my way. I just stopped by to give you this."

Arik offered Cam a handheld laser projector. The handle and trigger were large enough that the device could be operated while wearing gloves. Cam looked down at Arik's hand before accepting it.

"What is this?"

"Instructions for what to do while you wait for me. Once you get out to the door, look into the optics and hold this down. It'll project an inverted image onto your visor that you'll be able to read from the inside."

Zaire had stepped out from behind Cadie. "Why don't you come with us now? There's nobody here. Your distraction worked."

"There wouldn't be enough time. If I don't show up at the Public Pod in the next few minutes, they'll start looking."

"Here's your locker," Cam said. "Number eleven. Everything you need is inside. I put duct tape over the latch to keep it from locking."

"Duct tape? Another high-tech Wrench Pod solution, I see."

"I trust duct tape more than I trust an electron computer." Cam looked at Arik's eyes. "Are you sure you're up for this?"

"I look a lot worse than I feel." He looked at Cadie. "Does she have audio drops?"

"Yes, she can hear you."

Arik turned toward his wife. "You don't have anything to worry about," he told her. "Everything will make sense very soon. I promise."

Cadie nodded inside her helmet. He saw her say that she loved him.

"I love you too," Arik said. "Both of you." He put his hand on her belly and tried to feel the baby through the layers of micro-fiber, and she covered his hand with her glove. He could see that she was crying. "There's no reason to cry. This is a good thing. I promise. I'll see you very soon."

Arik turned to Cam before he left.

"Take good care of her," he said. "No matter what happens out there. Don't ever leave her."

He could see a flash of confusion in Cam's eyes—a question forming on his lips—but Arik was gone before his friend could stop him.

• • •

A ping notification appeared on a nearby piece of polymeth as he walked through the shop. He waited until he was close to the door and accepted only the audio portion of the connection.

"Arik? Where are you? We're ready to start." It was the woman from the Juice Pod who had coordinated the event. She sounded irritated.

Arik leaned against the wall and tried to slow his breathing before he answered. "Go ahead and get started. I just left the Dome. I'll be there in five minutes."

He closed the stream before she could respond.

He was able to rest on the maglev, but it wasn't enough. It occurred to him that he should have given Cadie the laser projector the night before to give to Cam in order to save himself the trip to the Wrench Pod. He was much weaker than he thought he would be, and he even questioned whether he would be able to climb the stairs up to the stage. He needed another stimulant, but there wasn't time for it to take effect.

As he stood outside the Public Pod and caught his breath, he was aware of his skin pulling tight against his ribs, and of the slack elastic of his pants hanging from his hip bones. He hadn't eaten in two days, and he had been shedding increasing amounts of blood. He'd tried drinking water, but even when the anti-nausea medication kept him from vomiting it back up, his body wouldn't absorb it. The blood vessels in his arms had constricted and receded to the point where he didn't think they would accept an IV needle anymore, and the dehydration had caused oppressive and pounding headaches that required double and triple doses of painkillers to control. The taste of iron was always in his mouth from raw, bleeding gums and cracked lips.

When he opened the Public Pod door, he saw a huge image of Subha on the polymeth above the stage. The lights were down, and Kelley was standing next to the podium below her, looking up. The borosilicate tube she was holding was still shrouded.

"—typically a one-to-one ratio, meaning six molecules of carbon dioxide will yield six oxygen molecules. The process also requires twelve molecules of water with half of those recovered as a byproduct. That's what it took evolution 1.2 billion years to do. And *this* is what *we* were able to do in just a few months."

She removed the shroud and presented the tube. The absorption disk began to turn blue in the sunlight, and the oximeter immediately began to move.

"Our version of photosynthesis yields exactly twice as much oxygen as natural photosynthesis, requires only six molecules of hydrogen, no water whatsoever, and needs half the number of photons. I think it's safe to say," Subha said, pausing for effect and smiling self-assuredly, "that we have thoroughly outdone Mother Nature."

The audience erupted in applause. Someone stood up, then someone else, and eventually all of V1 had risen to their feet. Subha beamed in the yellow light from the dome, turning so that her sari winked and glittered. Kelley saw Arik in the back of the room and extended his hand. He wasn't smiling. He looked at Arik with a quiet and intense gratitude that Arik found unsettling. He could see the pride in Kelley's heavy eyes all the way from the back wall. The audience followed Kelley's gesture, turned, and their ovation intensified as they watched Arik advance up the aisle.

But when he struggled with the steps up to the stage, the applause subsided abruptly and was replaced by a confused murmur. The spotlights accentuated Arik's ghostliness. His sunken red eyes glowed against his pale and gaunt face, and patches of baldness showed through his cropped black hair. He shuffled to the middle of the stage, bent with pain. The audience remained standing, bobbing and craning to get a better view.

Kelley had stepped off the stage. Arik touched the podium to open his workspace, then looked up. He saw L'Ree in the front, more confused than concerned. He found Darien farther back, standing with Priyanka, Zorion, and Fai. Most of his peers, Gen V, were sitting together to the far left.

"Thank you for coming." He cleared his throat and squinted into the glare. "I think you've already seen what you came here to see today, but I have one last thing I want to show you."

He looked at his watch. By now, Cadie, Cam, and Zaire should have reached the wall, and Cam would be reading his message. He would be learning all about the secrets contained inside the baby, and how important it was to protect her life. He would know how much Arik loved them all, and how sick he actually was. Cam would relay to Cadie and Zaire how sorry Arik was that he would not be joining them, and then he would tell Cadie directly that Arik's biggest regret was that he would never have the chance to hold his baby daughter. They would all be thinking about coming back to V1, but before they could move, the door in the wall would open, and they would begin to understand that they were no longer alone, and that their lives were really just beginning.

Arik touched the podium and cut the power to the Public Pod. The lights went out, and Subha's face flickered and disappeared. There was a moment of silence, and then a tremendous bellow as the shields against the windows detached and fell away. The room was flooded with natural green light, filtered through the lush teardrop leaves of the thick vines clinging to the outside walls of V1.

The audience began filling the aisles, surging forward, advancing as a group toward the windows and pressing themselves against the glass panes. They climbed the stairs of the stage and spread out along the entire wall to get as close as they could. Nobody noticed that Arik had sat down behind the podium, then laid down facing the windows, then closed his eyes and lost consciousness. They knew only that he had shown them the impossible.

ACKNOWLEDGMENTS

I WOULD LIKE TO THANK my wife, Michelle, my daughters, Hannah and Ellie, and my friends, Ben Yaroch and Ben Rossi, for their love, friendship, and support during all my schemes and endeavors.

ABOUT THE AUTHOR

Photograph © Michelle Cantrell

Christian Cantrell is a software developer from Northern Virginia. He writes the technology blog LivingDigitally.net and is the author of several self-published short stories, including "Brainbox" and "Farmer One." *Containment* is his first full-length novel.